from the
BLUE

— A Novel —

PAUL ALLEN ROBERTS

authorHOUSE®

AuthorHouse™
1663 Liberty Drive
Bloomington, IN 47403
www.authorhouse.com
Phone: 1 (800) 839-8640

*This work of fiction has no intended reference of any kind to any person, living or dead, or
any geographic place, or any public, private, or government owned company, or political
or organized entity whatsoever. References to known individuals and locales are used to
illustrate the time line of the story and interaction of fictional characters in the story.*

*No other inference is intended. Historical references in all categories have been
modified to fit the characterizations and are therefore not intended to reflect
accurate or actual historical events nor the actual timing of such events.*

Published by AuthorHouse 01/30/2017

ISBN: 978-1-5049-5954-4 (sc)
ISBN: 978-1-5049-5953-7 (hc)
ISBN: 978-1-5049-5955-1 (e)

Library of Congress Control Number: 2015918197

Print information available on the last page.

*Any images depicted in stock imagery provided by Thinkstock are representation,
and such images are being used for illustrative purposes only.
Certain stock imagery © Thinkstock.*

This book is printed on acid-free paper.

Dedication

I am forever grateful to my wife,
my mother, and her mother.

To my two brothers,
I couldn't have done this without you.

Finally, to my father:
you, sir, are my hero.
Thanks, Dad.

About the Book

A primitive, loving society is thrust
out of isolation by foreign invasion.
Overcoming the odds, they learn
of their own unbelievable past by
exploring one of their own islands.
It's a story of the inevitable, of
survival and the overlooked. The life
changing events for the island nation
and those who invaded, their intense
emotional response to unforeseen
events. A journey of loving, the
anguish in the loss a loved one.
And the power of intuition.

All done "in the BLUE".

Map Room

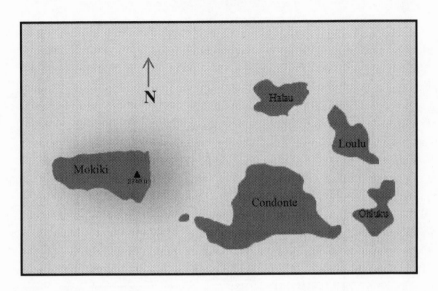

The Condonte Islands
(the five largest with many
other rocky islets and atolls)

South Pacific Ocean

Map not to scale

North orientation

150 miles east to west among the five main islands

Lowest elevation: sea level

Highest Elevation: 2,740 feet on Mokiki Island (two miles inland from its eastern coastline)

Coral reefs to the north and east of Halau Island and east of Loulu and Ohluku Islands

Geographically similar to Bora Bora and Moorea

Pronunciation Guide

The language of the island group has certain similarities to other Polynesian and Oriental languages. Every letter in a word is pronounced succinctly. The word order is verb, noun, and subject. Commonly, the last syllable is dominant in all words other than a noun. In a person's name, the emphasis can be placed on any syllable.

In any name with four or more sounds, the emphasis is put on the second-to-last syllable. The simple act of putting emphasis on a different syllable, other than a noun, changes the meaning of the spoken word. A native speaker's conversation ends in an elevated tone with the last word of a sentence. The language also includes a *guttural stop*. With fluency, the guttural stop softens somewhat. Translation is challenging due to the myriad of metaphors and historical word origins.

Character names

Iliakahani: ee-lee-ah-ka-HAA-nee
Pohiꞌi: pō-HEE-ee
Hoꞌuolo: hō-uu-Ō-lō
(Note the guttural stop shown as an underlined apostrophe)

Place names

Mokiki: moh-KEE-kee
Condonte: kōn-DŌN-tay
Ohluku: ōh-LU-ku
Loulu: loh-UU-lu
Halau: ha-LA-oo

Chapter 1

"There were so many questions and too few answers," Ihilani said to herself. Her toes sampled the soft sand as she walked on the beach on the northwestern tip of her island home. She loved the early morning hours of calm breezes on her skin and her hair. This beach was always her favorite. She sat in the shade of the palms and reflected on the island's history she knew so well.

Her mother, Iliakahani, was greatly admired and respected. She had lived a truly inspired life and had evolved into a real mother figure for almost all residents on the island—always loving, always humble, always smiling, and always caring for all others. Her father, Pohii, the adored leader of the islands, was ill, although it was not a life-threatening illness. His pain progressed slowly, and he rarely talked about his stiffening joints until recently.

Still, Ihilani worried with gut-wrenching sorrow every time she looked into her father's eyes. She forced elevated courage each time she talked to him. She had been there when he took over as the leader of the island nation when she was just eight years old. She barely remembered her grandmother. Her grandfather's death when she was just seven—and his traditional weeklong funeral—sent her into a spiral of sorrow that she could not forget. It was such a harsh time for her. Life itself was still a mystery to her, and at eighteen, she was just discovering a broader meaning of truth and honesty, of life and death, love and trust. She and her brother had been groomed in their early childhood to be upright citizens.

But she was not sure what her place was.

Now she had to face the prospect that her brother, Kai, would succeed their father. She loved him, but she couldn't bring herself to fully trust him. Her mother tried to reassure her that God would guide him to greatness, and at twenty-three, he was a respected son, brother, husband and father of two. Still, Ihilani had her doubts.

The ancestral council had discussed Pohii's current health at the last two meetings. At forty-six, his rise to power, his status as leader, father, and grandfather was a testament to his true calling in life. But now, Pohii had to set all that aside.

Since the three other island factions united and invaded Condonte (and were soundly defeated just after Ihilani was born), the island had not been prepared for war.

That war, the second in a decade, had seen wave after wave of raids. And for Pohii, even in the shadow of his father, those times of horror and death on both sides forced a buildup of defenses and spears. It was his leadership that caused the enemy to cease without surrender. His subsequent invitations to his enemies finally persuaded them to unite under his father's leadership—but not without caution.

The ancestral council's lifetime members came from all four islands, two each from the other islands and three from Condonte Island. It was a sacrifice the others agreed to, not in defeat but because Condonte Island's population was twice that of all the others combined.

In proposing this option, Pohii masterfully convinced the others to join him in peace. He explained the benefits of acting together and ending the fighting forever. With a greater population, he made it clear that their ambitions would be easily defeated once more even if all three acted in unison against Condonte again.

Pohii, in one of his frequent moments of diplomacy, conceded that the Council of Elders, as they were initially called, would be the place where the other islands would be heard and respected.

Since the council's creation, Pohii had honored that commitment. His decisions were his alone—not out of vanity or overconfidence, but duty as he saw it.

Just before the day's first meal, a ship arrived just off the western shore of Condonte. The anchor was dropped, and a small boat was lowered and rowed to shore. The men aboard had never seen these islands before. It was their first excursion to a landing. The island guards, hidden in the foliage, saw them coming.

Ihilani was farther north on the beach, sitting in the palm shadows as she felt a break in her thoughts. As she calmly turned to look south along the beach, she saw the large vessel and the rowboat. Terror gripped her soul. She bolted up to assess, quickly walked into the shadows of the palms, and ran up the hill to the compound she knew. She hoped she hadn't been seen. Two of the guards ran up the trail to the center of the community, where Pohii was already awake. The guards were ordered to capture the invading force alive and bring them to the outdoor compound just below the ceremonial grounds.

Condonteans had developed a sort of sixth sense about invasions. The alarm sounded with incredible speed throughout the island. Four guards were sent by canoe to the other islands to alert them.

Pohii arrived in the shadows near the beach. Eighty warriors with spears were ready. Hundreds more hid in the darkened jungle. They were armed with spears and blow darts and standing to hear the orders from him. Pohii thought that with such a large vessel, other invaders might be hiding within the ship, but he couldn't be sure. He had known deception from others in the earlier raids between islands.

The Islanders watched as Pohii whispered the command to his guards who swiftly surrounded the eight invaders with spears, ready to defend the island.

The intruders instantly knew the odds were against them and wished they had brought hand cannons. They dropped their daggers and long knives into the sand. Surrender seemed the only option.

Pohii ordered that the invaders be tied to the trees just below the ceremonial grounds.

Their weapons were confiscated and would not be returned, he ordered. That's what he had always done in times of conflict.

After the nearly incoherent interview and shouts for death from the assembled crowd and his son, Pohii proclaimed that he would voice the fate of the outsiders in three days' time.

He needed time and God's guidance. He hoped that his decision would follow history and protect his subjects, but for the first time, the future—along with the past—challenged him. He ordered his guards to remain on the beach and watch the vessel offshore. It silently rocked in the waves all day without further sightings of warriors aboard. They knew from experience that complacency could be an unstoppable advantage to the enemy, especially with such an enormous and strange vessel. The small caravel was among the first to be built for the Spanish Armada.

But if they were invading, why would the entire force come ashore in such a small number?

In times like these, Pohii's subjects and his family knew to trust his judgment. They left him alone for such a monumental decision. One by one, he pondered each element. Then he made his choice.

As dawn broke on the third morning, the Islanders grew anxious to hear their beloved leader's announcement. Rain could be seen crossing an adjacent island across the eastern channel; it threatened a deluge here. The overwhelming reverence they felt for the weather was deeply steeped in their culture. The weather was a deterrent to a ceremony, especially if lightning could be seen in the approaching storm.

Weather observation, although primitive, was the responsibility of the palace guard. No lightning was seen.

Kai had voiced his absolute hatred for these invaders to his father. "How dare they come to this island?" Kai had not been allowed to fight in the raids between the islands almost a decade ago, but he had always said he would defend his island home to the death.

Pohii made considerable effort to calm his son. He asked him to wait for the decision he would make.

Kai's blood pressure remained at maximum.

Pohii left the only home he had ever known. As he walked, he went through the list of his duties for the day. The reclining guards jumped as he stood in the doorway.

His wife moved quickly across the room to stand behind him, on his left and in the sunshine. "What must you do today?" Iliakahani asked with deep love and respect.

"Feel the power of the sun," he said, "and then kill or not kill."

As Pohii took several steps forward, the morning sun wrapped him in warmth.

A breeze from the east seemed a bit irregular. *An ominous sign,* he thought before discarding the notion. Inspiration from the sun, the moon, the stars, and the rain were critical and masculine. That was emphasized from the beginning in all forms of education, training, and most importantly, raising a child. The ground they walked on was of equal importance. They took a slight pause to honor the earth as feminine. The sun, moon, and stars were powerful reminders to the women of the island that the men were always above them in physical strength, prestige, and law.

Ah, but the wind, the wind was female. It was calming and soothing but only rarely had might.

An elder from the eastern island appeared in the sunlight. He saw Pohii pondering his duties. He slowly moved closer and said, "It is now. It is you. We are waiting."

Pohii, the pleasure of the moment broken, said, "And you, my priest, what must you decide?"

"You will hear it, but you must be patient, Pohii. Your duties, your decision, and your wishes must come before mine."

His confidence with his announcement was never in doubt; Pohii walked along the path to the gathering in the ceremonial grounds. The entire population of Condonte Island and a contingent from the three other islands had arrived overnight to hear his decision. They had been given a signal that he was on his way from the palace. Everyone was silent when he strode to the center of the vast grounds. His guards had assembled near the six others astride the restrained prisoners.

His wife took a position with the other women next to all the children in the outer circle—to protect the children's eyes from the spectacle if the men so wished it.

Pohii's personal guards were ready. The priest gave him the nod. "The prisoners may speak!" Pohii said.

Fairness to all was a familiar hallmark. The apparent leader of the prisoners was walked several paces forward and forcefully stopped.

"Majesty, I've come to explore, to learn from you, to introduce the world to you!" he said with a nervous stammer.

His interpreter finished the translation.

"What have you learned?" Pohii said. He had known the man for only three days. He had heard it all before; it was a blatant plea for leniency.

"Your Majesty, I have learned just a few words in your language, but I hope to respect you and your people."

Pohii remained unmoved. "Are you ready to hear my decision?" he said with his customary calm.

With all the humility he could muster, the prisoner spoke. It was a calculated risk that he hoped would save them from death. "Your majesty, your history, your people, your family—I respect them all, and I will respect your decision."

Pohii paused. He was surprised by the prisoners narrowing of fate and understanding of the morality that had been violated.

A beach guard ran into the ceremonial ring and shouted, "More canoes come, big canoes!"

Chapter 2

After learning that larger vessels were moving into position, Pohii looked at the lead prisoner with an intensity no one had seen before. "How many warriors are on these canoes? How many more canoes are coming?" He tried to suppress his anger.

"Majesty, I have told you the truth! We are not warriors! We are explorers!" the anxious prisoner said.

"Tell me the difference," Pohii said bluntly.

"Majesty, we are explorers who have been looking for new countries to trade with, to learn from, and grow with ... nothing more," the prisoner said.

The unfamiliar words didn't sway Pohii.

Iliakahani watched the interrogation. She wondered about the stark differences between the Islanders and the invaders. The majority of the islanders typically wore one garment regardless of gender. The invaders, all but two, wore something on their feet she had not seen before. Their clothing was different also. Multiple items, one for the chest, another for the hips and legs, finally the feet. It was evident that their clothing was in need of cleaning, but their facial hair was what fascinated her. She had not known of male facial hair, certainly not among the islanders.

"You have kept one truth from me: more canoes arrived this morning," Pohii said with mounting anger. "I do not believe you!"

"Your Majesty, they will patiently wait for me to tell them we are welcome here or must leave at once. I regret that I didn't tell you," said the prisoner.

"You haven't answered my question. How many remain on your big canoe and the others?" Pohii asked.

"Twenty-eight remain on my ship, and four hundred are on the four others. They will all wait for my word," the prisoner said.

"When will they act if no words come from you?" Pohii asked.

"They will come today when the sun is at its highest, Majesty," he murmured.

"How many and for what reason?" Pohii demanded.

"Two boats of fifteen men each from one of the four other ships, and they will search for us," he said.

The morning shadows were still long, Pohii observed. Not much time. He had seen the unusual weapons that had been seized from the prisoners. The capture of the prisoners had been all too easy. No one had been injured.

Distant claps of thunder were heard from the East. The audience gasped. It was an unmistakable omen.

Iliakahani sat in the outer ring and could hardly suppress her smile. She had seen Pohii in action many times, but this was different. Pohii had changed course. Her smile had not gone unnoticed.

Ihilani saw her mother fidget and asked, "What is it, Mother?"

"Just wait. You'll see," Iliakahani said.

The storm moved northwest over the open channel in an apparent course that would just touch the north coast of Condonte. It would bring increasing winds to the center of the island.

Ah, the wind, the power, the omen, the feminine, Iliakahani thought.

Iliakahani knew that Ihilani felt the emotional jump. She also knew it would take time for her daughter to understand it like she did. She would be patient.

Pohii stood silently for what seemed like an eternity. The dramatic events were racing through his mind. He knew his silence added considerable tension to the moment—a classic way to induce meaning to his decisions in the past.

Iliakahani stood from her seat. The wind had boosted her confidence to break the protocol. Slowly, all in the audience stood in support for Pohii. He was moved to think they had known his decision before his lips parted.

Addressing the population as a whole, he said, "We may be standing on the edge of a cliff. If we surrender to the past, we invite God in war. If we allow the prisoners to convince us of the present without question, we may be ending our families and all our tomorrows. But if we listen to the men bound before us, we may see our tomorrows. I believe this is not safe without trust and respect. So, to avoid war is true. To use caution is also true. We shall welcome these men with caution and watch them carefully. They will each have a palace guard as they talk to us and as we listen. They will not have free movement, but they will remain with us until we trust them or leave unharmed. We now go to the western beach and watch the others come to our land. We will be ready to protect ourselves."

The silence lasted for several moments.

The elder from the eastern island entered the ring, and all eyes remained upon Pohii. "We shall prevail. We shall continue, but now we learn."

With the protocols observed, Pohii exited the ceremonial ring.

The audience began to whisper to one another out of respect for him. The ring emptied in a quiet, orderly fashion, but Iliakahani noticed the wind picking up.

Eight hundred warriors took their positions in the shoreline foliage out of sight, and fifty guards waited on the beach for the invaders. Pohii and the thirty palace guards stood in the shadow of the trees on the beach.

The prisoners remained bound with their hands behind them. They watched intently as nothing happened.

Pohii reassured them. He gazed up, and the time wasn't quite right yet.

In the distance, two boats were lowered from one of the larger ships. The crossing would be difficult with the winds and ocean swells. The boats seemed as though they vanished when they reached the bottom of the swells, but they reappeared when the waves crested.

Three of the bigger ships raised their sails and begin to creep to the south—away from the storm.

Three leaving, but two remain, Pohii thought. *They will return.* His warriors would stay in position.

Pohii started to believe some of what the lead prisoner had said. He was getting used to half-truths from this man. Pohii asked that the lead prisoner be brought forward. "Remove his bindings," he said.

The guards instinctively doubled their watch of the prisoner and held their spears in threatening horizontal positions.

"Go ready," Pohii said.

The guards returned their spears to vertical.

"Invite your men to come here before me. Tell them that you will talk to them. I will speak to you," Pohii said.

Four guards escorted the lead prisoner and his trusted translator to the edge of the beach. The others stood a few paces away.

Iliakahani and her daughter stood well away from the events about to unfold, yet they were able to see most of the beach.

"This is good, Ihilani. Watch carefully," Iliakahani said with ease. "The wind is speaking now."

Iliakahani watched as the boats reached the halfway point from ship to shore. She felt an odd unease among them. She knew they were tiring quickly.

The storm moved past the northern tip of the island and then turned southwest toward Mokiki Island, the uninhabited island some twelve miles due west of Condonte. It's steep northern cliffs, and nearly vertical peak could be easily seen from the western beaches of Condonte.

Deeply entrenched in many a sinister mystery, Mokiki was the focus of many an evil story. No one dared to even think about going over to the island. The devil lived there. In the specter of an invasion, they witnessed the storm increasing in intensity. There was an expectation of an extraordinary event in the making. They knew it. They felt it.

The channel between the islands took on a whole new tone as the invaders grew more fearful of the storm and wearier of the proclamations that brought them there.

The winds swirled the sands on the western shoreline as the two boats finally reached the landing.

Pohii could feel an advantage brewing. The windblown, stinging sands added misery to his desire for calm diplomacy. He remained focused and strong. With his bravest guards at his back, he said, "Wait for my word. See that all know." Two guards moved to relay the message down the length of the beach.

As they all watched, the two boats stopped on the beach. Unseen by most, the two remaining ships had slipped out of sight—and out of harm's way. The storm was poised to close in on the northern cliffs of Mokiki.

The beach was long and wide. From the north end, it gracefully narrowed along the coast. A stream emptied into the ocean at the south end of the beach, just before the heavily forested cliffs that jutted out into the channel.

The cliffs ended with a separate high rocky prominence to the west, which was known as God's Finger. At a little more than twice the height of the cliffs, it proved that they were all living within the hand of God.

The lead prisoner motioned to the men in the boats to step up onto the beach. They did so slowly and nervously. They did not speak. They could see many more warriors, but their exhausted expressions didn't reveal the flood of terror they felt.

One invader fell to his knees and then face-first into the sand. He was entirely spent. He moved an arm in agony and turned his head to breathe. The waves were reaching his feet and occasionally lapping at his shoulders.

The others were motionless, barely taking the breaths they so desperately needed.

"Tell them they are welcome today," Pohii said to the prisoner, "for tomorrow has not come."

The lead prisoner said, "We are welcome, but caution is needed with the grace and dignity of the islanders' culture, which we do not yet understand."

The silence was broken as the men sighed in relief. They helped the fallen sailor to his feet.

Ihilani watched a sudden increase in the lightning, and a vast explosion sent a terrifying column of fire into the clouds. The intense brightness took the entire population by surprise. From twelve miles away, they watched the spectacle and were frozen in awe. Were they seeing God's wrath? Were they seeing the devil?

Some of the women and children screamed and retreated back into the jungle. The Warriors had revealed their numbers as the event unfolded, but they were unable to move.

The invaders turned to see the distant explosion from the beach. As the clouds parted above the blast, the lightning abruptly stopped. They could see the scorched cliffs near the central peak on Mokiki as it continued to smoke from the vaporized foliage. The severe heat added steam to the changing environment, and the clouds seemed to roll away from the center. Rays from the sun illuminated the peak and revealed the power of the storm. Plumes of steam rose from the island.

Fierce winds arrived on the beach and dissipated in an instant. The winds calmed, and debris fell to earth. The sands no longer swirled, and the sounds returned to normal. A faint, foreign, ugly smell lingered and slowly dissipated. The jets of steam continued rising from the island. The foliage continued to smolder.

That distant event seemed over, but the trauma felt by all would send most to the priests for answers. They thought, *Did God stop the violent storm? Had the devil invited it? Why had it happened right then?*

The priests could not explain the power it revealed.

Pohii said, "God and the devil have fought. We all saw it together." Turning to the new invaders, he continued, "We shall welcome you to our land. We will honor you, and you us, during our first meal together."

The audience was taken aback as Pohii spoke. It was as if nothing of any consequence had happened across the channel.

Iliakahani felt the very essence of the distant clash had to be revealed. She would be patient. She had witnessed the event as she stood next to her daughter. She smiled and gazed at Pohii and the island across the channel.

In the crowd, some whispered, "Pohii." Others said, "Pohii, Iliakahani."

Pohii felt the needs and the calm.

Sunshine returned to Mokiki, but rough waves crashed on the beach. People sprinted away from the massive wave and reassembled when the waves subsided. With one unspoken and unknown element, the storm had put the final touch on the event.

When it was over, Ihilani and Iliakahani stood in stunned silence.

Iliakahani took her daughter's shaking hand.

Ihilani said, "Mother, I don't understand. I am frightened!"

"I, too, am afraid, Ihilani," she said. "This is not ended. There is much more we will learn together." Iliakahani's smile returned.

Iliakahani's guidance was usually enough for Ihilani. She had learned patience and courage from her mother, but it was at its limit.

With a tilt of her mother's head, the blink of an eye, and the touch of both hands, Ihilani felt the reassurance she needed.

Her mother's smile meant so much to her. For the first time, it was mixed with her mother's respect for her as an adult. She fought back the tears as her mind searched for meaning. Did her mother really know what would happen today as she claimed on this and previous occasions? Was her fear genuine? Was there something about her mother she didn't know? Was the newfound respect for one another enough? She waited for the answers and smiled.

Iliakahani said, "I trust you now more than ever. You will learn how to lead in your own way—just as Kai will lead in his."

Ihilani placed her arms around her mother, and her fears evaporated. It was genuine. It was very good.

The four guards took the weapons from the invaders, and the procession moved to the trees below the ceremonial grounds.

Chapter 3

During the first meal together in the ceremonial grounds, the awkwardness slowly eroded as more and more words were understood. Pohii reserved judgment if mistakes were made in his language. He allowed the unknown words from the invaders' language to ease in. They were the only ones speaking, although the translator whispered to both of them.

Pohii learned his name and overlooked the fact that he had two names rather than the one name commonly found in leadership roles in the islands. It was typically insulting if his family name was not already known and unspoken, but he continued without any further inquiry. Perhaps it would be a topic later on.

"What is this word *trade* I hear?" Pohii asked the lead prisoner.

James Cristo said, "If you have a fish, and I am hungry for it, and I have a coconut, and you are hungry for it, we might agree to give each other the fish or coconut."

Pohii thought about the answer. "Why would I give you a fish for a coconut?" Since each was plentiful in the islands, he thought the concept was laughable.

James felt embarrassed by the example and refined the answer. "Where I come from, there are those who cannot come to the sea. They take food from the land far from the sea."

Pohii listened, but the idea that this man's people could not walk to the ocean from where they lived was inconceivable.

James chose his words with great care. "On this island, everyone works together and moves the food to one location or their homes and shares the food. Where I live, there is more than one community with a distance between them. Perhaps it is like moving food between islands here."

Pohii had never heard this before. The islands had been mostly self-sufficient for as long as anyone could remember. The roots, berries, fruit, fish, and coconuts were all they had ever known. Pohii would tend his garden with his family just like everyone else did. They were more than willing to share with anyone else on the island.

Some dedicated their lives to neither fish nor coconuts, but they were fed just like anyone with a purpose other than collecting food. No one was ever left hungry. There were legends to the contrary, but food collection and sharing it completely was the standard by which they all lived.

"We have words that tell of our love for one another," Pohii said, "I work for all. I gather more than I can eat so that all can eat. We know all know this."

James understood. Trade was in their culture, but no one had refined it for profit yet. There was no trade, bartering, or currency. They had no need for it. It was a doctrine to them. Greed was never the issue, but pure, basic, ground-level survival was.

They didn't see themselves in the same way he had seen them. To them, the primary emotions served them well. They all had boundless love and worked hard. James could hardly believe the utopia on the island. It didn't matter to them. Superstitions aside, they absolutely loved living there. Hospitality had never been defined. The Islanders elevated the meaning well beyond any scholarly sense—without being the least bit aware of the concept.

James said, "Your Majesty, your love for each other is something I admire in you and your people. I can honestly say my people enjoy love the way you and yours do. I just wish it were as complete and as wide as yours." He smiled.

When the translator finished, Pohii smiled too.

Jacob Abbottsford had learned much of the language quickly, but he was not yet fluent. As the hired linguist for the mission, even in this total immersion, he had not yet mastered it. He carefully chose words for both sides and was committed to the quality of his translations.

He was the perfect aide for the job. Being among those captured on the first days focused his role and terrified him.

As he was tied to the trees those first days, he listened to the guards intently and watched them respond to each other. On the first day, he gained an understanding of the language.

Though he was fluent in dozens of languages, this language was a Polynesian language he'd never been exposed to. The uniqueness of the language kept him enthralled. He had learned earlier in his field that comparison to other languages would have to come after fluency.

He focused on the translation; it brought about an intensity he had never felt. When he translated the words for *leader* on both sides, he took the risk of not concluding Pohii was thought of like a monarch within his culture.

For now, he would allow James to hear it, but he used *leader* as he translated for Pohii. The immense responsibility expected of him, the desire for clarity, and a sense of courteous diplomacy in translation was paramount to him.

On the third day, he asked for a momentary pause to relieve his self-imposed pressure for excellence. He had become aware of Pohii's personality early on and began to admire him with great depth.

Never far away from the mission or his role, he liked Pohii almost from the start. He had been warned against it, but he couldn't help it. There were others with the very same impression. He was a dedicated, loving leader with a mild, fun-loving side. He was wise beyond description. He talked about it with James. They compared their own impressions and agreed about the leader of the islands, but James was more cautious. "A prudent position while negotiations continue," he said.

The meal lasted several more hours. When the invaders could not eat anymore, they asked to retire for the evening. Although visibly disappointed, Pohii agreed. He granted the request until the midday meal.

Iliakahani and Ihilani were among the many women who brought the morning meal to the new guests. Their smiles were just what the invaders needed.

The women began eating even though it broke tradition, and the men cautiously sampled the feast after watching the women. There were no embellishments to the food. There was no salt. The raw vegetables and berries were especially welcome. The fire-roasted fish was new and tasty. The spring water went down with ease.

The women watched in amazement as the guests inhaled the meal. The women had left starvation behind several generations ago. They thought to eat without enjoying it was unusual. Many of the men would pay for their indiscretions, but that would wait a few hours. Some napped where they sat.

The general satisfaction the women felt in presenting the meal was fleeting in the presence of these new people. They would be patient.

Chapter 4

During the morning meal, a palace guard interrupted Pohii.

The five ships were rounding God's Finger, but the light breezes made the journey to the channel much longer than the invaders wanted. His stance remained cautious, but he was less nervous. He summoned the warriors to stand ready.

Iliakahani walked down to the edge of the beach with her daughter. The guards were already there. The first prisoners were under guard in the compound.

Pohii sent for James and the interpreter. "What will the men on the ships do today?" he asked.

James turned and said, "Two more boats will come. The crewmen on the other ships will wait for word."

Pohii wasn't sure why the procession was so slow. "Why don't they all come now?" A war party would certainly do so.

"We have done this to be sure we are not all captured and killed, Majesty," James said.

Pohii was not confident about their intentions.

The ships stopped and dropped anchor. Sails were lowered, and all was quiet. Two boats entered the water and began coming to shore. The Warriors saw the weapons and instinctively got their spears ready.

"They must be told, James," Pohii said. "Tell them to come on the beach without weapons."

James ran down to water's edge and shouted, "No weapons. Beach the boats—but no weapons!" He shouted twice more as the sands stopped the boats.

James talked to the invaders and assured them that negotiations were good. They left the weapons in the boats, but a few of the men hid their daggers inside their britches.

James knew a few would not comply. They had been trained to protect themselves and their comrades, but two or three daggers against a hornet's nest of spears would be suicide and not bravery. "No weapons! If you have a blade, walk back to the boat. Leave it there—and don't let any of the warriors see it. Your life depends on it!"

He paused for a moment. Eighty spears were focused on them. As all eyes raced back and forth to grasp the moment, one man backed down to the boat in compliance. His naughty little secret was revealed. Three more men sheepishly returned to the boat.

Pohii saw the lies and called James.

Abbottsford stood by.

"Tell the four to return to the big ship as I watch. The others may stay," Pohii said.

"Yes, Majesty."

"No more men may come today. Tell them now."

James relayed the message and the warning. One of the boats with the offenders rowed back to sea.

"James!" Pohii said. "Do you know why you and your men are still alive?"

"Please tell me, Majesty," James said.

"I know you have the first foot of trust with me. I do not have it with you. That will come. The others on the ships—what will they do now?"

James knew any pause would be suspicious. "They will wait for us to return to the ships and then depart for other lands far away … if that is your wish, Majesty. I told them you are very patient and gracious with us, and you are alert and cautious of us. I told them I hope we haven't offended you at the first landing."

Pohii had hoped he would hear this to avoid all-out war, but he remained steadfastly vigilant. He was not convinced at all. "Tell me, your men with you here, what each one knows. Point them out to me."

James went to each man and carefully described what they did, their specialized knowledge, and how they fit in with the others. They smiled in ignorance of the true meaning of Pohii's request.

Pohii knew the value of introduction and how it established his own position. At times, Pohii would stop him for clarification from the translator. He politely acknowledged each of the twenty-six men in the lineup.

When James got to Ferdinand—a Catholic priest—he carefully described his role without mentioning the religion. He explained that Ferdinand kept spiritual order among the men.

Pohii made a mental note of Ferdinand as the sixteen remaining men were introduced. The newest invaders were escorted to the inland community. They would be kept separately from the first who had arrived three days earlier. The guards tended to the new invaders, and Pohii asked James to give them a briefing about the events he had already witnessed.

When the four offenders reached the ship, they tied the boats with the ropes flung down from the deck of the ship. When they climbed up to the deck, the first mate was waiting. "The captain wants to see you. Right now! The four of you!"

They reached the captain's door and reached for the knocker, but the door opened.

"Get in here, all of you. And shut the door!" the captain bellowed. He knew who he wanted to talk to first. He stood in front of his elaborate desk. Four other armed crewmen were in the room.

"Disarm them." The crewmen removed the weapons. "Claudio, what have you to say?"

"Captain, we returned to avoid beheading, sir," Claudio said.

"Beheading? Are you lying to me, Claudio? Tell me the truth now so that I am not the one to behead you this instant!" he roared.

Claudio's mouth opened and closed.

"Yes, Claudio. I know you well! Anyone else willing to lie to me?"

"How about you William? Will you be truthful?"

"Yes, Captain," William said.

"Then tell me what happened on the beach!" he roared.

"Captain, if I may?"

"Yes, Marcos," the captain said. His intensity could burn through the ship and the men's skin and bones.

"Um, yes, sir." Marcos swallowed and shuddered. "Just before we landed, we saw the large force of warriors on the beach. And when we landed, James Cristo ran up to us."

"James Cristo? Are you sure?"

"Yes, sir. He told us negotiations were going well—but send no more boats until he says," Marcos said.

The captain found himself absorbing the news about his nephew with a stinging dose of astonishment. He looked at the other crewmen. "Is that what he said?"

The four men nodded.

The captain was aware of the reputations of the four men. He thought the brig was the best option for them, but he knew they would betray themselves among the others as the most fitting punishment. "Dismissed!"

The door behind them was opened, and they swiftly exited. The door slammed shut.

"Damn it! Why is he waiting? He should have sent the message." The captain stroked his beard, turned to look at the island, and thought of his men on the island. He looked at the cabin floor, looked at the ceiling, and thought of the mission. He had yet to consider a rescue.

"We will wait." His decision was frustrating but final. It was the third time he had had to wait. What a miserable agony waiting was. He loathed waiting. There would not be a fourth.

The captain moved to the door and grasped the latch. After he had opened the door, he summoned the first mate. "Bring my glass to the aft deck." He climbed the steps to the highest deck on the ship, took a position away from the rigging, and accepted the instrument. He surveyed the waters to the island through the glass. The boats were still empty on the beach. He saw the guards posted along the beach. He could not see the warriors.

"Tell the men we will reposition the fleet farther north and closer to the island—but still out of range. We will do so as the sun sets."

The first mate left with the order and filled in the sailors.

He still had roughly two hours of daylight left and hoped the trade winds would allow for the maneuvering. The waters had no visible obstructions, but one of the sailors was called.

He was given the precious glass, climbed to the top of the rigging, and scanned for reefs and rocks between the ship and the islands. He returned to report a rocky coastline at the bottom of the sheer northern cliffs to port, but there were no visible obstructions along the broad beach on the island to starboard. He saw some flat rocks just after the north end of the island.

The captain accepted the essential glass, dismissed the first mate, and rested in his cabin.

Two hours later, the sunset occurred with its customary lack of twilight in the tropics. One moment the sky was bright as the sun touched the horizon. As soon as the sun slipped below it, the dark night sky replaced it.

The captain knew the quarter moon would be in sight in about half an hour. He ordered a sail for the center mainmast only. The anchor was raised, and the torches on deck were hushed.

Three lamps were lit in the captain's cabin, and the port window curtains were opened. The fleet saw the signals and obeyed.

Chapter 5

One of the guards stirred on the beach at dawn. The five ships had moved sometime overnight, and he ran as fast as he could to the palace. "Pohii, Pohii, the big canoes moved!" he said, gasping after the sprint.

The Warriors knew the guards had the duty to notify Pohii and had remained overnight in the brush along the beach. As the sun revealed them, they saw that the ships had moved in the open channel less than two miles to the north-northwest. The considerable movement had completely reset the challenge to the island.

Pohii's eyes widened as he heard the news. He walked quickly to the beach to see for himself. The palace guards, never out of his shadow, followed him.

Pohii stood on the beach in the palm shadows and watched the ships for several minutes. He momentarily shifted his gaze between Mokiki Island and the ships.

The flat seas and little wind allowed him to listen to the ships. The ships were gently rocking, and the rigging on the masts slapped in the morning sun. He saw men on deck on the nearest ship, but only one or two moved. There was no flurry of activity.

Iliakahani had quietly followed her husband and stood in the shadows of the trees. She focused on his analysis of the channel. She had seen him move his eyes to Mokiki and back to the ships—and she knew. *Oh, the power—oh, the spirit—of this moment.* Her energy flew. She absolutely knew it.

Iliakahani sensed her daughter's arrival. She stood calmly and felt the flow of the extraordinary moment. She wanted to acknowledge her daughter's presence, but the information was still coming. With new confidence in her own assessment of the view, she whispered, "What do you see, Ihilani?" Her words were filled with the warm love she was famous for.

Her eyes were wide, and her heart was open. With each breath, she inhaled the warm feelings. She turned to her daughter. She knew that the young women standing next to her had felt the first level in her own mind. She knew the difficulty it would pose to Ihilani. She stood in silence as her daughter joined her in the new joy, love, and trust between them. Iliakahani broadly smiled.

She felt Pohii's eyes on her and turned to look at him. His focus on her had a purpose, and he paused to enjoy her warm smile. He slowly walked toward her. The palace guards automatically followed at a respectful distance.

Pohii slowed his walk as he came to his wife. He knew she had seen something important. He saw it in her eyes before he wrapped his arms around her. In the caress, he whispered, "Tell me what you see, my wife."

"The time is right, my husband, and the blue came to me again." The words flowed within every part of her body.

Pohii felt it from her. He knew she was right, and he was accustomed to her helping with his decisions. "What did you see, my wife? The love?"

"The love and the blue made me see, my husband. I saw the power we all have on these islands—and the new power of the guests we have among us." She took a few breaths, and Pohii knew there was more.

She said, "The blue showed me one more unknown power. I have not been shown from where it comes, but it is now safe to discover it." She couldn't have used any other words as the blue faded. And it was gone.

Pohii had heard about her mysterious blue in previous conversations and accepted it in trust and her incredible love. He knew to wait before talking about it with her.

Iliakahani sighed with a deep cleansing breath. Her daughter had a thousand questions, but she didn't dare ask any right then. Even though it was warming and soothing to experience, she felt frightened by the event. She was far from understanding it, and couldn't shake it, not to mention the ships just off shore. She backed away and walked back into the jungle. When she was in the jungle shadows, she ran to her room in the palace.

She rested her head on the bed and reclined with her knees near her elbows.

Her two guards needed to recuperate after they fought to keep up with her. They knew not to allow anyone else to enter her room—with one exception.

Iliakahani knew where she went as Pohii whispered her retreat. She knew her daughter needed time, but she would talk to her. "I will go, my husband. I will walk slowly."

Pohii understood.

She released her hands from Pohii's and turned. Her head lowered slightly since she had so many questions. The slow walk to the palace allowed her to review the morning. She hoped the answers would come, but she knew they would appear at their own time.

Chapter 6

Mokiki lay silent in the distance as Iliakahani watched from the west balcony of the palace. It was her favorite view.

The steam had stopped. The flora began its recovery. The insects returned to routine. The birds returned from their retreat. The ambiance was restored. The streams flowed to the falls and then into the ocean. But all things were not the same.

The rock and ground mumbled in its natural progression. The elements and physical structure born of Mother Nature and tectonics had changed slightly. The totality, the very breath of the island, needed time. Many thousands of years ago, this island had been the first of the five to appear above the ocean in a torrent of activities.

The island's east coast with all its beauty as seen from Condonte belied its true size and scope. The frontier of the island stretched for forty miles to the west from its iconic vertical peak. Its coastline was laced with high cliffs for nearly its entire northern flank running in an almost perfect line westward. Its southern cliffs in a long crescent were dotted with rockfalls and waterfalls. The terrain attracted daily rainfall and cloud mist on the cliffs.

Near the western shore of the island, the second of the two peaks rose to a nearly perfect crown for the island. A cone of dark rock emerged from the jungle and stood like a grand guardian. The western end of the island completed the map with gently curved cliffs in dark red, sheer rock faces. The waves were always small and continuously lapped the shore.

The high interior remained unknown and unexplored. The single access route on the southeast shore could be seen from Condonte Island's western beaches.

Iliakahani had always heard that Mokiki was a forbidden place, but she couldn't shake the quandary of beauty she saw in the view versus the evil stories always heard about it. She thought she could see a small beach from the palace balcony, but she knew she would have to wait for a change she felt was coming.

She looked away once more as the preparations for the midday meal began. She had visited Ihilani and offered her hope and love, but she would have to learn the answers as her daughter did. She had asked her to join her, and they would progress together.

Ihilani responded with innocent love and felt the relief and purpose that comes with the spirit of volunteering. Her mother also felt the relief, but her desire to learn more from the blue remained high and endless. She thought she was receiving the signals from the mysterious island.

As her focus was about to turn, the blue slowly returned. She felt its slow rise. She stopped and waited.

The blue leveled off, but it revealed nothing new. The haze was definitely there, but its full power had not returned. Iliakahani wanted it; she knew the blue and loved it, but she waited. She was fully open to it and felt natural and innocent love.

It felt good, honest, and inspiring. For a moment, she felt part of the focused blue. It was as if there was a partial invitation. She felt comfort in the blue. Her expression changed from love and confidence to wonder and acceptance. Her euphoria was about to peak when the blue slowly faded. She would wait for its return.

Chapter 7

Pohii asked James Cristo and his translator to join him on the beach. "What is the truth of the men on the ships? Why have the ships moved?"

"Majesty, the captain wants me to send him a message," James said. He realized his failure to communicate with the captain. He had neglected his fundamental responsibility of keeping him informed every day. He was to send a signal even at the cost of his life.

The captain was watching with his glass.

"What message will you send him?" Pohii asked.

"The first message was to be that we are still alive," James said.

"You will send him the message now!" Pohii pointed at the ships.

James walked to the edge of the beach with two guards behind him. He took off his outer shirt to reveal an undershirt that had not seen a decent cleaning in quite some time. He waved the outer shirt three times over his head from left to right. After a moment, he repeated the signal. This went on until he saw a mirror reflecting from the ship's deck.

Pohii said, "Return to me."

James obeyed.

"What is the second message?" Pohii asked

"That you and I are speaking to each other," James said.

Pohii waited for the translation.

Abbottsford said, "That your Majesty speaks, and I speak with high respect." He thought the gravity of the moment needed the added humility.

"Send the second message," Pohii said. He had decided not to include the fact that he didn't fully trust him yet. He had heard the translation. He was not impressed with it.

Finally, the mirror acknowledged the message.

James stood in front of Pohii. The captain's anxiety had come down a bit as the signals were observed.

"Who are you sending the message to?" Pohii said. He knew who James had said he was sending it to.

"To the leader of that ship, Majesty," James said.

His patience ebbed. "How many leaders among your men?" Pohii's expression changed.

"Majesty, there is a leader on each ship," James said.

"Five leaders? And are you a leader?" Pohii said.

"I am the leader of the smallest ship, Majesty," James said.

Pohii thought about the past three days. He considered himself equal to the elders from the other islands. He sided with calm after a vicious battle in his mind between deception and half-truths versus snap decisions that could end countless lives on both sides.

Pohii took a breath and let it out. "Who is the leader of the signal ship?"

"His name is Captain Gregorio Cristo. He is my father's brother."

Pohii heard the translation and what it revealed. He felt Iliakahani's gaze on his back as she returned from the palace. He turned to her. She smiled, but her message was unclear to him.

"What do you know, my wife?" he asked.

"The time is good, my husband," she said. Her message intrigued him.

"I am ready. Are they ready?" Pohii asked.

"They are ready, my husband. Ask them to come," she said.

"You smile for them?" he asked.

"Yes," she said with her ever-present smile.

He felt an unexpected new love in her answer. As he gathered his thoughts, he felt for the first time that he was in grave doubt of the outcome.

Iliakahani extended her hands. He felt her boundless love, and he held her closely to mask the swelling of raw emotions. She knew the man she was caressing and the weight of his yet-to-be-announced words. She softly moved her hands up his back as her eyes delivered the message. "It is very good, my husband," she said. Slowly, his good mood returned.

He was ready. He stood and paused for a moment, taking in the forces, the passion, the power, and the fear. He walked, and his confidence increased with each step. If the tropical heat and sun's rays weren't enough, all on the beach breathlessly waited. "Tell the ship leader to come. Tell him he will return to his ship."

The beach felt otherworldly to his audience. They all turned to James Cristo.

"Yes, Majesty." His eyes widened. His expression turned from the deepest dread to an exhilarating smile not seen since before he landed on the island. With Pohii watching, James moved quickly to a boat. Two more followed. They looked back to Pohii.

He returned their hope with a slight grin and a nod.

They rowed feverishly to the ship.

Pohii watched, and the waters in the channel calmed him.

Iliakahani felt the most intense sense of peace.

Ihilani shivered in fear, her fingers covering her lips. *What is going on? How can he do this?* Her fear increased.

Kai had watched the whole thing in disbelief and disgust. His choices would have been different. He had to hide his feelings, which he had learned long ago and was very good at.

The boats bumped against the ship, and James tied them to the ropes. Their bodies were filled with adrenaline as they reached the railing.

They were escorted without ceremony to the captain's cabin. The door closed behind them.

"Why do we wait, James?" the captain asked. "Why do we do nothing for four days without word from you?"

"Captain, the people on these islands, are so new to us—so innocent, ignorant, and intriguing—I guess I got enthralled with them."

"Stop!" the captain said. "Tell me exactly what this has to do with our mission since you have laid distance from it."

James knew that there was something about the Islanders and the islands that would change the scope of the mission, but the words were not forming in his mind. "The leader of the island has asked me to extend an invitation to you," James said.

"An invitation? To what? A mass execution?"

"No, sir!" James said. "You alone are invited—"

"James! In God's name, why would you think I should consider setting foot on the island with this savage?"

"You alone are invited to celebrate our coming. Pohii wants to meet you!" James continued.

"Oh, God! You haven't told him why we are here, have you?"

"Our mission has changed, sir!"

"By what possible authority can you stand here and say that, James? Of all people, with all the planning, with our commitment to Her Royal Highness." He paused for an instant and folded his arms over his chest. "Tell me."

"Captain, Pohii could have killed my men and me at first landing, but he did not. He could have killed everyone in the second landing party, but he did not. He is curious about us. His people are interested in us. They are weakly armed, but they can fight hidden from view. Any armed landing with the intent to defeat them would require may more ships and weapons that we don't have. It would be suicide to invade here."

The captain thought about the testimony for several moments. "So, I am invited to speak to him?"

"You are invited, but he said you will return to this ship before the others," James said.

"I go, talk to him, and then return? What happens to the rest of our men on the island?"

"That would evolve from the meeting, Captain," James said.

"So I am invited to a meeting? I have the freedom to land and depart without capture only to leave you as prisoners? Why should I do that, James? Why shouldn't I just set sail now and cut my losses? Why shouldn't I order the men to stand ready at the cannons? Why shouldn't I demonstrate to the island the will of the queen?"

But there was another option.

The Blue had returned with its own authority.

The ship was noticeably moved by something very big.

The sailors ran to the rails but saw nothing. A second, more powerful bump was felt. This time, the wood throughout the ship sprang back to position. The stern of the ship was suddenly raised eight inches, sending the ship's crew to their knees. The masts and rigging swayed from the impact.

The men flew to their command positions without orders from the captain. The rippling moved away from the vessel and subsided. Then, with the size of the smallest ship, a boulder fell from the northeast cliffs of Mokiki into the channel. Its descent was witnessed as a crack of sound reached the ship.

The massive wave raced across the channel. Even as its size diminished, its persuasion was clear. The sailors held on tight as the wave violently presented the side of the ship with its powerful over wash on deck. The ship swayed to starboard, rocked back and forth, and returned to calm center. The fear was not lost as the crew dutifully looked for damage.

But there was no damage. The sailors' fears had peaked and remained so.

The ship had survived the warning.

Those on shore retreated as the wave reached the ship and were out of harm's way when the monster wave moved the rowboats fifty feet inland.

The first mate was called.

"Check the crew and report," the captain said.

The first mate returned and said, "All accounted for, Captain."

"Any injuries?"

"None, sir."

As the waves retreated into the channel, the sun's rays evaporated the moisture from the sands. A faint fog momentarily covered the scene and vanished.

Iliakahani knew. Oh, she knew. Her smile beamed. There was no need for convincing. She knew it. She loved it.

Pohii saw her and knew it was good.

Ihilani felt it. Even as terrifying as it was, she knew.

Kai felt the good for the first time, but he remained defiant.

And then the blue left again.

Chapter 8

The captain left instructions with the first mate, and he climbed down the rope ladder to the rowboat with James and two others. They rowed at a somewhat subdued pace to the shoreline as the captain's mind prepared for the meeting.

James cautioned him, and the others listened to the interaction.

The boat stopped on the beach, and the men stood together on the sand.

"Take off your hat, sir!" James said. He had noticed the bewilderment of the palace guards as they looked upon the captain and his elaborate hat.

The captain complied begrudgingly. "I see, James, the insignia has not been previously announced."

"He already knows to expect the leader in this meeting. Don't reinforce it, sir."

The hat was returned to the boat. Of all his hats, this one had long occupied a utilitarian role. He had chosen it for this unnecessary and pathetic excursion. He thought he could afford to lose it in the waves. He had purchased it before he was elevated in rank, and it had the least amount of meaning, which was only known only to him and his wife back home. All others had been presented to him by his superiors in the Armada and were not expendable.

"I may rely on your knowledge and sensitivity, James," he said.

James said, "Pohii will offer his hand first—not to shake but to show you no weapons. Then return the motion exactly."

They walked together to meet Pohii.

The captain recognized his sailors, and they paused to let Pohii speak first.

"Welcome," Pohii said with a smile. He felt the captain's odd unease. He felt the hope and fear from James and the dedication from Abbottsford.

Pohii slowly extended his hand in greeting.

Abbotsford fidgeted and instantly knew the greeting wasn't meant for him.

James grinned and extended his hand for inspection.

Pohii shifted to the captain, and the ceremony was repeated perfectly. The captain was secretly patting himself for his performance thus far.

Abbottsford waited as everyone judged each other.

Pohii summoned a guard and dispatched him.

The guard ran behind the other guards and returned with something he was hiding behind his back. He stood next to Pohii, and the other guards remained silent.

Iliakahani and her daughter stood well back from the circle of men. She felt the meaning of what was about to happen and smiled.

Her daughter felt her radiance.

Pohii grinned once more. "James, please ask our newest guest to come here to me."

Abbotsford flawlessly translated the command for the captain.

For the first time since landing, the total focus was on the captain. He had no idea what was about to happen. He was ready to accept his fate with dignity and honor.

James feared the worst as he looked at Pohii and his expressionless guards.

The guards' eyes shifted back to Pohii to hear an order. One guard obeyed and used his spear to present the captain with his hat. The spear slowly returned to vertical.

"Your headdress belongs on your head," Pohii said.

Abbottsford translated.

Pohii knew the meaning; he had watched them on the sand. He was aware that this man was the leader of all the ships. The captain placed his hat back on his head.

The respect between them was established from the start.

"Now we eat," Pohii said.

The women moved quickly and returned to the gardens in the palace grounds. They had the food ready for the meeting. All they needed to do was present it.

James and the captain realized one more signal would have to be sent to the ship, and they asked Abbotsford to translate that need.

Pohii watched as they were escorted to the shoreline and dispatched the two sailors back to the ship. He knew they talked about what had just happened, and he would wait to talk about it until the meal.

James and the captain turned away from the shoreline and walked back. Before they reached the circle, Pohii, and his palace guards started to walk to the palace.

James and the captain walked up the path until the palace came into view. They stood at the gate and realized the size and grandeur of the palace were truly extraordinary. It was not like anything they had seen before. The polished stonework was intricate and immense with a slight beige tone. There were subdued decorative touches in the inspired design. There was a curious absence of support columns of the west entrance and the balcony above it. The tapered lines to the left and right edges were not truly vertical, and the height left them breathless.

It was the first time any of the guests had seen the palace. The clean, expansive gardens reflected a culture they had just discovered and wanted to learn more about.

"James, why did you not tell me about this?" the captain said.

"This is my first time here, sir. I've never seen it until just now." James looked around at the spectacular monument.

"I cannot believe it. Such stunning beauty in this wilderness was built by such a primitive society as this?" the captain said.

A palace guard announced the meal.

Pohii's family and those of the ancestral council had been seated around the north garden's largest stone table. As Pohii was seated, the guards offered the last three on the opposite side to James, Abbotsford, and the captain.

The women started to bring the food. And what a feast it was. The meal was presented in a regimen as grand a dinner in Europe, the captain thought. He couldn't quite place it. England? Italy? Greece? Perhaps Portugal? Spring water was brought to the table in large, round stone cups. An array of fruit from pineapple to coconut was first and last in any meal. The succulent roots and vegetables steamed as they were placed on the table. The leaf-wrapped fish was baked to perfection and set on the table. The aroma of mild sweet pepper was deliciously intense.

By the fourth course, the light conversation and further inquiries ended. The last delicacy was brought in. The drink had an aroma that was new. Its dark brown, and deep red tones didn't reveal its content. It's bitter aftertaste lingered. It was explained that the drink was exclusive to the meals in the palace. Fruit completed the meal.

Pohii's attention moved to James and the captain. "Tell me—tell us all—why you have come."

"Our reason has changed, Majesty," James said as he looked at Pohii and the captain. "We are interested in trade, as I said, but now we see so much more here."

"What do you see, James?" Pohii said.

"We see how you and your family love each other. We see how much you love and respect these islands." He paused. "We see your ways. We see your achievements."

But Abbotsford had translated it differently. He translated *achievements* as *traditions*. He hoped he could stay on topic.

Pohii sensed a confused word from Abbotsford and raised his eyebrows. He looked to his left and saw his wife's smile.

She squeezed his hand.

"Say it again—with true words," Pohii said.

Abbotsford said, "Majesty, I use words you know. The words I use have the true feel of the words I hear from you. Yes, at times, I decide to use other words, but the feeling of the words are true."

Pohii looked at his wife. Her eyes were ready for him. He felt the message and turned to Abbotsford. "Yes, I have the words. Please continue." He had the distinct feeling he had heard a deception just before the explanation offered by the translator.

Iliakahani knew her husband would proceed cautiously. She gently squeezed his hand. She completely adored him. She knew the purest love is independent of agreement or disapproval.

James said, "Please let me say, Majesty, that we have a new respect for all who live on these islands. We know now that you have much to tell us—just as we have to tell you. We look forward to that."

Pohii saw the sun above the western sea. He wanted more, but with night coming soon, he reluctantly paused. "Captain, tomorrow I want to hear from you, but now, you return to your ship." Pohii rose and moved to the left as his wife followed. Their guards carefully followed. They entered the palace.

The captain was clearly dismayed by the sudden conclusion. He looked at James.

The guards escorted the captain to the compound below the palace grounds. They walked with the guards down to the beach.

The swift and efficient movements were done in primitive silence. They reached the beach, and one of the guards pointed to the ship. Four sailors on the ship had been waiting for the signal. They quickly returned his boat to shore. The unspoken order from the captain as he climbed into the boat was clearly understood, and the four sailors rowed back to the ship.

The captain, clearly appalled, was thinking he had never experienced anything like the island's primitive society or its leader's awkward diplomacy. He was reforming his opinion of the meeting and Pohii as the boat reached his ship. He had not seen James leave the table.

The captain returned to his cabin and thought about his options.

The morning light was accompanied by light rain. The weather front had arrived well before dawn. They wrapped the bottom of the sails to fill the rain barrels after tasting the rain several times. It was routine at sea, and they had orders not to leave the ship. Within an hour of sunrise, the barrels were nearly full. The clouds broke open in the eastern sky, and the sails were lowered.

The captain opened his cabin door, stood in the sunlight, and breathed the ocean air.

What was his fate in this godforsaken channel? Where was James? What ultimately would he tell the queen?

The island guards filed onto the beach with James centered among them.

The captain saw the assembly as it happened. Just in time, he thought. He would not act yet. His frustrations had not been addressed. The queen's expectations and generous funding had to be forefront in the mission.

James sent the signal to return to shore. *This time, I do the talking,* he thought.

The captain gave the orders, and the first mate acknowledged. The wretched boat was lowered. The indignity of it all! The captain of the fleet descending the rope ladder to this outpost of heathens who could have—and perhaps should have—remained undiscovered and left to rot. What were they hiding? For now, that would have to do.

The captain and his crew began the short trip to shore. He had the time to put the final touches on the speech he had composed in his mind overnight. He would explain his actual mission and the orders from the queen. He thought about the setting he found himself in. There were certain events whose timing benefited the Islanders. He noticed their general lack of concern about the developments on the third day as the weather grew worse. Having had to circumvent the southern fringe of a monsoon on his way to these islands, he had initially dismissed any connection.

The boats reached the halfway point.

The guards on the beach watched with the sun at their backs.

Pohii arrived with the interpreter, and they stood next to James. They would stand for several more minutes.

Iliakahani held her daughter's hand as they walked to the shadows in the palms. Iliakahani, in fact, was surveying the beach and the mood of her husband. As the captain's face came into her view, she knew something was very different about him. She would watch him.

The boat landed, and the guards went to escort them. The captain and his crewmen walked calmly to the center of the beach.

Pohii was aware of the captain's mood. "We walk," Pohii said. He was certain his bluntness and quick move were the proper way to begin the day. They walked quickly to the palace grounds.

James and Abbotsford were already there when Pohii entered the grounds.

The captain was escorted to the compound—where his crew was to remain—and then to the gardens. He noticed the palace guards on the balcony in the west facade. Upon reaching the north gardens, he saw more guards. He was offered a seat at the grand stone table. The women entered with food.

Pohii and his wife sat on the opposite side of the table. The nine elders were also seated. The food was brought in. James, Abbotsford, and the captain were taken aback as they absorbed the darker mood that began with the long silence of the Islanders across from them. They waited.

The captain noticed the absence of Pohii's children. He felt a sudden rush of doom. James and Abbotsford had come to that conclusion hours earlier.

Iliakahani knew that her husband had made another profound decision. Her warm presence offered a mild balance to the meeting. She smiled effortlessly. She had waited for the blue all morning, but it had not come to her. She missed it, but she knew the timing was random. She knew that what she had seen in the blue was all she could have ever hoped for. The blue was a friend for her. That familiar feeling was widely held by nearly all the islanders—with the possible exception of the lead elder from the easternmost island. His legendary loyalty to the spirits and the residents of his home island was in contrast to his doubts about Iliakahani's boundless and unbridled intuition, but he secretly loved her.

Pohii was about to finish the meal, and he looked into Iliakahani's eyes with a warmth he couldn't disguise. She returned a broad and confident smile. She knew her place, her role, and her commitment, but her love was most important. Recently she had witnessed the first fading and broadening of the horizon she had always thought that love itself was born with.

The spring water was refreshing, cooling, and calming. Pohii motioned to a guard and waited.

The guard returned with Kai and sat him at the table. His eyes moved to the guests across the table. His expression showed his complete loathing of the invaders.

"My people were surprised and afraid of your landing," Pohii said. "God saw you land. The elders heard of your landing. My children and other children ran to their parents. I heard my people's words from your mouth. I learned about you slowly. I learned that the man who heard our words did well. I learned that I will know you and begin to trust you. I wanted to learn the reason for your landing. I listened. I asked questions, and I heard your answers. There is one among all who landed here who we invited to come to the palace last night. He had troubles with my words—as I did with his. I learned your reason for landing. I know you want more than respect and that you are all following the wishes of your leader who lives far away."

Pohii wasn't quite comfortable with that thought. He didn't understand it the first time he heard it. The actual scope of the world outside of the islands was a mystery to him.

"Now my decision. I know you want us to serve your leader far away. I know you are here to defeat us." Pohii fixed his eyes on the captain. "I know your ships have new weapons. I have seen the weapons you carried to the beach." His eyes moved to James. He signaled a guard, and the guard walked to the palace. "I heard your thoughts of us have changed. I do not believe you. This I know. One among you has told me the truth. He alone may choose to remain with us or return to your ships with you. You must return to your ships and go."

The elder's nod of approval was distinct.

The invaders were stunned.

Chapter 9

The guard returned with the one man who had been truthful.

The captain's eyes revealed the disgust he felt as Ferdinand entered. Had he revealed the mission of his own will or was he coerced? Did the overnight interrogation he endured force a choice between loyalty and religion? Or was this treason?

"This man has told me the truth. This man may stay here or return to you," Pohii said. "This man knows you well and told me of your leader far away. This man fears you and your leader. This man loves God. What is your decision?" He looked at Ferdinand.

"My dear leader, Pohii," Ferdinand said. "My loyalty to my queen and to God has not changed." His slow, deliberate delivery was confident and respectful. "My choice is to return to the ship with my captain."

Pohii stopped him. "Captain," he said in the captain's own language.

Abbottsford waited nervously. His eyes widened, and the smiling admiration arrived.

Pohii returned to his native tongue. "Your priest is good to you. I think he is good to all."

"Tell us now, Captain. What are you to do with your priest when he returns to your ship?"

Abbottsford listened and carefully continued his translation.

The captain wasted no time. "We will return to the ships, and we will leave. The priest will continue his duty as before."

Pohii thought for a moment.

Iliakahani felt a shiver in her bones.

"Will he live long?" Pohii asked.

"That will be his decision while he is on the ship," the captain said.

Pohii was only partially satisfied with that answer. "And when your queen gets the word?"

The captain swallowed. He knew the Queen would not be impressed. She was known for her fierce demands, narrow vision for trade, and brutal expansionism. Her realm was vast, and taxes were slowing the fill of the Treasury. She had enemies in Europe and Asia.

The captain's fleet was one of many that were sent to find new territories and treasures. These small islands and meager resources were anything but glory, but there was one thing he knew about the islands, which would intrigue the queen.

He was not prepared to explain it with any clarity. It would take them months to return home. By then, they might find a more valuable territory to offer Her Majesty. His mind was flying as he answered Pohii.

The armed palace guards stood ready.

"As we sail for many months to return to the queen, we will wonder what she will say. I fear her decision would be his banishment at least—if not much worse," the captain said.

"Say your decision again," Pohii said, looking at Ferdinand.

"I have not changed my decision. I will sail and meet with Her Majesty. I know that is God's will."

The gardens were quiet. The skies were changing with the slow arrival of another weather front from the east. *The time is now*, Pohii thought. His concerns for his people and the islands had to come before his concerns for any of the invaders. "Then we will see you go. You will leave with our respect." Pohii knew he would be invaded again. Time had always been his friend and his worst fear. Pohii whispered to one of the palace guards, and the guard moved swiftly to the gate of the garden and the compound below. Pohii stood at the table. Kai stood.

"We go to the beach," Pohii said.

The captain and his men were escorted to the entrance of the gardens. They stopped there for several moments. They could hear movement in the compound below them. They waited. Another smaller movement was heard.

Finally, Pohii started walking to the beach.

The palace guards escorted the remainder of the invaders to the beach.

The elders followed behind.

Iliakahani waited in the garden, and Ihilani joined her as Kai watched the invaders leave.

Iliakahani didn't want to see them go. She had feelings for those lost souls as they left the garden. She knew her husband, and the elders were doing the right thing, but she ached. Her sorrow changed as the approaching front touched the eastern shore of the island.

The wind abruptly arrived with a chill. Ihilani grabbed her hand.

Iliakahani's brilliant smile returned in an instant.

Kai said, "I don't like the cold."

Ihilani repeated the thought with a mild shiver.

Iliakahani's smile was dominant, graceful, and loving. Her mind was anything but still. The blue's influence was back with a power she had never felt before. She followed the route to the beach as if directed by the blue alone. Her children followed close behind.

They arrived at the beach, and the invaders' evacuation had just begun. The boats were brought to the water, the captain directed his men, and the guards watched their every move.

Kai ran past his mother and sister and stood next to Pohii. The women offered the invaders a small amount of food.

The wind had picked up strength as the first boat's oars swatted the waves. The captain entered the boat, and orders flew. Ferdinand was last to board.

The last boat was still empty.

James looked back at Pohii and his son. He smiled, waved, and entered the boat. The last invaders took to the boat, heard the orders, and rowed in the direction of the smallest ship. Its masts were rocking from the wind. Sails were raised on the lead ship, and the others quickly followed.

A reflection from the captain's cabin windows as the ship turned gave the feeling of an end.

Kai felt the invaders were justly humiliated and were retreating as he looked into his father's eyes. War had been avoided.

The sails were straining in the wind, and the ships moved out to sea.

The Islanders watched as they sailed away.

The winds continued unabated until the ships vanished on the horizon.

Iliakahani's smile was brimming as the blue fed her mind in a new brilliance. The feelings were not of good-byes or good riddance but of new, well-focused peace and discovery.

Oh the wind, the feminine. It was so very good to feel its presence. The cool winds slowed as the rain began cleansing the island. The islanders returned to their homes and duties, but the Warriors would stay on alert for several days.

Pohii looked at his son and said, "We must watch the sea. We must watch for their return, my son."

The two of them walked calmly back to the palace.

Iliakahani saw the blue as more incredible information came. She felt almost powerless to sort the powerful information. She saw the ships passing less than two miles northeast of Mokiki. Something had fallen into the channel near one of the ships; she knew it.

"What is it, Mother?" Ihilani said.

"I must tell your father. Let's walk." She offered her hand, and Ihilani clasped her mother's hand as they calmly walked back to the palace. The blue was still present—renewed and energizing. She could feel it from all directions as the sun returned to the eastern shore of Condonte.

Pohii was talking to Kai in the western gardens as the two women reached the gate to the compound. The two women paused for a moment.

Pohii said, "I know your fear and hatred for the invaders. I know your reasons for war, my son. I have those reasons. I have lived them. I know how to fight. I know how to protect my family and these islands. I know life, and I have seen death. I have seen many families and friends die. I know you wanted me to execute the invaders. We listened to them, we fed them, and then we said good-bye to them. They survive, and we live. They will return, my son. They will return. We will be ready."

Kai said, "But we will die from their new weapons when they return. They will come back after talking with their leaders."

"Some of those new weapons are still in the compound, my son," Pohii said.

Kai felt a smile creeping across his face.

Iliakahani saw her son's smile and knew it was from his respect of his father's wisdom. Kai still had a deep hatred for those who dared to invade. If given a chance, he would have executed all of them as soon as they set foot on this sacred island.

She stepped into the gardens, and the men turned to see her.

Pohii waited as she came to him. She offered her embrace. Pohii couldn't resist.

Ihilani felt the warmth, but she couldn't hold back her tears.

They all felt the blessing that God had smiled upon them. The battle had been averted, and life was sustained.

Pohii knew the time was right for a celebration and gladly made the order. A welcome calm mixed with the exhilaration of victory came back to the islands in the third crescent moon of spring.

Preparations were well underway when Iliakahani and Pohii retired to their quarters in the palace.

"My dear husband, I saw the ships leave as you did. I know it is good."

"It does feel good, my wife," he said with a brief smile. "We are right to feel safe."

"I want to tell you of the blue and what it said to me. I want to tell you what I know now," Iliakahani said.

"What did it tell you?" he said.

"The blue showed me a new path. It showed me a new power we can discover. I saw you and Kai in the blue this time. It showed you together with God's guidance leading these islands."

"It showed Kai?" he said.

"Yes," she said. "He is ready to go with you."

"Where do we go?" he said.

"You must go together," she said.

"Where did you see us going?" he said.

"The blue showed me you and Kai on Mokiki with fear and then smiles," she said.

Pohii felt astonished by the prospect of setting foot on Mokiki. It had always been across the channel and just the right distance away.

Iliakahani saw his smile disappear.

"You must go, my husband—now that James and the others are gone," she said. "The island is ripe. It is good. It is new."

He stood with his mouth agape.

"There is a new power on Mokiki. It is a good power. It is waiting," she said.

"We eat first. Then we will talk about it more," Pohii said. Diverting the thought was all he could do. He knew the legends about Mokiki. He knew of the dark fears. How would Kai take it? He set the thought aside.

Iliakahani knew she would see it come. The urgency was clear to her. She knew her husband would have to take her news and slowly chew through it at tomorrow's feast.

The palace's massive walls gleamed in the hours before sunset. The family walked in through the formal west entrance. The stone steps on either side to the second and third levels were cool. The first floor was home to the ancestral council. The oval room was the largest in the palace. It had a grand courtyard entrance and high ceilings.

The elders announced a celebration to honor Pohii's leadership, and the community shared a massive feeling of unity and family. The real scope of the party was not revealed to Pohii's family. The three-day celebration from many years ago was still a fond memory.

They stood in the west entrance and thought about their home. The leader's family retired to their quarters on the third floor for the rest of the day.

After Pohii and Iliakahani had spoken to their children and grandchildren, they settled into the modest bedroom Pohii had chosen for himself and his wife. The balcony in the "all-island-families room" overlooked the west garden and was too big in his mind. It didn't fit his feeling of equality with others on the islands. His insistence on equality—regardless of a person's position or duty—was second only to his wisdom and integrity. His kind, fun-loving attitude, and position of duty joined with his uncanny ability to dismiss fear. His challenges were always accompanied by the unspoken vision he possessed. The elders were frequently exposed to his astonishing decisions and positive outcomes no one else foresaw. The respect and honor earned from his accomplishments were always accepted with a slight embarrassment he could not outgrow.

He said that God expected the right decision, and his people deserved it.

Iliakahani and Pohii had talked for several hours before they fell asleep, and all was quiet for the first time in a week.

Chapter 10

The sunrise was announced by drumbeats and singing on the northeast shore. The celebration had begun. The celebration was the largest seen in years. The smiles, energy, food, and anticipation increased with every inhalation of the aromas. The leaf-wrapped fish, fruit, roots and rare spices produced glorious smells that lasted long into the afternoon. The ceremonial torches were set ablaze.

With just one hour of daylight remaining, the drums announced the start to the festivities. The efforts of so many were coming along nicely. The elders had invited many citizens. The parade of people who sat even for just a few moments with their beloved leader was very special, and to be asked twice in a lifetime was exceptionally rare. The smiles and tears were something no one would forget for a long time.

Those who came to the celebration expressed their thanks and love for a job well done as they sat with Pohii. He made a point of tirelessly thanking each individual.

Ihilani and Kai were tired of the traditions but dutifully remained at their mother's gentle request. Iliakahani absolutely loved the celebration from start to finish. Before she was seated, she had reviewed her childhood, her adolescence, and her marriage. She felt truly blessed. Her mother and father always knew she had something special that she would discover. They would constantly tell her to find love, and it would come to her. As the guests exited the ceremony, she was able to see their admiration for her husband. She felt their unconditional love.

Two hours into the ceremony, the Pohii family stood. The elders guided them to the palace for a brief time. Then the family returned to the event.

The elders seated them once more. Iliakahani and her husband reflected upon the love they felt. He agreed that the love was high. It was important that the celebration brought the community closer together. His duty to the Islanders was among his first thoughts every day.

As the celebration ended, Iliakahani reminded her husband of the events she had witnessed on the western beach. She answered his questions about her impressions of the last four days as best she could.

He gently asked what she saw beyond what he had witnessed. "What is the new power on Mokiki?"

"I saw a power that is ready for us to discover. It isn't a new God, but there is high power. It's a good power. We must discover it. We know the legends, and we must be brave."

Pohii knew the resistance would be fierce—and the elders would stand against it. "I will talk to the elders about it tomorrow, but I want you with me. I will tell them after the celebration."

She hadn't seen such determination since his oratory in the ceremonial ring two days earlier. So much had happened since then. Her husband had just agreed to make the most important decision of his career. She would stand beside him as he spoke to the elders.

As the islanders returned to their homes for the evening, the elders were notified that Pohii wanted them to assemble in the ancestral council room. He gave an order to two palace guards.

The family returned to the palace, and Ihilani and Kai returned to their own quarters. Pohii and Iliakahani said good night to them and returned to the first floor.

The palace guards lit the torches in the courtyard as the elders arrived.

Iliakahani felt the inescapable power returning. The blue entered slowly and deliberately.

Pohii took her hand and walked into the council room. The elders' eyes were on her as she followed him. They sat on the long side of the table opposite the elders.

"Pohii, you called us. What will we hear?" said the first elder from Condonte Island.

"I have come to talk to you about our fears," he said with his natural confidence. "The fear is that we are threatened by invaders from far across the sea. The fears of legend. The fears of the unknown."

"We are listening, my leader," said the elder. "We know of the new threat from the sea. We believe they will return. They will have a long journey. We now know there are others."

"They will return," Pohii said. "They will come back with many more warriors. They have new and powerful weapons we do not have. We have some of their weapons at the compound. Their elder told me about more weapons, bigger weapons. Weapons on the ships." The elders were stunned.

"We could see an end if we do not act swiftly. I have said so to the citizens in the ceremonial ring, but we must talk. We must plan. We must meet our fears. We have two advantages. We have the benefit of time. We have time until they return—to prepare and add to our strengths and our will." He looked at his wife. "We have one more advantage," he said with a small smile. "We have the love for each other. We have a good life. We have our traditions. Each step we take, I will remember these two advantages."

Iliakahani felt the blue in a moderate glow. The warmth was relaxing and empowering. She was silent and respectful. She grasped her husband's hand. He looked at her and offered his calm, loving gaze.

"We can live beyond our fears. We can keep our traditions. If we find new traditions in our efforts, we can build upon them. Just as our ancestors long ago built this palace out of the unknown, we can search for and build out of the unknown. The only thing we need to do is to talk about and end our fears—slowly, one at a time."

Iliakahani beamed. She knew his words were shocking to the elders. They would have serious doubts.

"We will talk about this in council," the lead elder said. "We will need to talk about this carefully. We will not ignore God. We will listen to our leader. We will help you when we can. We must have faithful discussions."

The elders stood to signal the meeting conclusion. They would talk among themselves.

"We will talk again tomorrow," he said.

Pohii and Iliakahani left the room and returned to the courtyard. After a moment, they walked upstairs to their bedroom.

Iliakahani said, "What will you say tomorrow?" She knew the discovery was yet to be addressed.

Pohii knew that her question had much more behind it. "Yes, I will talk about discovery, my wife. They will be opposed to it because of legend and fear."

Iliakahani looked in his eyes. His answer had so much of the blue. Did he see the blue as she did?

"We will talk about the legends and the fears first," he said. "We will move slowly. We will wait for them. We will listen. When they know, we will tell them about the need for discovery."

Iliakahani felt that her husband had thought about it much longer than she had realized.

"Have you seen the blue, my husband?"

"I don't know, my wife. I have not seen the blue, but I think I have felt it. I know you see it now and in the council room. I think I feel it when you see it."

She knew his honesty. She knew he had felt it. She couldn't have wished more for him. She knew it had advanced for him. It was good.

"I love the blue, and my love for you, my husband, is so very good," she said.

On the bed, they looked at the ceiling. They sighed and fell asleep together.

Chapter 11

Iliakahani awakened and looked at her sleeping husband. She walked through the all-families room and onto the balcony. She watched the view to the west as it slowly changed with the rising sun. The beauty of these islands was revealed by the sunrise. It was her time. She loved to watch the start of the day. She would wait for her husband to wake. She had to tell him. She absolutely had to. She took in the fresh air, the hint of the ocean, and the flowering vines in the gardens. She heard the flocks of birds beginning their days. She cherished the morning calm and the slightly cool breezes.

She heard soft footfalls behind her and knew it was Ihilani.

"The morning is good," Ihilani said.

"My daughter, yes, the morning is good." Iliakahani offered her arms. The embrace of greetings was the most welcome.

Ihilani smiled. "I know there was a meeting with the elders. Can you tell me about it, Mother?"

Iliakahani thought it was time. She felt something new. She had dreamed about it. She needed to share it. She moved her hands to her daughter's shoulders. The blue was with her all night, and she felt it this morning. "Ihilani, we are going to see many changes with time. Those changes that come from fear will be hard. The changes that come from love will be easy. All the rest will surprise. The dream I had last night had a new love, a new power, a new fear. I trust it, but the words have not come. I love it, but my eyes could not quite see. I saw a new palace, I think, but I know not where. I saw big canoes that were going there. I saw a great storm there and felt the suffering." There was too much—the events came too fast. "Good will come here. It will be very good. That is what happened. Yesterday, your father told the elders what has happened and about the new days coming. I will tell him about the dream. Then he and I will meet with the elders again."

Ihilani didn't know where to begin.

Pohii walked out to the balcony and embraced them.

"The morning is good," Iliakahani said. They smiled as they embraced.

"Let's talk as we eat," he said.

They walked down to the west side of the courtyard. The first beams of the sun had begun to move down the wall. The morning meal was already on the family table on the first floor. Kai joined them.

The women in duty to the family returned to their own families.

Pohii always insisted that his wife was seated first, and he sat beside her. Ihilani sat at her mother's side. Kai sat next to his father.

"What will be said in the meeting today, my husband?" Iliakahani said.

"I will take the first step. I will talk about the first fear we must jump. I will talk about our first duty to each other. I will speak of the first plan we must do together. I must go slowly."

The conversation lasted for an hour.

A guard entered the room to announce that the elders had assembled in the council room.

Pohii sat for a moment longer to gather his thoughts. Ihilani and Kai knew it was time to begin their days.

Iliakahani looked on as her children left the room. She looked at her husband. "I saw the dream, my husband. I saw that this meeting will be good."

"Then we must meet with the elders," he said.

The ancestral council room had an elegant table, a high ceiling, and pristine walls that were lit by elevated torches. It was the most dynamic and beautiful room in the palace.

The spiritual center of the islands was occasionally open to the general population. The elders filed in with a traditional greeting to God and each other. The mild and warm feelings were present as Pohii and Iliakahani entered. Guards took their normal positions after the swearing-in tradition.

Pohii started with the background issues that were familiar to all islanders. The citizens knew the fears well. There was an agreement that each fear was justified in tradition. The elders knew this buildup would lead to a challenge to fear. They listened with skepticism and steadfast resistance.

Pohii's skill and adept oratory were a fear to many in the room. His well-known power of persuasion was precise and easy. Pohii mixed it with a sprinkling of love and diplomacy that made his work a success. He would not address more than one or two fears. More would come later.

He talked about the invasion as a fear of the unknown and unpredictable. He said that the fact that the invaders had departed without incident was temporary, and he felt they would return. He talked about the weather over Mokiki as a living fear.

He carefully crafted a plan for their survival. Showing their fears would be an advantage for the invaders. The concerns could be overcome with planning, preparation, and discovery.

Iliakahani knew what he was doing. He was preparing the elders for positive actions. He was convincing them. She felt good. It was confirmed in the blue. It was not easy to conceal her smile, but she did it. She knew it would betray the moment.

The elders listened carefully and independently. Although they knew Pohii very well and respected his guidance, they had skepticism, doubts, and scenarios that needed answers. They needed time to form one opinion among themselves. They needed to weigh each word and agree. How much time did they have? How much time would they need? The fears were identified and replaced by new fears.

Pohii knew a new set of rules, and unknowns would place them in a new quandary. He continued his persuasion out of duty, trust, and commitment to his new goals. They had no choice but to prepare for war. No amount of planning could spare them from war. They must plan and discover ways to meet the inevitable return of the invaders.

Time was an unknown element. It would dare the leadership to prepare and discover. The ultimate plan was to think of new ways to prepare, plan, and discover. They must do so with deliberate and careful speed.

Iliakahani heard his words and his goals. The elders had been exposed to the plan in its infancy. The blue had shown her that the next few days of meetings would rally them and focus the population. She saw it was very good. She fought back the tears of joy as her mind filled with the blue. She had no fear for the first time in her life. She wanted to say that she had seen it, but she dared not. It was too new and too joyous. They would not believe her.

The one thing she hadn't foreseen was the blue itself. It had penetrated the minds of everyone in the room. Like a shiver, it had entered every nerve. Some were experiencing it for the first time. She remained calm as she received the message from them.

Dear God! This is so very good, she thought.

"Now you know!" Pohii said. "Now you know what we must do. Now you know we must plan. Now you know we must prepare and discover." Pohii's astonishing words had come at just the right time.

Chapter 12

The meetings went on for several more days. As each session concluded, the elders graced Pohii with cheers and applause. Each thing had been laid out and agreed upon in step-by-step presentations, but the details of the plans were still vague. More and more citizens were briefed and invited to the meetings to spread the words of their beloved leader.

First, there would be extensive efforts to make spears and gather stones. They would collect leaves and make fire pits all over the island to prevent the entire island from burning. The scale of each project was enormous. The men did the preparations for war, and the women and children did the gathering of food and water.

Several groups made ropes, and others made wooden barricades. Torches were made and stored in caves. The tree sap for the torches was harvested into stone containers and hauled to strategic hiding places.

Thousands of darts were readied and set aside for dipping. Bamboo was harvested from the northeast jungle and set out on the beach to dry.

A trail up to the top of the southern cliffs was cleared for the lookouts. The views along the south coast were important. They provided the ships a hiding place just beyond the south side of the cliffs that could not be overlooked again.

Warrior training was ordered with emphasis on individual fitness and ferocious intensity.

The women and children were included in their own training. Everyone had to train and participate. The elders encouraged the citizens to voice their concerns along the way. There was no need to suppress, decree, or dictate.

A week into preparations, Pohii knew it was time to meet with the elders. He was aware that the focus could be lost without a real threat from the invaders. He was pleased that his people rose and were determined to survive.

The invaders had not returned, but they had to be ready. The preparations were going well, but there was more to be done that he had not told them about.

When it was time, he asked the elders to select eight of the bravest men from the islands to join them at the meeting. The elders would hear a major announcement, and the special guests would be assigned a special mission.

Kai had already volunteered. Pohii knew he was ready—no matter what the challenge.

Iliakahani couldn't wait. Her heart pounded as she entered the room with Pohii.

The guards performed the swearing-in protocols for all who entered. They sat around the table in the traditional way—first the elders and then Pohii and his wife. The others stood along the walls in the room. The guards remained in their positions.

The elders made room for Iliakahani at the table. Something about her presence helped them—even though she had never said a word in the council room.

The lead elder rose. "We are here now to listen to our leader. We know there is a mission. Please speak of the mission."

Pohii waited for the elder to be seated and then rose. "We saw the ships in the sea. We saw a storm come to Mokiki. We saw what the storm did. We saw God protect us. I know that God has come to Mokiki. He showed lightning, fire, and steam to warn the invaders. He told them to leave. He told us how to make them go. He told us he loves us. We all saw. We saw it together."

The elders wanted to believe. The traditional view was that Mokiki was the forbidden home of the devil, and it was not resolved. The first crack in the granite belief had just been thrust upon them and did not show any signs of crumbling. They were speechless.

Pohii continued his assault on the fear. "We all know that God has helped us. God has seen the devil and pushed him back out to sea. We all saw how he did it. God is powerful. God knows what to say. God knows how to help us when we don't know what to do. We know we are living in the hand of God. God spoke to us." Pohii raised his left hand and pointed to his palm. "We all know the thumb of your left hand is God's Finger. We all know it well. It sits at the end of the cliffs on the western beach."

He gestured to his palm again. "The space between the fingers is the channel between the islands. The palm connects the islands as one people. God's hand is grand indeed. Mokiki is God's home now. He has taken it from the devil and sent him far out to sea. We saw it happen. We know it."

The elders listened with courtesy and disbelief. The traditional evil stories still burned into their minds. It was going to take some time to change.

"Now we go to Mokiki to thank God for his guidance, his help, and his wisdom. We go to return our love for God." It wasn't easy to say, but Pohii had to say it. It was true.

The eight brave volunteers knew what the mission was. The elders were considering the revelations and the new plan. They remained uncommitted to the changes they had just heard.

"I too will go," Pohii said with all the confidence he could muster.

The elders were shocked. One of the elders raised his hand to speak. That protocol was the highest of all they had agreed to long ago with the formation of the ancestral council. The graceful transition between them occurred without objection.

"My dear leader, you have visited all the islands but one in your duties. I am not ready for you to go to Mokiki. The people are not ready. I see you want to go. The people on these islands don't want you to go to Mokiki. I cannot send you unless the people know it is good."

The elder from the northern island was right. Pohii, Kai, and the eight other brave men felt the good.

"I believe you when you say that God is good. Our traditions tell us so. I believe you when you say the invaders saw—as we saw. I don't think the people see it the same way."

Pohii raised his hand. "For everyone in this room, we must all tell them. We must thank God that we survive with his hand upon us. I thank God here, and I will thank him on Mokiki. I must go to Mokiki." The decision was absolute. It was final.

Iliakahani was beaming. The blue was luminous and glorious. It was filling her heart. She knew the elder had been correct.

Their support and understanding were crucial—even if it meant an extended commitment to campaigning for it. It would take some time, but she knew it was very good.

Everyone in the council room agreed. They would talk to their families and neighbors. They would tell them that the elders knew that God had come to Mokiki. They had seen it with the lightning, fire, and steam. That event protected them from the invaders and convinced them to leave the islands. Their leader would go to Mokiki to thank God personally.

A vast majority cast their support for the mission within a week. The elders also voiced concern for Pohii.

Iliakahani had seen the sign and seen the evolution. She told all the women in the palace that the elders knew Mokiki was much better than they had ever thought.

The day had come. The canoes were ready. The women packed food for a little more than four days, even though the mission was planned for three days. The men had prepared themselves with prayers and convictions. The elders blessed them with a special high ceremony.

The canoes had the capacity for six men, but only four were assigned to each one. They divided the food packs for the excursion. The prepared food rested in the hull at the third position.

The canoes carried the men's spears and some of the captured long knives. Each canoe had one open seat to express the belief that a spirit rowed with them.

After the ceremonies, the men stood with their families on the western beach. The elders bestowed the traditional high prayer of good will upon them.

The men walked out into the sea and entered the canoes. The winds were calm, and the morning sun was at their backs. The men dug into the sea with their paddles.

Iliakahani and Ihilani stood on the beach and watched the canoes disappear from sight.

Ihilani had the greatest of all fear: that the men had only a small chance of returning.

Iliakahani had no such fear. Her tears of joy were filled with the respect she had for both of her men and the current that flowed through her nerves. She knew that the most challenging of all fears had just been crushed by both of them, and she couldn't have felt prouder. The blue was constant as she watched them.

Iliakahani waited for hours. She knew they would be safe and would land, but she waited for the signal. In the third hour, she was relieved to see smoke rising from a fire on Mokiki. She knew Pohii would light it himself; it was just his way of saying he loved her.

Chapter 13

Mokiki was much larger than Pohii had ever imagined. The peak was much grander and beautiful. It felt spiritual and invigorating. He could see the inspiration it evoked, and he felt no fear.

What could this steep mountain, this island, and this place reveal?

The small fire's purpose was ended with a dousing of seawater.

The men moved the canoes to the high crest of the tide. They unloaded the provisions, gathered palm fronds to build a shelter for the evening, and built a fire ring. They began to prepare their first meal on the island and settle in.

One of the men said that he felt the eyes of God were looking over them. Several of the men took note of the changes to their own beliefs. The fear was gone. A new reverence was easing in. They felt that Pohii was right in saying that God had come to Mokiki. They were relieved that it was true. They knew something more would be found on the island.

Pohii and Kai talked with the volunteers after the meal. The conversation included discussions about the remarkable calm they felt. The winds were heard atop the island, but the beach breeze was almost nonexistent. The sun was brilliant and intense on their skin. It was warmer and more humid than their home island. Their energy returned much more quickly—even in the heat.

Pohii and his son saw a faint white haze. For Pohii, it was mixed with a slight light blue. For his son, it was entirely white. Even in the glare of the sun, they both noticed it.

It reminded Pohii of conversations with his wife. He grabbed hold of his son's arm and whispered, "So it *is* here."

Kai said, "What is here, Father?"

"The blue. It is here. I can see it!" It had entered very slowly, very calmly as if by design.

"My sight is a very bright white, Father. I don't see blue." The hue was changing for Kai. It left him slowly.

They stood together and felt the first traces of power and calm from it. They hadn't noticed anyone else during its appearance, but three others also saw it for the first time.

Ihilani found her mother by the railing of the west balcony. Iliakahani was sobbing.

"What is wrong, Mother?" she asked.

"Oh, Ihilani!" She turned to her daughter. "I am so very happy. Your father is safe, and he has seen the blue. Kai is safe and has seen it too."

Ihilani wrapped her arms around her mother. "What is the blue, Mother?"

"I see the blue when it comes. I am not seeing it just now, but I did see it. It showed me they are safely on the island, and I saw the blue come to your father." Her tears subsided. She felt her strength return.

"So that's what I saw!" Ihilani said. "But, Mother, it wasn't blue. It was white. It was very bright, and it almost filled my sight—like a dream when I am awake."

Iliakahani embraced her daughter with the strength of revelation, pure love, and exhilaration. "I am so happy. Ihilani, it is so good that you have seen it. I can finally talk to you about it. There is so much to tell you. There is so much you will see. You will feel so much love. I can't wait for us to see the blue together."

They talked about the blue for hours. Their excitement grew into a new bond they would cherish together.

The men talked quietly and enjoyed a meal in the afternoon sun. They had planned for the exploration of the island well before the crossing.

As they reviewed the plan, several branches cracked in the jungle behind them.

They waited for several minutes with frayed nerves. Then the calm returned.

As the meal concluded and the shelters were started, Pohii talked about the haze they had seen.

Kai asked why he saw it there and not on Condonte Island.

"The first time it came to me, I didn't see it. I felt it. And when I felt it again, it was stronger. Your mother feels it and sees it, and she has for a long time."

"She has?" Kai said. His mind swirled with thoughts. His mother had not discussed it with anyone, but her reactions were always filled with extraordinary insight. She always claimed that love was her guidance, but now he knew she was carrying these facts in secret.

"Yes, my son. She has talked to me about it a few times—softly at first—but she doesn't always see or feel it. She says it comes when something important is happening or when something is about to happen. But only rarely has she told me about anything that *will* happen."

They heard a muted sound in the valley behind them. It was getting closer. The motions seemed overly cautious. The movement slowed as it got closer. The sounds increased, and the pauses between them also increased.

They stood at attention, with spears ready, as the blue subsided. The blue followed them even as the unknown was confronting them.

A figure in the shadows stopped, observing them.

Is this God? Kai felt incapable of moving in the close-range presence of God.

Pohii put a protecting arm across his son's chest as the figure moved in the shadows.

Silence.

The figure moved again, and the men gasped.

A pale, thin man with a beard walked into the sunlight and stopped. He elevated his arms in a welcoming fashion and said, "Pohii!"

Pohii didn't recognize the man at first and said nothing. He was torn between God knowing who he was and something else he could not have foreseen.

"Pohii, I am so glad you are here!"

Pohii recognized the voice. *How can this be?* "Ferdinand?"

"Yes, Majesty!" He walked toward them with outstretched arms and collapsed in front of them.

Pohii and Kai raised him, offering him food and water. His legs were frail, but he was acutely aware of the rescue. The men found a new and unexpected aura from him.

The blue was back.

Pohii knew that Ferdinand's presence on the island was so much more than an unanticipated advantage. That thought surged and peaked. The blue had just centered. He had just felt the blue's first level. Pohii knew they had to stay on the beach while Ferdinand recovered. "We will stay here today. Tomorrow, we meet God," Pohii said.

They talked about their plans as they prepared the final meal of the day. The women had made the meal of berries and roots and dried fish. It tasted very good, but it also offered life-renewing sustenance to the one invader they had trusted.

"Thank you, Majesty. You've arrived at just the right time," Ferdinand said.

"Thank you, for being here for us, my priest," Pohii said.

The rest of the men saw his welcome to the population as graceful and humbling. Kai knew it was an advantage for Ferdinand to be on the island with them. He saw the blue as its hue changed from bright white. Its flow turned from a small invasion to full freedom. He didn't feel he was accepting it. He was allowing it to enter without objection.

The blue was doing much more. It was always doing more.

One of the brave volunteers came forward. Koiku had been watching Pohii, Kai, and Ferdinand. "Pohii, I can now see white light. It is good here." His courage to speak to the leaders about the blue was a testament to his own honest life back on Ohluku Island. As a father of five and a son of one of the elders, volunteering was automatic. So many things in his life seemed automatic, but they weren't as essential as doing the right thing without a definition.

Kai said, "Yes, it is good. How have you seen the white?" He wanted to hear about Koiku's experience—and anyone else who might have seen it.

Koiku said, "The white is changing for me. So much is here. And it is all good. I want to be here so badly—for my family and us."

"I am honored by all of you," Pohii said. "We know what we must do here for our families." Now that the blue was out in the open, it was okay to talk about it.

Ferdinand said, "The blue comes when I see the good, but it doesn't always come. And the blue doesn't come when I see the bad." For him, the blue was a very centered natural blue without other hues. He knew it was evolving for him. It was only a week or two old for him.

Pohii and Kai were preparing for the evening meal as the shadows slowly covered the beach. The men made a fire in the ring in the sand and readied the shelters.

Just after sunset, the quarter moon rose over Condonte.

And the men fell asleep.

Pohii stirred as dawn arrived. Only one other person was awake.

Ferdinand was deep in thought as his lips mouthed the morning prayers. Reverence for God was much more than a secular requirement to him. His faith had saved him. He gave thanks to God for sparing him from meeting the dark angel.

He prayed for the men and asked God to watch over them and keep them safe. He knew they had other beliefs—and they had an unnamed God that had apparently served them quite well. He would not risk trying to convert them to Catholicism. He would use his faith, education, and spiritual guidance as they needed it. He would wait for them to ask his opinion or offer answers to their questions.

His education crossed many international borders and natural barriers in Europe. His early education in Spain was followed by the seminary in Italy. He had a two-year commitment in France and numerous pilgrimages to Rome. Along with his constant learning of the faith, he had many interests in the sciences and arts. Math, engineering, and architecture mixed with a small dose of medicine. His mind was in a constant search for the next improvement in all those fields, but adventure grabbed him by his feet and dragged him in.

The discovery of new lands across the open Atlantic intrigued him. He had sailed to the Azores and the Canary Islands for the bishop. With his encouragement, he would take the next step with a rumored mission for the queen.

At thirty-three years old, Ferdinand's physical stamina was truly challenged by the verdict aboard the captain's ship.

The captain had declared him treasonous. Ferdinand knew he had to act quickly and flung himself overboard.

When his head came up for air, the lead ship was well beyond rescue. One of the ships cruised by within feet of his head as the fleet continued in the winds. He saw Mokiki and began his escape with a slow, deliberate swim. To his surprise and great relief, he made it to the rocks.

He raised himself to one of the rocks where he could recover away from the waves. Three hours later, he felt a little better and moved over the rocky shoreline to the beach. He rested in the shadow of the palms. The blue had come to him for the third time. He had felt it on Condonte twice before.

He thought God was calling him, and he gladly accepted the feeling. Then it brightened and calmed him.

On the second day, his search for berries and fruit in the valley kept him from absolute starvation. His story of survival was incredible and inspiring to the men around him. They had a mutual understanding of a limited number of words in each other's languages. Even though the words he used were still foreign to them, they welcomed each one.

The blue was making it easy in the calm.

Ferdinand walked out of the shelter. His overnight dream was still fresh and nurturing. The fire in the sandpit had burned itself out, but the embers were still warm. He could barely make out the smoke from them. He turned to look at the valley and the mountain behind him. Just as the first beams of sunlight reached the top of the peak, he saw its glow. The dream had come true. He would have to take them there.

Pohii stood out from the shelter, and Kai soon followed. The other men exited their shelters and brought wood for the fire. The morning meal was soon ready, and they consumed it during the conversation.

"We now go to see God," Pohii said. As the men assembled, Pohii noticed that his pains were absent for the first time in two weeks. He felt energized. He wasn't alone.

All of them felt the energy rush. As Ferdinand stood, his recovery felt astonishing. The energy they felt didn't reveal the stamina required for their first day of real exploration.

Ferdinand pointed the way. The men carried their confiscated long knives into the valley. The deliberately moderate pace, although frustrating at times, was needed for the bare feet of the islanders. As they inched their way up through the valley jungle, snapping twigs and limbs along the way, they knew they could do it. They climbed five hundred feet to the escarpment behind the peak. With nearly every step, they convinced themselves that they were meeting God. They felt the presence as they crept ever nearer. They wanted it. They could feel it. It was very good.

The energy was increased with each step. The approach leveled off slightly as they neared the escarpment, but they were nearing exhaustion.

Chapter 14

Kai felt the increase of energy as the men neared the top of the valley. The clouds cooled the men as they assembled and recovered in a small clearing at the base of the peak.

"I have something to show you," Ferdinand said. He turned and walked, and the rest of the men followed with enthusiasm. The footpath followed the mountain's contours until they reached an intersection.

Pohii noticed the footpath had been cared for.

Ferdinand said, "We will take the path to the left and return here."

The men moved slowly and carefully along the path, which descended thirty feet below the intersection before it leveled off and continued in an arc. There was a hip-high wall on both sides of the foggy path.

Pohii peered over the side and watched the fog race down into the valley as they walked along the path. His focus on thanking God was mixed with countless questions. They reached the far side of the path, and it ended at a sheer vertical wall. On the right, an unusual rock rose at least twenty-five feet. The rounded column at its base tapered up to a blunt point at the top.

Koiku said that the path circled the rock, and he walked up to the large boulder. He touched it, and it was moist and cool. He walked around to the other side. As he walked, he took note of several symbols carved on the sheer wall beyond the curious rock.

Three of the symbols were larger than the others. Koiku wondered what they meant. He stopped for a moment behind the rock and tried to figure out the symbols. He moved beyond the halfway point in the path as the first break in the fog began. When the fog finally retreated, the sun revealed a flat meadow.

Koiku stopped. "Pohii, what is it here?" His nerves were taking over as Pohii appeared.

"What is it, Koiku?" Pohii stopped next to Koiku at the wall. The fog continued to withdraw as they stood there.

"What is this place?" Koiku asked.

The sun, still behind the mountain, beamed on either side of the truly grand spire. Two thousand feet above them, the peak seemed as if it disappeared into heaven.

Pohii was convinced more than ever that God was there. The sunbeams rising up behind the mountain were beautiful.

"God is coming," Pohii whispered.

The Blue had returned and amplified the whisper. Koiku and three others heard him.

Kai heard it and wanted to believe. The contagion moved swiftly, and all but one believed.

Ferdinand felt the moment but hesitated. His own religion was still irresistible, but the relentless blue was filling him. His struggle was far from over. His commitment to his Savior was still paramount to him—even though the blue offered a new, incredible experience. He had never felt it before. He knew love, but the blue was so pure.

Pohii moved from behind the large boulder and returned to the group.

Koiku's foot landed on a sharp pebble in the shadow of the boulder. The temporary pain caused him to shift his weight. He slapped the boulder to maintain balance, but he fell to the ground. He landed on his back and felt a mild vibration along his back. His instinct told him to wait and assess the situation before moving. He moved his hands to his stomach and raised his knee. He noticed three squares of rock in the shadows below the boulder. He shaded his eyes from the glare of the sun and saw that the stones had some sort of symbol carved into them. Indeed, the inlay was different on each one. Had he seen the same symbols just a moment before? "Pohii, what is this? Look down here—and these rocks." Koiku dusted himself off, rose to his knees, and pointed to the first stone.

Pohii placed his hand on the huge boulder. Almost effortlessly, he turned it slightly. He withdrew his hand instinctively. The sudden movement caused Koiku to raise himself abruptly. In doing so, he stubbed his toe on one of the rocks.

The vibration increased, and they all heard it. The sound of rushing water within the wall below their feet was unsettling. It stopped, and the large boulder returned to its original position.

Ferdinand was still in the blue—even as the others lost it. He knew the answers to their questions, but he waited. He waited in the blue, the awesome blue. "Come now. We return to the other side," his said with a broad smile.

Pohii and Koiku felt something familiar, something right. They had seen it before. Pohii knew where he had seen it. Ferdinand had been there at the Palace on the last day. He had enjoyed Iliakahani's smile.

Ihilani saw it, and her mother beamed her famous smile on the palace balcony. "Mother, I see them!"

It was so much more than seeing them. There seemed to be a new understanding among the men. The powerful images were coming quickly as if she were there with them. The progression within the blue was a surprise to her. The men were still behind the mountain, and it no longer seemed to matter that they were in her line of sight. The pure images were beautiful and in full motion.

The facts were now clear. Iliakahani saw a thin man with a beard, but she didn't recognize him. There was something familiar about him—something new and something old. The ten other men were following him and talking to him. Pohii and Kai were following him, talking to him, and learning from him.

Ihilani said, "Mother, are you all right?" A chill replaced her calm.

They stood on the west balcony and watched the developments unfold.

"They are entering the masculine where there is no feminine," she said softly, breathlessly. She was not sure what the blue was revealing to her. It was still coming. It was still the familiar blue. The masculine and feminine had been brought to her in all her experiences with the blue. This time, the feminine was fading as the masculine was building.

She didn't understand, but blue's intensity was rising. She couldn't let go of it—even if she had made a considerable effort.

The men reached the end of the path and climbed back to the intersection. They couldn't help but look up at the mountain. They paused for a moment to assemble, and Ferdinand pointed to the wall below. Now that the fog had temporarily cleared, they were able to see the wall.

"Majesty, what do you see?" Ferdinand asked.

The Blue had returned, surrounding them.

Pohii said, "A flat trail with a small wall on both sides. On one side, it sits at the top of a cliff. On the other, there is a wet jungle floor. I see trees along the steep slopes on the far side of the jungle floor."

Ferdinand nodded and smiled broadly, but he knew differently. His education in Europe told him what it was, but it wasn't time for explanations. "Thank you, Majesty. Let's move along the trail." Ferdinand smiled.

The other men encased in the blue turned and walked with him. Pohii had some new questions, but he wasn't sure why. He had answered Ferdinand's question about the view, but there was something about it that needed further exploring.

The meeting with God was more important.

Their movement slowed as the trail curved along the base of the mountain. After several minutes, they arrived at a clearing.

A white stone monument stood before them. It was serene in its nearly untouched appearance. The men froze in awe. Twelve steps surrounded it. A wide raised platform surface, in a perfect circle, protected by a round stone canopy from the rain. Twelve columns supported it.

The feeling of grandeur, stateliness, and purity overwhelmed them.

Ferdinand had seen it four days ago and still had no idea what it was, who may have built it, or how long it had been here. He had walked up the stairs and placed his hands on the cool stone. He wondered how the others would react. He was still contemplating its effect on him. He couldn't arrive at any logical conclusions, and that frightened him the first time he saw it. Ferdinand signaled them with a wave, and they followed. They didn't say a word.

Pohii stopped. "Is this the entrance?"

"No, Majesty. It is something else," Ferdinand said.

"What is it?" Pohii said.

"Come see it, Majesty. There is much more to see. I do not know it myself even though I have seen it before."

As they approached the first step, the perspective loomed larger. The monument was increasing in size with each step they took.

Pohii stopped and waited. A light breeze on his back calmed him for a moment.

Kai moved closer to Pohii. The men stopped with him.

"What is it?" Pohii asked.

"I know not," Ferdinand said. "But, Majesty, come with me to the top of the stairs." His hands motioned the invitation.

The two of them moved together, and the other men waited behind.

As they reached the first step, a sensation on their very skin stopped them. They smelled just a hint of sulfur. Pohii wanted to abandon any further exploration, but Ferdinand motioned for him to follow.

Ferdinand was first to reach the first of the twelve steps. Time was slowing down in his mind. Each step up was more laborious than the previous one. He had been there once before and felt no such sensation.

Pohii felt the strain and stopped on the eighth step. They knew to take it slowly. They felt light-headed.

"What is it?' Pohii whispered.

"Come and see," Ferdinand said with a friendly smile.

The last four steps were grueling. Pohii began to feel exhaustion in every muscle and ligament.

Ferdinand was nearing the absolute end of his strength.

When they reached the raised surface, Pohii saw that it was a wall with a darkened interior. He stopped and looked at Ferdinand, who was already returning a slight and friendly smile.

Pohii was intrigued. Ferdinand cautioned him; his own curiosity had almost cost him his life on several occasions. He had seen the monument and had yet to understand its real purpose.

The monument's bright exterior, dark interior, and boundary wall created a perfect circle. The sixteen-foot diameter and its perfectly smooth top casement further complicated his assessment of its true purpose. Exhaustion was reducing their ability to experience the monument.

Pohii was hungry to give his thanks to God and grew weary of the need to find out what it was. His curiosity faded.

The blue took things to a new spiritual level with a faint glow from deep down within the monument. A new element entered. The new sounds were building from what they thought was the wind, and vibrations accompanied them. It was building and intensifying. The glow was moving closer.

Then silence. Darkness.

The two men stood in the shadows, shaking. The monument was murmuring, and the sensations were slowly decreasing. A balance had been reached as the tensions eased.

"Ferdinand?" Pohii asked. "What is this? And why do we stay here?"

"It is part of what I saw. I don't know its true meaning, but I feel it is important to see." Ferdinand tried to peer down into the opening.

The vibrations returned. A rush of air came up the chamber—followed by a bright flash and a nauseating odor. The birds took flight, and both men ran down the steps to the other men.

Flames briefly flew from the canopy and dissipated with a loud rumble.

The men were sprawled on the ground. They couldn't have been more afraid of proceeding with the dream of meeting God.

Ferdinand stood and offered a hand to Pohii. The other men slowly rose too. Ferdinand knew that the men needed a spiritual return to normal, and his training in scripture helped him. "God is power. God is grace. God is good. God has just shown us his power. God knows we are here. He will welcome us in his grace. He will show us what the good is. He will see that we are humble, that we love him, and that we want to live our lives in his love."

Pohii and the others were staring at Ferdinand. They heard the words, but the understanding was not present.

Ferdinand realized they had never heard some of the words he had just used. He smiled. He moved his right hand over his heart. "God loves us. God wants us to come."

The calm was inching back.

The Blue returned with a force they had not felt before. The effect was most welcome, and the power was intense. They felt calm and refreshed.

The ease, calming, and centering was coming so fast. It felt as though it had been there for centuries.

Iliakahani wept openly, and Ihilani couldn't contain her tears. The good had become the most important feeling they shared together, but its broad focus was so new and genuine. It was something they did not understand. The totality of it all was so consuming and honest. They couldn't sort it all out. They both felt that the experience would take a long time to completely absorb and understand. They loved it, but they didn't know why.

"Mother, this is so good—and it is so much!"

"Yes, my daughter," Iliakahani said through her own tears. "I cry best when I see good in the blue, but this is the biggest I've seen so far."

Her feelings about her past were slowly fading as the blue virtually swept them aside: her mixed emotions about the founding of the Council of Elders, her grief when her mother passed away, and her pain in the war with other islanders. She touched the scar on her left arm. She had only recently noticed the reminder of violence. Then she noticed it for the first time, she felt no pain. There was no pain to overcome. The scar remained as the only memory of those truly dark days.

Ihilani said, "Oh, Mother. It's so beautiful."

"And there is more," Iliakahani said as a breeze swelled around them. The timing couldn't have been better.

The blue for the women—and for the men on the distant island—began to fade.

Iliakahani was getting a new impression about what she was learning. She would have to think about it and absorb it. She looked at her daughter and said, "Ihilani, I think I know what the blue is teaching us. I know this good. I have seen it before. It has become important. I know that I believe it. There is more—so much more. This is good, but it has just started."

Ihilani was dumbfounded. "Is it God talking to us, Mother?"

"I don't hear words, my daughter, only strong feelings. They come to my eyes, and I feel it in my head and body."

"That's what I know too, Mother!" Ihilani said.

"It's not just us," Iliakahani said. "I feel ... no ... I know that many others have seen what we know. What we have just seen. Oh, God. Thank you. I know this is so big and so good."

The powerful message was still coming. It formed a gap in her mind. The boundary of good had just crossed beyond the ocean's own horizon, and she couldn't see it in her mind. The shore of the island and its physical impression of a border were no longer valid in her thoughts. Everything she saw or recalled in her dreams came into question. Had she lived with common borders all this time? Were they less important now? Did they have any true meaning? What about this community and its boundaries?

A million questions and impressions were racing and shocking her.

The blue intensified—to the point of burning.

She froze as images came to her with incredible speed. She was seeing it for the first time. Her emotional boundaries were being moved. The blue had shown her, but the blue wasn't moving it—she was. She was moving the boundaries, and the blue had shown her that she had done it countless times.

She didn't know it with absolute certainty, but this first exposure was so overwhelming that she was at a loss. It was so powerful, enlightening, and spiritual. She stopped to capture it, but she couldn't move.

Ihilani knew something had happened. Her mother was seeing something new. She saw the look on her face. Was it doubt? Was it disbelief? "Mother?" Something was definitely different. "Mother?"

Iliakahani didn't respond. She was totally enveloped and didn't let anything distract her as she recounted the vast expanse of emotions she had lived all her life. She saw what was now important, but at the same time, she dreaded those elements she would have to discard. They included some of her most cherished moments. She now knew the truth—the absolute truth. She knew the love in truth.

"Oh, Ihilani," she said. "You are here with me. Thank you!" She wrapped her arms around her daughter. The moment was so different. It was capturing every nuance and pore of her daughter's skin. The communication had evolved to a new closeness. It was almost a silent transfer of knowledge.

And then it happened. It was electric. They both knew—together, as friends—for the first time.

"Mother?" Ihilani said. "How long have you known?"

"The very first time I saw it, my daughter, I was about your age."

"You mean the blue?" Ihilani's own self-confidence was building, but it was nowhere near the level of her dear mother.

"No, my daughter. The blue shows me the good. It has shown me that good is what love's own strength is." She had heard the words come from her mouth. They had bounced in her mind for years. For the first time, she heard the truth in her own words. It was so easy for her to say it, but she was just becoming aware of the very pinnacle of truth.

She thought about the phrase several more times. She knew her difficult past had built the very foundation of the concept in her mind. She knew that truth and love were forever intertwined. She knew that other elements are often steps up to the top. She was sorting out those elements in her adult life, but nothing had prepared her for hearing the top first. She whispered, "Good is what love's own strength is." *Oh, the tears of joy, of revelation. The purity. Oh, the simplicity. The truth, the good, the love. Oh my God, the strength!*

The blue quickly faded, and Iliakahani fainted.

"Mother!"

Women came running from the courtyard. They brought water and the rarest of cloths from the palace. The women dutifully attended to Iliakahani with the moist cloths and a pillow. One of the women brought out a palm frond to shade her eyes from the sun.

Ferdinand gathered his courage and every ounce of strength as he boldly moved back to the monument.

The others watched silently, not knowing why they stood there.

He walked with purpose and experience back to the trail.

The others walked swiftly to catch up.

A breeze swirled between the monument and the base of the mountain. *An omen*, Pohii thought. *The wind moving directly toward us is a warning to slow down.*

The Islanders slowed, but Ferdinand's pace remained steady.

As they passed the monument, the sense of discovery—of its placement, of its very existence—fell behind them. The questions mounted with every step.

Was Ferdinand guiding them to God?

A smaller square monument appeared as they walked. It was more like an entrance, Pohii thought. As they approached, he asked Ferdinand to stop. "What are you doing, Ferdinand?"

"It is important that we all see everything that is here. This is the third of seven." Ferdinand said.

They had only seen a fraction of the island's history. Ferdinand had seen everything, but his own heritage and training were not enough to fully determine the actual use of the structures—much less who might have placed them on the island. He had suspicions but no knowledgeable theories. All of the books he had read over the years had not prepared him for this—or even the palace on Condonte Island.

The style of each building on the islands was unique. Nothing came close to the style, although he thought the architecture had a Greek or Roman feel. Overall, there appeared to be no positive way to say that any other culture, from the primitive to the advanced, had any influence.

He had given some thought to it on several occasions. Why did they have such a need for massive verticals and relatively thin horizontals? In the curved trail, the verticals were so tightly arranged without the appearance of mortar, yet they curved down and out from the center of the wall. It was the one site where function over grace appeared with such glare due to the finely polished downward slope.

Two days before his rescuers landed, Ferdinand had explored much of the island in a hunt for food. He found a steep trail just before the intersection at the base of the mountain. It led down to a deep valley where he could see several small ponds and a small stream cascading toward the ocean.

At the point where the trail leveled off, he took a moment to consider the stamina required to climb back up the trail. Could a shelter be arranged right there? He turned his gaze up and realized what the trail was leading to. The arched wall above him was so much more. He stood there in complete amazement and knew what it was. An earlier civilization and its gifted engineers had built themselves a dam. Why? What did the other buildings provide for this unknown culture?

A bird flew from west to east, and he saw its reflection in the polished surface of the wall. The curvature of the wall had magnified the image tenfold.

He ducked and grasped a tree to steady himself. With nerves on high alert, he took a breath. Then he saw the bird fly away in the sky above him. He realized the extent of the perfection and the mammoth effort put into the construction of the dam. The structural calculations alone were astonishing. It was all too much. It was gleaming before him.

He felt a minor vibration and a low, steady hum. He heard a rush of water in the valley below. A jet of water under high pressure flew out from the dam at a nearly horizontal angle. Its roar was deafening as it coursed into the second pond. When the water jet ended, the vibrations stopped.

His instincts took over, and he retreated up the trail. At the top, he looked down at the power he had just witnessed. He sat down. Where are they? Who are they? The questions mounted with each breath.

He wondered if they were still there. His fears were elevating with each detail he pondered—even with his scientific background and his religious training.

Pohii walked up beside Ferdinand and said, "What will you show us now? Is God really here?"

"I think so. I know God watches us all," Ferdinand said. "Oh, yes. God is always with us!"

Iliakahani awoke with a start. She gasped. Her eyes were wide open. She sat up with her hands raised. Ihilani offered her hands, and she stood up.

The relief was felt by each woman on the balcony as Iliakahani returned. She looked into her daughter's eyes.

"What happened, Mother?" Ihilani asked.

"I saw so many new things in the blue. I think it was just too much." She saw new images, faces she couldn't recognize, and distant places she had never been. She saw the good, the bad, and the middle all at once. She wanted to put herself in the good, but the bad and the in between were in competition with the good in her mind.

"What is the blue?" Wainani said.

Iliakahani realized her innocent question was going to take some time to fully understand. She and the others attending to her could be shocked by the answers.

Wainani's mind was always filled with a joyful innocence that others loved about her. Her husband was constantly protecting her, shielding her, and worrying about her. She prayed to the spirits and to God every day. It was one of many things about her that carried her and guided her from moment to moment. Her devotion had not gone unnoticed by the elders on this island. She had all the necessary elements to be an elder, but all the elders were men. It's the way it had always been, and she knew it without the slightest question.

"The blue is like a dream when you are awake," Ihilani said. "You may feel it at first—or see it. Mother knows both."

For Wainani, the questions didn't bring any clarity. Her mind was always fully open to God and his inspiration, yet this blue was something different. She opened with innocence. She was hearing about the blue for the first time.

Iliakahani said, "Yes, the blue is good. The blue is here. It's all around us. It comes with the good." Her audience, including her daughter, listened in silence. "I always feel it coming, and then I see it." The blue was with her as she spoke. "I remember the first time I felt it but didn't see it. It was a year after Ihilani was born. The war was over just a month before, and I went to bed after a good day." The details were still crisp. "I had just closed my eyes to sleep when a new feeling slowly found me. I had seen it many times as I was falling asleep—white, blue, and sometimes red. They moved together slowly when my eyes were closed. But this time, I felt something." She stopped for a moment. Her feelings were honest and real. They welled up as she burst into tears.

Her audience was transfixed. The women around her were silent.

Ihilani moved to touch her mother's hands. It was trusting, reassuring, and loving. The confidence was real.

Iliakahani looked into her daughter's eyes and knew. Her smile gleamed in her tears.

She took a deep breath. "It is time. The feelings I am having now have grown with time." Her memories were reinforcing her words. Her confidence peaked as she recounted her evolution. "I knew it wasn't just me having them. Others had seen it. I know that it is good and that some in my family have seen it."

Her words flowed with no sign of abating.

Ihilani nodded. Two other women nodded.

Wainani was still frozen; her spiritual battle had just begun.

"Most of the time, I feel the blue. Sometimes I see it when it is very important. I have grown to love it and know it. It comes in the good—but not in the bad. For this past year, I have seen it in daylight and at night. It is beautiful." Iliakahani stopped. Something in the blue alerted her. *Oh, dear God!*

The feeling was coming from Pohii and the explorers—from within the blue. She could see it and feel it. Something was about to happen, and she wished she were with him.

The women in attendance watched as Iliakahani walked to the railing and looked at the island. Her feelings were in a desperate mismatch. The good and something else was at odds—in a competition. Her husband and her son were standing in the good, but an element of worry deflected the experience for her.

For the first time, the blue had shown her two uncertain outcomes. One was overwhelming, and the other was a feeling of relief mixed with dashed hopes.

Ferdinand motioned for the explorers, as he now thought of them, to gather again and continue.

"I want to thank you for my rescue, but I know you have come here for a different reason."

Pohii said, "I am the one who gives thanks, my priest. It is you who are walking with us now."

Ferdinand felt a slight embarrassment that Pohii would place so much on him at that moment. "Let's see more and discover more together."

They moved to the small monument. In the shadow of the mountain, they assembled at the new building. It was much smaller than the round monument they had just left. It had four columns and a slightly pitched canopy. The wall on the mountain was different. There were seven carvings on the wall—three in the top and four in the bottom line. Each had a different design. The dominant colors had exclusive hues. The largest was about a third bigger than the others. It was centered in the top row and was a deep, brilliant blue. It shined in the shadows.

A shelf about a foot below the bottom row—tilted away from the mountain—had its own carvings. They were arranged differently than those on the wall, and each one had its own scale. The red one was in the lower right part of the shelf—about six inches from its edge. Something about the symbol looked familiar.

The simplest of all the carvings showed a white background and a light green circle inlay. The carvings were presented in a gentle arc—with equal distance from the blue carving.

A light brown carving was the smallest. It had six distinct hues, and its background was light brown. A dark brown border highlighted white squares. Light blue designs were in each corner. A large blue circle was slightly above the center. A smaller yellow dot, touched the brown square.

All of the other colors were represented in various shapes, but the red one was a semicircle with its crest pointing to the northwest.

Ferdinand pointed to the light brown carving. "We are here!"

Pohii looked, but the thought of arriving at God's door overwhelmed him. "God's door?" It was the moment he had been waiting for.

The other explorers stood in reverent silence. The power, majesty, and reckoning were finally at hand, and they trembled and waited with humility.

Chapter 15

Pohii waited for the answer.

Ferdinand thought about it. He had yet to be tested in his newly adopted language. The daunting task of announcing his answer was tempered by the ultimate respect he had for everyone standing with him. So far, the discovery and the exploring were his focus. He knew they didn't want any of it. They wanted to say thanks to God. That was why they had come. His rescue was a mere coincidence. They had trusted him to lead them to God.

Ferdinand's eyes filled with tears. "My friends, this is not God's door, but God is always with us. It is your ancestors' map of this island."

"Our ancestors?" Pohii realized his dream was at stake. This news was not what he had expected. The blue was fleeting for him, but a turning point had not yet arrived in his mind.

The blue couldn't leave now—even if he made an effort. Its intensity had not wavered.

The thought that Ferdinand had been something other than truthful had never entered his mind. He was posing many questions that had no obvious solutions.

Kai had a famous look on his face as if in witness to fraud.

Pohii looked at Kai and said, "No, my son. This is God's island."

Ferdinand heard every word, but the tears were still coming.

Pohii never swayed from his position that Ferdinand was a friend who had been honest with him. He turned back to Ferdinand. "What is the word *map*?"

"A map is, in God's eyes, the island as he sees it from the clouds, looking down upon us." He smiled, crouched down, and drew an oval in the soil. "Here ... something like this ... as God looks down."

Kai and Koiku said, "I've seen that!" They looked at each other with big smiles

"Where have you seen it?" Pohii said.

"On the side of the palace!" Kai said.

"On the stone in the bay. In Ohluku!" Koiku said.

Pohii knew each island had something similar that had been overlooked for as long as anyone could remember. It was never explained or included in a conversation. It was just there. It was not threatening and was just part of the landscape. It was a design, an embellishment. They didn't see it as a representation of something else.

Pohii's mission had not changed, but a new path had been opened. He was intrigued by the illustration and the answers his two volunteers had given. He was thinking about this new element even as his desire to thank God remained.

The sun was a little more than halfway down in the western sky. It was the second day of the three-day mission.

Pohii said, "The sun will give us a little more time. We will need some to get ready to sleep."

Ferdinand knew there were only a few things left to discover. The concept of time was measured for him—but not for the Islanders. They felt it but had never had the need to measure it with any precision. Ferdinand thought that timekeeping down to the minute had a purpose in a complex society. This group of islanders was blissfully unaware what hour it was— not to mention what day of the week it was.

They had relied on a brief annual announcement from the elders of the first full moon and then started a new year again. The progression of time for them occurred like a constant breeze from the ocean. The abruptness of timing anything raised emotional expectations and fears they had apparently learned to avoid. They were used to advance notice for just about everything. For the most part, they lived calmly.

Life on the islands—except during war—was relaxed and passionate.

Ferdinand had only made his discoveries during the past two or three weeks. He had lost track of time and was still at a loss for any scientific or spiritual conclusions. "Let us go now—as God watches—to the next place I want to show you. This way now."

The group moved silently along the trail for two or three minutes. The feeling of God's loving surveillance wrapped them.

As if a curtain had been lifted they saw the fourth monument. Its size and shape were eclipsed by its purpose. It was the one Ferdinand dreaded the most. He had entered it when he was nearing starvation. His fears were in charge—even as the blue crept in. That memory sent pulses to his nerves.

It was square with beveled corners and edges to the roofline. Someone had taken a lot of time and effort to develop that building. Ferdinand evaluated his own attendance in the art of architecture. His formal schooling ended eleven years ago in Milan, but this was as close to perfection he could have ever imagined.

He would come to think about it as the "hall of the senses." The islanders saw the building as slightly more imposing than the round one. It's dark gray stone facade was in contrast to the brilliant white of the round monument. As they walked closer, the dark gray revealed a shadow of violet. The beveling was gray from every direction. The small entrance was light violet. The monument was due west of the mountain, and the entrance faced due east.

Once inside, the explorers found themselves at the top of a staircase. They paused. Kai and another explorer were fighting nausea as they reached the carved railing at the top of the staircase. Looking down into darkness was not helping them recover.

"My priest, what is this?" Pohii said as his eyes adjusted to the dark.

"I believe this is meant to show each one of our basic senses. There are five senses: sight, touch, hearing, smell, and taste. There is only one large room we will see."

"But we have no torches!" Pohii said.

"We won't need them," Ferdinand said with a smile.

Ferdinand noticed something very strange about all the buildings. They were all in pristine condition: no dust, spider webs, leaves, or debris. How could that be? The ancient site was so clean and bright, but it had been dark inside the building for years. What was forbidding the encroachment of the dense jungle all around them?

During prayers at the seminary, he gazed up at the stained glass and noticed a spider crafting a web. On this tropical island—inside this and other buildings—he inspected the entrance, the floor, the walls, and the ceiling. There was not a single insect. He remembered the entrance was open. There was no door. His other senses elevated as his fears returned. The absolute stillness of the air was another thing he felt uneasy about.

Pohii said, "Ferdinand, my priest, what will you show us here?"

"Oh, yes. Of course. Follow me. This way please." He tested each step as he descended. He counted the steps as he went. From his classes in Milan, he remembered the normal number of steps was twelve or more.

This staircase was long. It had thirty-six steps down to the landing. He held on to the railing with each step. The stairs were wide enough for at least six abreast. It was unnerving that he could only reach one of the railings.

The others stopped on the eighth step. Ferdinand could see their outlines in the dim light above. In the darkness of the landing, he called to them. "I am here at the bottom."

"I can't see you," Pohii said.

"It is only the first of two staircases. It is very dark here, but you will see again at the bottom."

The men were filled with fear, but Ferdinand had seen it before. Even in his own renewed anxiety, he knew they should all see it.

Ihilani was holding her mother's hand as they stared toward Mokiki.

They had lost them—all of them. No new feelings were coming. It had taken only a few seconds to change everything. The blue was still present, but it wasn't helping. The good was as close to absolute as she had ever seen, but its considerable advantages weren't enough.

Iliakahani knew differently. She had confidence in her husband. He was always close to her heart. Even though she couldn't see him in the blue, she could rely on other things. He made decisions that affected his life, his family, and his people. She remembered the moment he changed his mind in the ceremonial grounds with the fate of the entire population in his hands.

She had no doubt that her husband was safe, but she also knew that her daughter had a new fear to assess on her own. She worried that she was about to live in a new fear. She wasn't sure she should confront her about it. For just a moment, nothing else mattered. Her daughter was suffering.

"Mother, have they gone to heaven?" Ihilani asked.

Pohii's father, the soft-spoken, gracious leader of Condonte Island, had always made time for her. Even though he had other children and grandchildren, he was her calm before the storm. She had witnessed his long battle with pain.

She loved so many, and the loss of someone she loved frightened her the most. When his spirit departed for heaven, her first experience with grieving began. She was not expecting her own reaction to being so emotionally devastating. She retreated and sobbed. She couldn't speak to anyone without thinking about him. She floundered, rejected, and avoided. Her feelings had only recently leveled off and reopened to life and loving. *Now this, not this, please let it not be this.*

"Ihilani, your father is safe. Your brother is safe." Iliakahani's feelings in the blue told her so. Her own experience with them told her so.

"Oh, Mother!" Ihilani said. "I hope so. I will be sure when I see him." She wasn't ready for the blue. It had shown feelings without images, but that would soon change.

When the men arrived at the landing, they silently regrouped. Their fears eased somewhat as the camaraderie and guidance reassured them.

In the silence, they heard each other breathing. Kai had never noticed it before, but he heard them all breathing. Their breathing was almost synchronized.

"I think I can hear my heart beating," Koiku whispered.

They all heard it. He had never been so scared. His mouth was wide open. Like the beat of a distant drum, they heard it.

Ferdinand knew they had never heard such detailed sounds before. He couldn't see their eyes, but he could feel the tension. It was time to descend to the bottom. "Look back up at the top of the stairs. See the light coming through the door?"

The dim light beamed across the ceiling and ended.

The temptation to run back up the stairs and out the door entered everyone's mind, but they waited for instructions.

"There is a reason we can't see the middle of the ceiling," Ferdinand said. He had them back from the brink. The teaching had begun. "The ceiling is round where you can't see it. It goes up on its own wall and arches to the middle."

"What?" Pohii said. "How do you know this? We can't see it."

"We will see it at the bottom of the next stairs." Ferdinand moved cautiously along the railing on the landing and found the turn to the next stairs down. *Some twenty feet or so of the railing,* he thought. Walking through total darkness—even with the dim light above—had been terrifying. He could not see the floor, the railing, or the stairs. The floors and the steps offered no confidence. They started down on the second set of stairs.

About halfway down, the texture of the steps changed. Their feet told them of the pleasing, rounded, and slightly bubble-domed design of the next few steps. Every step had its own unique texture.

Ferdinand had certainly noticed it before. It was the essence of touch in such an utterly new way, and all the emotions it revealed were inspired. *Just who designed and built these structures? Who the hell were they?* His spiritual training, never too far away, had been violated by the question. He cringed at his momentary indiscretion and humbly promised God to confess and pray about it soon.

The texture of the last two or three steps caused modest pain. Ferdinand knew it was the sense of touch in its full range. It went from neutral to pleasure and then to pain.

The silence and darkness within the building would deter any considerate barefooted person, but touching the steps after the landing with their feet was another barrier.

They were bad experiences for him the first time; his memory had overcome him again. Was something hidden in the building—something the builders had been trying to protect?

"I can see my feet!" Koiku said.

They all could. The floor was highly polished stone. A faintly illuminated mist was disturbed on the floor, and it felt odd to stand in the mist. They saw a quickly moving current within the mist. There was no temperature change. It wasn't building or evaporating. It was just moving swiftly in one direction toward the walls and the bottom step.

Ferdinand noticed how the eddies in the mist behind them were slightly more luminous. They darkened and withdrew into the bottom of the wall.

Without saying a word, Ferdinand allowed his instincts and memories to take over. He quietly took a step toward the center of the room. He took several more steps and stopped.

Koiku raised his hand above his head. He could see its silhouette against the dim light. He noticed a greenish tint to the light entering through the entry above them.

The sunlight was reflecting from the mountain into the entrance. The foliage on the mountain provided the tone. Koiku noticed the dim light in the green mist. *What have I done?* He was spellbound. Ferdinand raised his hands and took another step forward. He wasn't there yet. One more step. *Ah, there it is!* The next step was crucial. "If you can see my feet, come here now," he said softly.

They moved cautiously forward, bumping into each other.

They stopped just short of Ferdinand's feet.

"Look here. Hear my voice," Ferdinand said.

They couldn't see anything but darkness.

"Look here. Hear my voice." Ferdinand took one final step and raised his hands together.

The mist glowed green as his hands penetrated it. It was much faster than the mist at their feet.

Ferdinand was careful not to stand in it as it fell. He allowed the rest of the men to see it flow around his clasped hands. He remembered it differently, thought it was violet.

He brought one hand to his nose, and it smelled differently. It tasted bitter. "We entered at the top of the stairs." He was teaching, and what a master he was. His experience modified his knowledge of the room, and his fears diminished as he spoke. He had not yet come to a final judgment about the purpose the building. "Then we went down the stairs, and we couldn't see anything."

The men's heads bobbed in the darkness. They couldn't speak a word as they trembled.

"We heard with our ears, and we felt the floor and the steps with our feet and hands," Ferdinand said. "We touched the floor with our feet and the railing with our hands. We all touched them as they changed. When we couldn't see, we used what we could hear and touch … to … get … right … here."

The words were entering and absorbing, but they were far from understanding. Standing in emotion as close to shock without losing consciousness was about all they could muster at the moment.

The men were terrified by what they had seen. They couldn't believe it. They forced deep breaths as if they were about to confront an unseen, vastly superior enemy. Then it hit him between the eyes: a return to spiritual thinking, the sharing, and the caring. *Of course! That's what it is!* "No, you are not about to see the house of the devil. You are not about to see God's house either."

The abrupt statement worked. The men added uneasy curiosity to their reduced fears. The change was so natural for all but one. Kai added the element of annoyance to his spectra of feelings. His own curiosity had always been in the balance with duty and honor, but humility was further down in his personality. His patience was always limited. He decided to avoid expressing himself, and that had inflated his anxiety, fears, and blood pressure. For him, the blue had almost entirely exited.

Ferdinand's hands were no longer in the mist when it returned to black. He moved his hands back to the mist, and the green color returned. It was reflecting the darkness on one side and the green on the other side. When his hands entered the mist and disturbed its flow, it mixed the two sides. He moved his hands cautiously into the thickness of the mist— perhaps three or four inches. Its thickness was three or four times that.

"Pohii, Koiku, come here," Ferdinand said.

The men took two steps forward and stopped next to Ferdinand.

"Koiku, move your hand into it," he said.

The green appeared, but Koiku withdrew his hand quickly as if he had touched lightning.

"Smell your hand," Ferdinand said.

"Oh! It's got a bad smell!" He smacked his lips. "And a bad taste too!" The remnants of the mist fell from his hand to the floor.

"Now we know four of the five senses. To get to the last one, we must walk through the mist to the green side."

"What green side?" Pohii asked.

Ferdinand said, "Take a breath in—and hold it. Breathe again on the other side."

The instruction was almost entirely rejected by the men. It was all they could do.

Ferdinand knew they were frightened and had not expected them to refuse to move—or was it that they couldn't move at all in this fear? He thought about this situation for a moment. His scientific training brought the answer.

"I have shown you that you can hear, touch, taste, and smell. And they felt strong here in the dark. You know what you see is most important. The other four have just barely taken its place here. All your abilities are important—all five. We all know that seeing is the most important, but the other four are just as important in this room. Never forget this!"

The men's fears momentarily switched to shock.

"But what will we see, my priest?" Pohii asked.

"First, I must tell you how to move into the mist, how many steps you must take to reach the other side, and when to stop. You *must* do this with your eyes closed. Even when you have reached the other side, you must wait for me to tell you that it is all right to open your eyes because it is very bright on the other side. The first time I walked through the mist, I did so with my eyes open—and that was a mistake. My eyes were dried in the mist, and the tears burned for several minutes after I saw how bright it was."

Ferdinand flashed back to when he'd first entered the strange chamber. When the mist touched his skin, he instantly held his breath as it enclosed him. He had blundered straight into the mist with terrified eyes wide open, and it burned his eyes. He had coughed in a panic for several minutes as he stood in the bright light.

"You can only take two steps past the mist. You must stop when you see the light with your eyes closed. You will see the light with your eyes closed. Keep them closed until I tell you to open them. It will be very bright. I will also tell you when to breathe again. I will be the first to go through the mist. I will go with my eyes closed and holding my breath. You may not hear me for a moment. I will slap my hands together four times when I have stopped. I will not speak again until I slap my hands together a second time. I will need the time. Please wait for me."

Slowly and quietly, the men assembled in front of the mist.

Chapter 16

"Remember to listen for me to tell you when to open your eyes and breathe again." Ferdinand stepped slowly into the mist, and it enveloped his body.

As he moved in, his outline closed behind him—and the mist returned to black.

"Pohii, I want you first. Remember to keep your eyes closed and hold your breath. Just two steps and you will be here with me," he said.

"I can't hear your words!" Pohii yelled.

Ferdinand knew that light was not the only thing the mist was reflecting.

This time, he yelled at the top of his lungs. "Pohii, I want you first. Remember, eyes closed and hold your breath. Just two steps and you will be here with me."

Pohii exited the mist just as he had been told to do.

"Keep your eyes closed and breathe. Shake your hands at your side. Cover your eyes with your hands until you get used to the light and open them only when I tell you. I must move you with your eyes closed, so no one will bump you when they come." He moved him two steps further in. "I will call the others in now. I will have to be loud."

"Let me call Kai," Pohii said.

Kai obediently entered.

"Keep your eyes closed!" Ferdinand completed the instructions for Kai and the remaining men. All eyes were still covered.

Ferdinand had told them the truth, and they obeyed him. They all arrived safely on the other side. "Pohii, please tell your people to open their eyes."

"Open your eyes!" Pohii said.

And there it was: the luminous room for all to see. They could see it all reflected in the mist. It slowly faded into the mist just before it touched the floor and retreated into the darkness they had just left behind.

A knee-high step led to a platform that gently curved up to a narrow vertical point. The glare, as bright as the noonday sun, prevented them from seeing it. Its awesome power, a focal point in the room, was projecting the images on the mist itself.

The temperature in the room was about the same as being outside, even though the air was absolutely still. The mist had just a hint of its touch as they walked through it. It was like an extremely fine dust on the wings of a moth. It didn't adhere to them for more than a second or two before it had returned to the current.

The images were green and blue, and they felt something completely different. It was something new, something beautiful, and something they had never witnessed before.

"Oh my god!" Ferdinand shouted. "I know what this is!" He strained for the words and moved around the whole room to be sure. "Oh my god!" He danced. He ran.

The other explorers began to giggle. They wanted to share the knowledge, but the infection was spreading quickly. The joy they saw in Ferdinand was much more than he had shown at his rescue. They rejoiced at the unknown—like children on the beach for the first time. The fear was reduced to wonder, and the relief of tension was more than obvious.

"Yes! Of course! Yes! Yes! Yes!" Ferdinand ran back and stopped at Pohii's feet. He realized that his exhilaration was not ordinarily part of his role as a priest, and he forced himself back to calm.

With a few deep breaths and a broad smile, he said, "It's a viewing room—an observatory unlike any other I have seen in my life. That's what this is! Oh my god!" A million questions entered his mind as he raced around the room. *Yes. There it is!*

He pointed to the images as he went below each one, but only a few stood out. There was one he hadn't seen before. The one image he was looking for wasn't there where it should have been. It just wasn't there. It wasn't anywhere in the images. "Come over here with me. I will tell you what I see."

They all walked to the left in the room. Ferdinand stopped them and turned back to see the images they had stood directly below only moments before. From this distance and angle, they could clearly see Condonte Island.

"That is the island you came from—the one I first landed on." Ferdinand pointed to the second largest of the green images on the mist.

"And that is Halau on the left and Loulu behind it," Kai said. "And we can't see Ohluku island at all."

The image reminded them that the island of Ohluku would be behind Condonte, and since Condonte Island had a small hill centered on it and cliffs on the south side, they wouldn't be able to see Ohluku's flat terrain anyway.

"Now turn around and look at this one over here." Ferdinand pointed to it. In the green along the bottom, a reddish brown cone of a hill could be seen. It was barely noticeable from the northern side of Halau Island. It was thirty-seven miles to the west end of Mokiki and could only be seen from the escarpment at its base. Its graceful peak was a sharp contrast to Mokiki's eastern peak.

He hadn't seen the western peak before. At the bottom of the image, there was a partial arc and a bright green area. Next to a white circle and a gray square, there were an odd bluish hexagon and a muted orange triangle.

Ferdinand had seen it before in the violet—he was sure of it—but why was it different in the green? The images were there before his eyes, but something was missing. He pondered it for a moment. He checked each image again. *Oh! It's the eastern peak!* He checked all the images again. It was not there. He had not seen it in the violet either. *It was never there. It couldn't have been.*

He turned around to look at the western images, including the red rock cone mountain and all its prominence. He surveyed the image from top to bottom and left to right.

He watched for several more seconds. A flock of birds flew from the south to north. For a moment, they flew behind the clouds—but they weren't behind the clouds in the classic sense.

In a flash, he thought he knew the perspective the images were projecting. It had to be a highly elevated source for the images. The birds had flown below the clouds.

He shuddered, his nerves elevated and overwhelmed him, and his mouth opened. He turned slowly to verify his theory. The birds had flown under the clouds. There were the clouds, but for the first time in his life, the sky wasn't behind the clouds; the island was.

The horizon is very high in the image, he thought. As he looked up at the projections, he noticed there were no images on the ceiling. He could see the physical ceiling despite the glare in the room. For the first time, he saw the source of the mist. The edge was all around the room, thirty feet above them.

He shifted his gaze to the bright images. He saw everything, like from the top of a staircase. Where were they coming from?

His mind, working harder than ever, was being challenged by the perspective he was witnessing. He was looking up at the images, but they were looking down. They were looking down. "Oh God!"

They all looked at him.

"It's from the top of the eastern mountain. That's why I can't see it!" Ferdinand said.

"Just like you can't see your own eyes—it can't see itself. The mountain can't see itself. Oh God!"

"What?" Pohii asked.

They had innocently identified the images, but the fact that they were witnessing them from inside a building had not yet sunk in. They were like paintings, but there were subtle movements in the images. The images were alive, moving on the mist and changing slightly with the movement of the sun and the wind.

Ferdinand was seeing things in the images and believing them, but the rest of the men weren't figuring anything out for themselves. To them, it was unbelievable. God had done this. He alone could have done this— and no one else. For the moment, that was all they could believe. To them, the only explanation was that it must be through God's eyes. After all, the elders had always preached that God was looking down on them from the clouds, the sky, and the stars.

Ferdinand had already said the key words as he described the word map. The source of the images was irrelevant. Its placement had no meaning. This is what God could see. The place they lived. That's all it was. The power of knowing what God could see was much more than a spiritual experience for them. They felt humility before God, standing with God, and seeing what he could see. Ferdinand had told them that it wasn't God's house before they entered the room.

The explorers knelt on the floor, enveloped in reverence. Automatically, in unison, they prayed silently. The blue entered their minds in full: the good, the pure, and the loving embrace.

Now they knew the blue and its tenderness. They felt safe in the new knowledge. Oh, it was good.

Ferdinand joined them, never questioning their religion or their conclusions. He had his own overdue praying to do. It was a very long list indeed.

Chapter 17

Iliakahani stopped talking. Something had happened. The emotions were riding a wave of information in the intense blue. Like a sudden loud drumbeat, it entered as the breeze at their backs gained speed.

The purest blue wasn't presenting images—only the raw feeling of the moment. She was sure of it. Her men were praying in the blue. She couldn't see them, but she felt it. Her smile was lit. The joy, the spirit, and the awesome beauty the feelings were filling her mind. The blue told her that all her men were safe, including the unknown man they were with.

Wainani was the newest to feel the blue. She wrestled with it. The spiritual guidance she had always lived with had been shaken by recent events. The conflicts were confusing for her. The arrival of the invaders had sent her to her favorite hiding place. Her safe place was in the tallest trees on the island. She had climbed them many times as a child.

Her husband knew it well. He had found her there a handful of times, much to her relief. Now she couldn't run to it, and she didn't know why—even though she wanted to. Something was telling her to stay. She couldn't resist it. She felt the mild burn in her soul that so many others had experienced, and she finally knew what they were talking about. She felt like she was falling deeply in love within the blue. It was a new love.

Up to that moment, she had disallowed it. Even as she longed for her husband's kindness and his caress, she felt that she had just expanded her love for all things. For her, there had been no turns, reversals, substitutions, or boundaries. There was just expansion. The blue had a mild, elevating feel that eased her fears. The feeling convinced her. She cherished it as much as she questioned it. Her fears had been softened, and she knew it was the beginning.

Wainani accepted it and relaxed. *Why have I waited so long?* Her tears flowed quietly, softly, in her regret. It was slowly ebbing. On this—her first day of knowing blue's exposure—the good was replacing her self-described weaknesses. She didn't know that she had never had any weaknesses—only conflicts.

Her adjustments were difficult in the beginning, but over time, she would grow and learn. For the first time, she felt that life had passed a landmark. She knew it, and she felt it. Her endless questions were changing to the positive. She felt the rise in love overtake her other emotions with each nuance, event, and experience. It was new for her, but the blue had an influence. The good had begun.

She didn't know that God had just blessed her and her husband with a new life to love. That feeling had already entered without definition. She would celebrate the private moment in due time. She would celebrate it with effortless love.

The women felt relief as they looked toward Mokiki. Wainani was motionless in the blue. Ihilani held her mother's hand.

Iliakahani knew it was an important moment for the men as the blue aided her mind's eye. She saw them kneeling in prayer. The traditional moment lasted for what she knew would defy patience in any other situation. Their gentle prayers thanked God.

The words were practiced and important. She didn't know that Ferdinand was thinking the very same thing. He felt like he was in the last few moments of Mass.

The iconic mountain on Mokiki and the one tall bush on Condonte shared the same name. In their language, the term was interchangeable with "fear at a distance." When used in a different context, it could mean strength, resilience, and protection. The name came from the unfortunate experience of touching it. The bush's natural defense would penetrate any skin or feather coating upon contact, and the pain would escalate into a lasting purple rash. Insects avoided it or perished.

The bush and the term were a warning. To the islanders, the menacing word was enough to cause fear. Since Mokiki was twelve miles away, they had always lived with a balance before the invaders arrived. They called it

Thorn Peak. It's spectacular elevation, and narrow, vertical rise was used by the elders and leaders for spiritual guidance.

Pohii felt his dream was satisfied; the power of being in God's presence had convinced him. The experience among the other explorers was identical. An absolute had been reached for them: complete humility before God and feeling his acceptance. They finally knew him, his paternal love for them had them mesmerized.

"Thank you, God," Pohii said. "Thank you for helping us! Thank you for loving us all." He knew for the first time that God had heard his prayers at the ceremonial grounds, the Palace, and the beaches.

Pohii formed his own opinion of the room they were standing in. He thought of it as the "judgment room." It's frightening entrance, and the beauty and brilliance of the room had convinced him.

Ferdinand was first to stand. The blue had shown him the impressions of the other men. He knew their conclusions were more important than his own. He knew the moment would last a long time. His own education had begun.

The struggle softened. The truth had many more layers than the absolute. From the moment he made his own discoveries on the island, he enjoyed the unexpected layer the most. The newest and the most innocent for him was the conclusion in reverence.

The spiritual commitment and training had convinced him. This truth—even if could be otherwise explained—was more important. His path was more certain than ever.

Pohii stood, closed his eyes for a moment, and raised his arms slightly. He had found what he was looking for all along: his love, the softening, and the truth. He opened his eyes.

All the men in the room had quiet tears in their eyes. It was God's parental love.

"We must go," Ferdinand said softly. "I must prepare you to go. It will take some time to leave here." He had shown them how to enter the room, and now he had to return to the spot in the room where they had entered through the mist. *But where in the mist had they entered?* The references in the images were vague. *I think it was Halau above us as we entered.* In the dark, he would have to search for the stairs. "I will go first again. This time, I will need more time to get my eyes ready in the dark." *I can do it. I must do it.*

"Let me go first!" Koiku said. His natural voluntary spirit told him that he could do it. They all knew he could. He was the only one who had remembered the first thing he saw when he opened his eyes: a mark on the platform that told him where to exit.

The four marks on the platform—with their own unique symbols—represented the cardinal directions.

Ferdinand knew the platform offered the answer. He had overlooked the compass; the beauty of the markings and their very existence erased his fears.

Koiku walked to the first one he had seen and moved two places to the left. "This is where we came in."

"Stand there for a moment," Ferdinand said. He knew he would have to reassemble the men in the dark. "We know how we came in. Stand next to each other like before."

They assembled and faced the center of the room.

"Now turn around and face the mist."

They knew he was right. They formed a line and looked at each other.

"We must take one more step than we did before. This time, we can all go together ... three steps with eyes closed. Hold your breath. I will say the word *now* one more time. When I do, we go. Wait for me to tell you to breathe and open your eyes. Ready? Now! One, two, three. Stop! Breathe!"

The particles had yet to rejoin the current in the mist.

Ferdinand moved one hand to his nose, and there was no smell. He moved it to his lips, but there was no taste. The timing was good. "Open your eyes!"

They stood silently while their eyes adjusted to the darkness. They knew Ferdinand would search for the bottom step in the dark. They followed the sound and watched his feet in the mist. The blue was helping them.

Yes! The relief of finding that painful first step! "I have it," Ferdinand said. What power he felt in his words. The "painful first step" had become an inspiration—a true force for him. "It is here. Follow my voice."

As they climbed, they all felt the meaning of their experience in the building.

Chapter 18

Pohii was last to the landing, and the others waited for him to recover. He stood with them for several minutes, still entranced and shaken. Pohii felt like his duty was complete. He had reached the goal of his mission. He knew the feeling of accomplishment. He was grateful to God and knew the spirits had been with him in the judgment room. The unforgettable experience was all he could think about.

They turned toward the door and walked out into the sunshine.

Kai said, "Father, we must go back to the beach."

Pohii knew they had to return to the beach, but seeing his son offer the direction made him proud.

They cautiously climbed down to the beach. The thought of the evening meal on the beach made their stomachs growl. They had not had a meal since morning.

It had taken almost three hours in the square monument, but it only felt like a few minutes. Where had all the time gone? Pohii thought about it as they descended. The four monuments were only one hundred feet apart. Crossing the arced path was farther than all the other paths together, but something had consumed the entire day. He wondered, for the first time, about time itself.

When they finally set foot on the beach, they felt physical and emotional relief. They hurried to start the fire and pulled new leaves for the meal.

Ferdinand blessed the meal, and every bite was intense with flavor. They thoroughly enjoy it and saved some for tomorrow. They retired to their shelters and fell asleep with humbled ease.

Ferdinand woke in the morning rain and knew they would have to wait until the rains had stopped and the trails had dried.

He focused on the three remaining buildings, but would there be enough time? What would the others want to do now that they were certain they had concluded their mission? Were the things he had shown them enough to prompt them for a second climb?

Anything he said would not be convincing. Convincing his rescuers to wait to return to Condonte would be difficult. They had formed their own visions of the island. They had not yet come to a single explanation. They needed guidance.

Ferdinand peered out of the shelter. He could see the first signs of sunrise in the rain. The singular beauty—the quiet rain and the quiet sea—made him feel calm. *Oh, dear God, the blue.* It entered his shelter, and he sat up and sighed. The blue started gaining on him. The advantages were coming. The reasons for returning, the answers, and the images were vivid, compelling, and soft. Each one was eclipsing any need to return to Condonte on this important day. The challenges in conversation during the morning meal were clear to him.

The blue was entering all the explorers with calm and quiet as they awoke. The last drops of rain fell from the leaves in the jungle forest and landed on their shelters.

Pohii and Kai emerged from their shelter. After a quick stretch, they surveyed the beach. There was something different about this sunrise. They had both slept soundly. Pohii was feeling very good; his pains were not paying a visit, which was a welcome surprise.

Pohii enjoyed the breeze as the sun crept up over the horizon.

Kai pointed to the southern channel and beyond God's Finger. There was an ominous storm along the southeast horizon. After several minutes, he noticed it moving westward.

Pohii hoped it would not come to the islands. The waves in the southern channel had a moderate swell from the approaching front. Only time would tell if this storm would come to Condonte or Mokiki.

A soft but sure rumbling under their feet changed their mood. Near Condonte's northern shore, they saw two giant splashes. They heard a thunderous sound from somewhere above them in the escarpment and water rushing down the valley behind them. They watched the huge cascade fall into the sea near the southern end of this beach. Even at fifty yards away, it was too close.

The natural pressures were again in balance. The blue's influence had returned in earnest, and the calm was restored.

"Let us eat," Ferdinand said. "Today, we see the rest."

Pohii knew Ferdinand was right, but he longed to return to Condonte. However, it wasn't safe to cross the channel. Waiting, relaxing, or doing nothing were options best reserved for tomorrow. The mission would be extended by one day.

Ferdinand requested a silent blessing for the morning meal.

The fire was lit. The morning meal was readied. The meal enjoyed by all. The conversation was friendly, reverent, and lasted more than an hour.

"We can see the last three before we go to the canoes tomorrow," Ferdinand said.

Pohii said, "There are two advantages to keep in mind: the short advantage of time and the advantage of love for each other."

"Yes, let's go," Pohii said. He thought of his people. Their future had to include the exploration of Mokiki. His own mission had ended with the highest reverence he could have ever imagined. He longed to return to Condonte, but he knew that the island had to be seen in total. He knew he had to explain what he found to his family, the elders, and all the citizens.

All of the men stood for a moment and waited for Pohii. He gathered his thoughts as they watched and took a step. He suspected that there could be an advantage in the knowledge found on this island if they faced another invasion. He motioned to Ferdinand to take the lead to the escarpment. Duty was on his mind as the slightly moist, shaded trail came into view.

They started up the trail with caution. They followed Ferdinand but had numerous questions.

Iliakahani stopped for a moment. Something had changed. She saw the blue in a subtle but inviting hue.

For the first time, she could see the cluster of explorers on Mokiki. An undulating line moved up the trail from the southeast coast. Even at this distance, she saw a magnified image in the haze. The images seemed as if she were standing beyond the halfway point in the channel.

Oh the wind, the feminine. Her hair moved in the light breeze.

"Please come," Iliakahani said. She was still facing west. Her daughter joined her at the perfect moment.

They stood together in silence for several minutes and enjoyed the breeze and the blue.

"Mother, what do you see now?"

"I see them about halfway up the mountain."

"I am worried, Mother," Ihilani said.

"What do you see, my daughter?" Iliakahani said.

"It's something I can't see, Mother. I feel it." The blue had faded slightly.

"Last night I had a dream, Mother," Ihilani said, her hands shaking.

"Please tell me about it," Iliakahani said.

"It came to me, and I don't know where I should start." Her fears had progressed during the dream. The increase in velocity of the images was the most startling: her childhood and her memories of her grandfather and grandmother.

Her grandmother was so tender, loving, and mellow. She couldn't think of a single fault or negative feeling coming from her. Oh, how she missed her. Her grandfather was so wise, softhearted, and loving— even with his enormous physical strength. She knew that her father had inherited most of those traits.

"I saw them together. Gran-papa and Gran-mama were sitting together in the garden and talking to each other as I listened. They were talking about old times, I think, but they were saying things I'd never heard before. They talked about the ancestors—who they were and how they were protecting them now—in the dream." She had to gather more images as she stuttered. "Gran-mama said yes." She realized she was seeing her grandmother for the first time in years. She had forgotten what she actually looked like until then. "And I saw her." The tears fell openly. She couldn't go on.

Without a word, Iliakahani embraced her with a new and special kindness. She held her daughter's shoulders and brought her so she could see her face. Iliakahani lowered her head. "Yes, you did, my daughter. I saw them last night too."

"You did?" she said. "Oh, Mother, why did I see them? Why did they come last night? Why does the good hurt so bad?"

The morning breeze had fully enveloped them, and the blue felt new to them. The feminine elevated them.

Iliakahani calmly explained that women feel memories—both good and bad—on a higher level than men do. Men and women *feel* memories on a higher level than what they *see* in memory. For women, the feeling and the visuals are more intense than men could ever imagine. Men could not come close to understanding the clarity and truth. It was a gift and a curse. The gift of conversation and the curse of having to keep a delicious or horrendous secret. The gift of commitment and the curse of keeping a vast archive of good and bad feelings. The gift of caring and listening and the curse of hidden distrust while remaining loving and open.

"Yes, they spoke of our ancestors. They had the knowledge," Iliakahani said. "The blue was showing us the path before we walked it. They built this palace and other things on these islands. It showed us who had been here before us. They protected the islands with the high spirit of love and purpose."

It was more than Ihilani could handle. It was difficult to completely understand. The concepts were too high, too much, and too soon.

The blue entered like a typhoon. For the first time, it shook them like thunder in the night.

It had arrived at just the right time. They had seen it coming in their dreams, but the power of the blue was stunning. Even though they couldn't see it yet, they knew a new discovery was about to unfold for the men on the distant island.

The blue color was dominant in their visual images, foreshadowing all others. They barely made out the outlines of the men they loved so much. Iliakahani finally realized who was with them. He was no longer an unknown influence on the men; he was familiar and different. She couldn't hear them, but she saw them receiving spiritual guidance from him.

Was he a spirit brought by God? She remembered the ships as they left the islands. She had seen something enter the channel during their departure. He had been there only about two or three weeks before they landed. He had walked out of the channel to the southern beach on Mokiki. He had flung himself from one of the ships as they left in disgrace.

The spirit? The ships? She was convinced it was Ferdinand. It had to be it. She knew it without a doubt. It had to be him. The blue around him was different; his outline was not quite what she remembered, but it was him. *Oh, dear God, it is good.*

The blue slowly declined and leveled off.

Iliakahani saw that the blue had different levels. The first was feelings. The second was visuals. The third was revelations. She knew it had to come in that order. Each level had its own truth. Each one had been elevated into the next. She hadn't expressed it to herself that way before, but she suspected it was so. She didn't know that she had been born with it.

When she saw it for herself, she had accepted it without fear. She was coming nearer to the realization. Time was slowly revealing it, but she was doing it without knowing it. The blue was always present in the good for her, and it had always been present. She lived in the good. It couldn't have been otherwise. She didn't know any other way. "One more thing, my daughter," Iliakahani said. "Ferdinand is with them."

The look on her daughter's face transformed from shock to a broad smile.

Chapter 19

The men reached the plateau and rested. They were reclining near the arced path over the dam.

The time was right. Ferdinand had to tell them. He gathered his thoughts and used his spiritual guidance training and scientific training to explain it. "Your ancestors built what we saw yesterday—and what we will see today."

The men focused on him silently. They did not know what to say even though they had heard the reference to their ancestors yesterday.

"I must tell you what this is and why I think it was built. I don't have all the answers, but some of them will be new to you. I will use new words. I will tell you what I know."

They were silent.

"I believe your ancestors built the monuments we have seen and have not yet seen," Ferdinand said. "Each of the buildings we saw yesterday was built for a reason. Each one is connected to all the others. Come with me to the small one, and I will tell you more." He walked toward the smallest monument.

When they passed the trail to the dam, Ferdinand knew he had to explain it. They passed the white monument on their way to the third one.

They assembled at the smallest monument, and Ferdinand said, "We have seen this before. It is a map of this island." Ferdinand pointed to the map on the lower shelf. "The map is what God sees from above the clouds. The same pictures on the map are on the wall above the map in different order. The map shows where each building is, and the wall shows how they connect to each other." With extraordinary care, he showed them that the differences between the map and the wall were necessary for knowing what the ancestors had built. It was important to know how they worked together.

The ancestors had stumbled across a discovery that vibration could be controlled and modified. The intensity could be adjusted from zero to unbearable. They discovered how to limit it, isolate it, and use it in many different ways. They learned how to count each move of the vibrations— from one pulse to hundreds of thousands of them. They had discovered ceramics and used it in many different forms, but the men would not see the ceramic ovens that day.

Ferdinand knew that the last three monuments were not going to be easy to see. His explanations had apparently passed them by with such innocent ease that he wasn't sure if explaining anything on the island would make any sense at all.

They were listening, absorbing, and learning the knowledge and essence of the island. The blue had shown them the images and placed them squarely in the explorers' memories. They had volunteered and committed to it long before they landed on the southeast beach. The blue guided them to this moment.

The women stood on the palace balcony with a mild sense of fear as the images burst in. The Blue was sending them an element of danger, but they couldn't see it. It wasn't time. Their beloved men had not reached anything to fear, but the women knew that they would. The men did not know that they could experience something bad in the blue. They could feel it, but they didn't see it. They waited for the blue to tell them.

The blue changed and showed them something new. The only thing they knew was a reference to their mutual dreams last night.

"Gran-papa is here in the blue," Ihilani said.

"Yes, I know it is him."

The blue was showing them the dream they shared last night in intimate detail. It played over and over—from start to finish—and then it slowed to the point where they thought of it as a live conversation.

"Mother, Gran-papa said our ancestors built something that protects us, nurtures us, and keeps us."

"Yes, my daughter, but he also said they had left it for us to discover again," Iliakahani said. And then she knew the fear was the discoveries.

A rumble in her mind told her there would be a great deal of work to do when the men returned. They would have discussions with the elders, explorers, and Islanders.

She was forming the process in her mind. It would be the most important, most grueling challenge ever attempted by this population. It was more important than any war or invasion. It would take a long time to train her mind to accept it all. She took a deep breath, stood next to her daughter, and watched the blue.

"Mother, what is the blue showing us?" Ihilani said.

The blue showed them so many images: the reverent, the beautiful, the unknown, the fierce, and the loving. It was like hundreds of dreams.

Iliakahani said, "We are being shown what to do, I think."

The blue showed them a transition from a dark, primeval period to a few days in the future. The time after the men returned from Mokiki was so brief in the blue, but it was so important. The women stood on the balcony with a new fear—the fear of commitment to the grand scope of Mokiki Island and its monuments. Another fear was that Condonte's citizens would not—or could not—believe any of it.

"I see the ancestral council with us all in the room," Iliakahani said.

"Yes, and I am with you too, but I don't know why."

"We will have much to talk about, my daughter," Iliakahani said. She knew certain decisions would take days to agree to. They would be of the highest importance.

Ferdinand said, "We saw the round, white monument. I think it is a vent where air can move up from beneath the ground. Like the heat moving up from a fire, the air comes up through the vent. I don't know why it is there and what its true purpose is."

The blue offered them an image. It was a vent, but the timing and rhythm were not shown.

"Now we go to the second one I saw." Ferdinand pointed to the base of the mountain.

They walked a hundred paces.

"Here is the entrance." Ferdinand pointed to eight arches that were perfectly aligned over a walkway to the turquoise structure. The jungle was just feet from either side of the colonnade and the octagonal building.

They found the stone walkway Ferdinand had seen before and walked to the building.

The walkway had perfect, eight-sided alignments. Small square stones filled gaps in the design.

Each corner was decorated with double columns and elaborately carved footing and ceiling caps. The symbols reminded Ferdinand of something he had seen in Florence and Pisa. He thought it was decoration with some sort of astronomical influence. He saw the stars and the moon, but the others were completely foreign. The exterior walls were forty feet long, making the building the second largest after the dam.

The southeast entrance was large enough to allow two abreast, but the double doors carved from the stone would only allow one at a time to enter. The doors pivoted in the center. Opening one door moved the other at the same time, but the wind prevented them from opening the giant doors.

Ferdinand had spent a good deal of time pondering the doors before he finally got the courage to open them.

He was most impressed with the doors and how they flawlessly touched each other along the full length from top to bottom. The absolute precision of the engineering had him awestruck.

Whoever built the structures had observed the night sky with great detail. There was a scientific feel in the cratered moon, stars of varying sizes, and the Southern Cross constellation, which was only discovered by European explorers a hundred years before. How long ago the ancestors had been there—and for how long—was anyone's guess. Just how long had the islands been abandoned before the current residents' arrival?

The men felt nauseous, but the blue calmed them.

"Why does this place make you sick?" Kai said.

Even though they hadn't felt it along the top of the dam or at the map monument, all the buildings had it.

Ferdinand was trying to put the pieces together, but nothing was coming of it. He had felt it before the explorers came to the island, but with much less intensity. "I don't yet know, but this building is next to see. We must see it together."

Ferdinand and Pohii touched the doors along the seam. As the doors parted, a slight puff of air exited the building.

They instinctively withdrew their hands.

The doors stopped moving for a moment, and then they began to close. With a bit more force, they pushed the doors open again.

The room began to slowly illuminate from the open doors and the interior roofline. Another passive system in the building began to brighten the room with indirect light all around the edge of the ceiling. The opening was at least four feet wide, and the light was constant. The ancestors had developed the lighting system to turn on while someone was in the room— day or night. It shined at roughly half the brightness of the sun at its peak. It left no shadows, which was new to the men.

They stared at the eight massive columns, the interior dome, and a hanging globe. There were eight sets of stairs. The floor below the globe was the most spectacular find. The globe was twenty-five feet above the floor, and a frail column hung from it, almost touching the floor. It was moving slightly and progressively pointing to various designs on the floor.

Ferdinand had not seen the interior with so much light before. He walked to the closest of the interior stairs and took hold of the railing. There were six steps up to the platform and eight strides to the railing that encircled the magnificent interior floor below them.

Pohii and the men followed close behind. The floor was twelve feet below. Its reds, yellows, greens, whites, and blues were fashioned as background among the golden inlays of gentle curves, long beams, and stars along the outer rings. The center of the floor was adorned with a gold inlay that depicted the sun. Four rings depicted celestial objects. The third one was marked with hundreds of small symbols. The eight larger ones along its inner edge caught Ferdinand's attention.

Koiku looked at the grand structure of the room. Kai looked at the columns. Pohii noticed eight massive arches between the floors. Three of the four doors on that level and no obvious stairs between the floors. Two of the eight columns had small arches at their bases.

"Father, over there," Kai whispered. He pointed to the arched doorway in the column to their left.

Just then, the massive entrance doors quietly closed behind them.

Chapter 20

Iliakahani felt two events: one in the blue and one from within. The blue was showing her feelings, but there were no longer any visuals of her loved ones across the channel. The feelings of emotional discomfort and discovery had her at odds with the streaming blue.

She heard sounds below the balcony. The women had assembled the midday meal in the north courtyard. It was the last day of the full moon. How could she forget the tradition of the highest meal to the spirits, especially since the moon could be seen during daylight?

The five-day celebration had been decreed by the elders many years ago to remind the population of their responsibilities to harvest the gardens and the sea—the sustenance of life.

This first of the two remaining meals had always been set in the north courtyard. The lavish quantities of food and drink were presented just after sunset. Many citizens came to the formal ritual. It was a cherished event.

The minimal meals for the next three days—before the lavish meals on the fifth—worried Iliakahani. Her loved ones were expected tomorrow. She turned to Ihilani and almost cried. "Come, my daughter. We must eat," Iliakahani said. She had to think of something quickly, but the blue was at her side.

When they reached the large table in the north courtyard, the display of food had just been completed.

Condonte's lead elder, Ho'uolo, led the prayers. He was like a close relative, and his presence evoked calm. In the paternal sense, she absolutely loved him. He had always helped her husband. His loyalty and centered spiritual judgments were legendary. His incredibly long life had been filled with the knowledge of the good and bad history of the islands. He had been blessed with a young appearance, immense spiritual energy, and a reassuring voice. At almost twice her age and over a foot and a half taller, his subtle, soft, smooth wisdom was just what she needed.

Her pace quickened, and she met him with outstretched arms. "I am very happy to see you."

"Yes, for me too. Good morning," Ho'uolo said with a smile. "You have a question, my daughter." He called all citizens—other than leaders and elders—his sons and daughters.

"Yes, please," she said.

"Please tell me, my daughter."

"What should be done about tomorrow?" Iliakahani said.

"We will rejoice in their return, we will feed them, and we will tell them to rest. They will join us in the fasting. We will keep them with us in the palace until the seventh day. We will have to talk about many things in the palace." His scholarly eyes focused on her.

The blue confirmed every word.

Iliakahani knew the meaning of every word. They were flawlessly chosen and expertly spoken. It was the moment she would never forget. She had no more questions. She knew the plan for the return of the men. She had seen it in the blue. His words defined the visuals. She knew that he too had seen the blue. She didn't know he had seen the blue since before she was born.

Koiku noticed that the doors had just closed. "Pohii, the doors closed!" he said.

Ferdinand stepped in. "We will open them when we leave." The first time he had entered, the symptoms of starvation had forced him to find a way out of this building. His discovery of the arched entrance in one of the eight massive columns had provided a miraculous answer. Kai had pointed to the first column on the left. Ferdinand questioned his own courage and methods of researching the building. His blundering had almost cost him his life on several occasions. "Come with me now. I will show you two ways to open the doors. This way." He walked to the arched door in the column.

A tiny room held a narrow circular staircase, and on its left, there was a hip-high column. As he entered the arched doorway, the arch over the stairs drew his attention. A smaller arch on the left had a decorative column with a sun symbol and a single hand design pointing to it.

Ferdinand touched it, and it moved down about an inch. The passive system responded. He looked back at the main entrance doors. The air pressure equalized between the exterior and interior of the doors.

Ferdinand broadly smiled. "Wait," he said.

And the doors slowly opened, there was no vibration or sound. Then the doors closed once more. The presentation was more than convincing, and his smile was more than captivating. He had them at the moment, and they knew it. "Now we must go down these steps."

They followed him and anxiously awaited his next words.

On the lowest level of the building, Ferdinand pointed through the massive arches. "This floor in the main room has a purpose you can see from the floor above, but here is where you can see the details. Start here at the edge." He slowly moved his hand and pointed toward the center. "You can see the design in the floor has five areas. They are in a circle around the room, and each one has a meaning and purpose. I have not yet discovered the meaning of this first dark blue circle."

It looked like the night sky with many stars in the inlays. Some of the stars were large, but most were small. They were oriented with the night sky at a certain time of the year—a reference point for the rest of the design.

"The next circle is the one that the long thin column points to. This one tells you what day of the year it is. It is known as a calendar," Ferdinand said. "This floor is the focus of the building, but the thin column doesn't move. The column is synchronized with the earth and the sun."

Ferdinand studied it again. The earth orbiting the sun was still a very controversial theory—to the point of blasphemy back home.

Ferdinand thought about it, but no conclusions were coming. He had more questions than answers. He reminded himself of the time remaining on the island and the two other buildings.

"Let us return to the stairs," he said, knowing full well that much more in the building needed exploring.

They dutifully followed him up the stairs. The blue elevated slightly as they exited the arch at the top of the stairs.

They returned to the railing and looked down at the magnificent floor. The blue raised the feeling of exhilaration and discovery.

"You were going to tell us the other way to open the doors," Kai said.

Pohii turned to his son and gleamed with pride. His son's leadership skills had been honed. It came with respect and honor.

Ferdinand stared at him for a second, and the image came to him. The blue reinforced the feeling of advancement in spirit for Kai. He was calm and centered.

"Yes. Of course. Thank you, Kai!" Ferdinand said with a humble and gracious smile. "I will show you now. Come this way."

They descended to the entrance level.

"Here is the second way to open the doors." Ferdinand took three steps to the right of the doors, pointed to the floor, and stepped on a raised stone. When it moved down an inch, he returned to the men.

The doors slowly opened and faced each other perfectly, wider than the column in the arch had done. The men regrouped in the colonnade, and nausea returned at a lower level. The men followed Ferdinand to the trail below the mountain.

Had they stepped to the right while on the lower floor, looking at the floor's design, they might have stumbled upon the raised stone, which was positioned just ten feet to the right. It unlocked the floor design. The delicate column above could be repositioned, and the individual elements of each floor ring could be manually changed.

Chapter 21

Iliakahani felt it. The blue was showing images again. This time, the faint images were so foreign that she was at a loss. She saw an interior descent, a gap in images, a faint dismissal, and then a wondrous view.

She saw elevated spirits and anticipation among her men. It was compressed in seconds after their outline returned. It was the first time the Blue had shown her the ups and downs in images along with an overall warm feeling. She saw their exit into the sunshine. She wondered if the blue was teaching again. The question remained unanswered.

The blue continued showing her the men on the trail. She knew the men had learned something new—a new concept or something useful. It would be a source of reliance, a new constant. The images were building slowly.

The images had shown her the grand natural progression and the movement of the moon and sun. The movements could be relied upon and measured. The feelings and images were so new that a name for it had not come. She waited for more. She knew it would be good. She could feel it.

She watched as the men stopped before another monument. They were standing in front of a broad, flat wall. The blue showed it as an almost out-of-focus, softer color. The detailed images had always come in variations of blue. The terrain, flora, structures, and men had slightly different hues. This one was outlined in light blue.

She had walked in the palace gardens. A hip-high wall marked its edge. The soft breeze near the south entrance reminded her of the feminine. The timing convinced her that her men were about to see the next structure on Mokiki. She felt a welling up of emotions. The good was coming.

Ferdinand and the explorers stood together at the latest intersection of the trail. He would begin his instruction here. The building's facade was orange. They had seen it for fifty paces before the intersection. The intersection was eighty feet east of the wooden entrance. The wall splayed left to right for one hundred feet. The walls were fifteen feet high. The shallow pitch of the roofline gave it a flattened appearance.

Ferdinand thought it looked like a storage facility. "This walkway is hard. The sickness will be hard. We must find the courage. This is the most important of all monuments. We will enter, we will learn, and we will leave. Then we will go to the last and largest." Ferdinand swallowed. "The sickness will be terrible, but it doesn't last too long. It is something I know. I have been in this building once before. When I opened that door the first time, the sickness ended." He pointed to the small door.

Less than a week ago, he had walked into the sickness and retreated from the effect several times before he finally opened the door and entered. In his mind, there was no way to overcome the nausea. He knew the sickness from the other buildings had different intensities. Just walking up to the door that final time had him wondering why he had blindly tested it.

The interior of the building was the reward. The blue had shown him. Ferdinand theorized that the building had been built first. "I will go first, but this time, deep breathing will be important. It will be difficult. I will walk quickly to the door, open it, and move into the narrow hallway to the first room." He ran for the door and moved quickly inside. In the narrow corridor to the first room, his nausea rose quickly. It slowly subsided, and he almost forgot to breathe. He would have to remind them as each one entered.

Koiku was first.

"Breathe!" Ferdinand shouted.

Koiku was running, and his elevated respiration began before he took a stride. He had asked the others if he could be first. He told them that he knew the others could do it. He had felt the sickness, and it was slowing down.

Kai ran in, and then Pohii managed to walk in quickly. The others made it to the room and tried to recover.

Kai held a hand over his mouth until the effects had withdrawn.

They breathed quietly until the last man had recovered.

"Thank you all for coming with me," Ferdinand said. "I am honored to have your trust."

"We are all thankful that you are here for us," Pohii said. "Please show us what you know."

The large room was a lobby of grand proportions. It was the center of all access to the rest of the complex. Ferdinand was aware of the advantages of the designed exterior, its eight-foot-thick walls, narrow entrance corridor, and arched doorways at both ends. From a military context, the building could be defended with ease. He initially thought the ancestors had enemies, but there was no evidence that war had ever come to the island. It was obvious to Ferdinand that the building had been remodeled several times.

The corridor extended into the room an additional ten feet. The interior door was offset to one side, and a visible remnant of an arched entrance corridor remained. That older corridor had been filled in to dramatically reduce its width. It was the last modification the ancestors had planned and constructed for this building.

The interior wall with the door to the corridor was the only thing the ancestors had not finished. The stonework had been completed, but the smoothing and polishing of the surfaces had not taken place.

This was when the ancestors abandoned everything, Ferdinand thought. He moved to the center of the lobby.

The men moved with him.

"This room is the center," Ferdinand said. "Each room we enter, we come back here. I want to show you the first room I saw." He moved to a doorway directly across from the door they had entered. He walked thirty feet to the massive wooden doors at the west end of the lobby.

He pulled the handle with both hands. The interior of the west room came into view. Its function was more important than its design. The walls were packed with shelving, massive tables, and benches. A platform and a single massive table were at the far end. Indirect and brilliant white light filled the room. Thousands of tablets on the shelves depicted the achievements of the ancestors.

"This is the sum total of their learning. This is the most important room in this building—and perhaps in the world," Ferdinand said. "This is the total of their knowledge, achievements, efforts, and dreams."

The room held the history of the islands. They found inspiration there and solved the engineering challenges. Ferdinand didn't know how much the explorers could take.

"We will come back to this room. It is too much now. We will return." Pohii said.

It was too important to discover and then abandon.

A look of understanding flashed across Pohii's face. Ferdinand was convinced that Pohii knew that the room would reveal the ancestors' past. This discovery would lead them all into their future. Pohii knew it.

The blue had shown him—just as it had shown Ferdinand. Neither of them felt the blue had anything to do with it, but the blue had a subtle level of influence that allowed them to accept it without being aware of it. The ancestors had not fully discovered the full range of the blue and its influences—from soft to intense. They only experienced three of the five ranges.

"The next room is what we will see." Ferdinand walked to the single door and opened it.

The ancestors resided in the modest quarter's room when they worked there. They were like military barracks with bathing, cooking, and lounge spaces. Wooden bed frames were at the far end of the room.

The men stood silently, absorbing the view. The ancestors had lived, worked, and slept there.

"We must go," Pohii said. He knew not to disturb the memories of his parents, grandparents, and all those who had gone before him. They hadn't seen the doors on either side at the far end of the room.

They all followed him back to the grand lobby, and Ferdinand closed the door. "Thank you, Majesty. You are right to honor them."

They lowered their heads for a moment to honor their ancestors.

Pohii was especially moved. His thought the term *majesty* was a simple substitute for the *leader*. When he realized the elevated meaning, he was embarrassed.

Ferdinand was instantly aware of it. The unspoken caring between them minimized the embarrassment.

A small yet important portion of the Blue had influenced it.

"Please follow me to the next room." Ferdinand walked to the last door on the left.

They paused at the entrance to the south room.

"This room is something I cannot explain," Ferdinand said. "It is another important room, but I don't know its purpose. There are large, beautiful columns in the room. They have only one design. I don't know why they were built or designed that way. We must not touch them. There will be a strong feeling in the room." He looked at them with a smile. He wanted them to see it.

Pohii and Ferdinand opened the doors together.

The floor space was dominated by two rows of columns in a graceful curve. The columns were decorated from top to bottom with a shine on eight angled sides. The light from the columns alternated between stone and shine many, many times on each column, floor to ceiling.

Ferdinand moved further into the room and noticed a slightly different color in muted tones, emanating from each column as he walked. *Why is it shining? The lighting in the room? Indirect light?* He felt calm and relaxed. He wanted to see it all. His mood changed, but his experience offered no explanation for the design. He stopped and noticed the change to fear in his emotions. He didn't want the emotion. He didn't like it. When he was halfway to the far end of the room, he turned around. He took several long strides toward the entry door. The fear was no longer present. "I still don't know why the ancestors built this room. There must be a purpose."

There is something about this room. It definitely isn't obvious, Ferdinand thought. There was a subtle emotional connection. There was no time to experiment. He walked up to the men. "We should return to the hall."

They pushed the doors open, exited and closed the doors behind them.

For a few moments, they stood silently in the hall.

Ferdinand's mind was pondering the building. They had entered the learning room, the quarter's room, and the room behind them.

The questions faded in. To Ferdinand, a conclusion wasn't coming. There were two other rooms to be seen. "I have many questions too."

The blue had sent him their feelings. They all knew they had to move to the next room.

Ferdinand knew that the next room was unpleasant. The water-operated, pivoting door was made from a single piece of granite. He wondered why the smallest room had such a massive door.

Ferdinand turned, smiled, and touched a raised stone on the floor to the right of the door.

It moved down an inch. The system began the process, and the door began to pivot.

The light in the room came up slowly. The men waited for the light. At a level equal to the morning dawn before the sun's appearance, they entered. The door began to close and caused them to move swiftly into the room.

The left wall had many storage cabinets. They had workstations along its entire length. Two feet above the work surface, there were more cabinets.

Ferdinand had a feeling that the hieroglyphs on the wall were important, especially the one beyond the fireplace. He found a scrap of wood and wrote it down with bits of charcoal. He put the scrap of wood in his satchel. He knew it would best be interpreted later—perhaps in the beach shelter.

They noticed a disgusting smell and retreated swiftly. They returned to the door and stepped on the raised stone until it opened. They wanted the door to open faster than it was designed to. They stepped out into the hall, and the door began to close.

"The bad smell is like cooking a long-dead animal!" Kai said.

The last thing the ancestors had overlooked in the room was the domed ceiling decorations. They drilled holes in the ceiling for ventilation, and stone caps prevented rain from entering the room. The wooden spacers had deteriorated years ago and sealed the room. The fireplace vents had been manually closed.

The true blessing of their exit from the room of experiments, as Ferdinand had thought of it, was a slow building of toxic gasses. The floor vents at the back of the room had been inadvertently left open.

When they had opened the entrance door, it allowed in a mixture of methane and other gasses from the basement below to once again flow into the room. It was nearly lethal potential. Had they spent any more time in the room with the door closed, it would have sent them all to heaven. They would have fainted and then suffocated.

The blue could not have helped them more. The blue had shown Ferdinand the putrid ashes on the fireplace floor as a way to solve the lack of writing material. He had disturbed the ashes, and the smell was filling the room.

The blue entered, and they stood together in the lobby. Pohii had a frightening coughing spell, and so did some of the other men.

"Big breaths," Ferdinand said. "Big, calm, breaths."

They were recovering. The blue changed to a moderate level.

Iliakahani bolted up from her seat. She automatically looked westward. The trees were in the way. She moved quickly through the gardens and went up to the balcony. She could see the island, but it wasn't helping at all. Something was happening. The blue eased her nerves. She felt a spike in the blue—a threat—but it passed.

She knew her men were safe, but she felt a retreat from fear. Then it faded.

She stood there for several minutes and then felt precious relief.

She waited. The blue spiked again with visuals. It showed ships reaching a place with other ships. Her visuals showed her familiar faces at a distance.

She was confused. She felt like screaming. She slapped her hands on the railing and steadied herself.

The blue returned to center.

She wanted to stop and recover, but the visuals were outpacing her feelings.

The blue was showing her the invaders' ships as they approached a far-off port.

Chapter 22

The captain ordered the sails on the forward mast lowered when they approached the port of Singapore at the tip of the Malay Peninsula. The Portuguese had held the port for the past two decades and protected it with a capable force of vessels. Ships from many nations would stop there for badly needed provisions. The risks were high, but the missions always came first. The harbor was ideally positioned for trade between the Far East, Sumatra, and India.

Before entering the straits, the captain anchored in calm waters just east of the landmass. He spent the morning briefing the crew about the need for absolute secrecy. He had done the same after the Condonte Island stop. It was especially important when entering this crossroads of trade. They were told of the gruesome consequences of treason.

The fleet spent the first day anchored just outside of the crowded harbor. The next day, they entered port after the harbormaster pirated the astounding dock fees.

They hurried their efforts and set sail just two hours before sunset with barely enough provisions for the journey to the next port.

The captain was aware of the long trip around the southern tip of Africa. They would sail westward and get provisions in a distant harbor. He hoped the seas would be calm and uneventful since the rainy season had ended.

The captain reflected on this excursion. The only thing he regretted was the decision that caused Ferdinand to plunge into the channel. He would have preferred to avoid that loss even though he knew the man was treasonous in the eyes of the Crown.

Ferdinand's greatest strength was his commitment to his religious faith, he knew about many more subjects than the captain. Abbottsford admired Ferdinand's flawless fluency with regional dialects in most of the Romance languages. Ferdinand admired Filippo Brunelleschi after the master architect won the reconstruction bid for Il Duomo in Florence. He was fascinated by bronze statuary and its mythical references within the Greek and Roman Empires.

As the captain momentarily thought of his own situation, he felt confident that he had reached for his own dreams after all.

The fleet set sail for the Mediterranean Sea, which was at least three months away.

Chapter 23

The explorers stood with Ferdinand in the grand lobby. "There are many things to see in the next room, but we must not touch anything."

They moved to the final double doors. Kai and Koiku walked to the handles and began to pull gently. The doors released and opened slowly. They heard an unusual sound from the hinges as they opened the thick wooden doors.

The light in the room began to climb slowly.

The walls were decorated with square columns. The floor had a pattern in the tiles. The ceiling had the appearance of the colossal artwork. The design overall had the feeling of centered authority. Seven large counters had decorative designs. The right wall had benches in four raised levels and space for two hundred or so. A lectern was between the cabinets and the first row of seating. The wall behind the cabinets was almost luminescent. Its textured surface was like pure salt. A globe hung from the ceiling about seven feet from the right wall, and a decorative structure in the ceiling surrounded the globe's thick support column.

They walked past the first cabinet on the left; its fascia design suggested flora and fauna. They reached the lectern and noticed its simple but noble design. *Someone of high importance may have stood there,* Ferdinand thought. He wanted to see the two stone tables at the back of the room again.

They stopped some four feet or so from the two tables.

"Please do not touch anything. Please wait while I see this again," Ferdinand said. He had seen raised circular stones on the horizontal surface of the tables before and wanted a moment to interpret them. He had noticed the carved symbols below the raised stones. The handholds in the raised stones were all pointed to the left. Each one had a unique symbol carved on the table's surface. *Why were there sixteen on the right table and nine on the left?*

The men watched his every move.

The soft return of the blue almost went unnoticed.

Kai felt an uneasy feeling. He wondered if eyes were looking at him from behind. He slowly turned his head, but everyone else was still looking at Ferdinand.

The blue had entered all of the men's souls, including Ferdinand. They stood motionless in the room. The power was overwhelming. The blue was vast and limitless. The challenge was absolute. Their minds filled with wonder, scope, and duty. The undeniable facts were entering with grace and dignity that empowered them. It had one goal, one purpose, and one meaning.

The blue showed them their ancestors' goals. The blue had guided them through the discoveries and the commitments.

They loved the kindness, the duty, and the tasks ahead. The blue had shown them that each of them was worthy and ready for it. Each of them mattered. Each one was an equal in duty. Each one knew what to do—and they would all do it together.

"The time has come to see the last one," Ferdinand said. "We must now see the last monument." He slowly walked back to the door, and the volunteers followed him without question.

"We must go to the trail one last time. I will be the first to go. I will wait for all of you there." He opened the single door to the corridor and walked quickly to the intersection.

The volunteers ran out of the room and gathered near Ferdinand. They had anticipated the sickness, but there wasn't any. A new sensation entered their bodies. They felt a light buildup of static—like just before a lightning storm. The day was cloudless. The sickness had returned.

"Now the last thing we must see," Ferdinand said.

Seventy feet to the north, they could no longer see the triangle building behind them. After another fifty feet, the trail turned sharply to the right. The trail darkened in the jungle and ended at a cave.

The ancestors had carefully excavated the cave, removing only the amount necessary to allow a tunnel into the mountain. There was no lighting—just the natural light from the north.

A shiny blue circle within a white circle was the only decoration on the door. Below it was the handle.

Ferdinand saw three marks above the handle. He turned it to the left. He felt the latch release, and the door swung open.

Ferdinand had selected the manual opening option. Had he turned the handle to the right, it would have closed three minutes later. The left option allowed the door to remain open indefinitely.

Ferdinand said, "Stand on the right side of the wall to let the light in please." They walked through the opening. Ferdinand considered asking one of the volunteers to remain by the door, but the blue reassured them.

They felt safe—even though they had never been in there. The tunnel curved slightly to the right. They moved slowly toward it, and their eyes were adjusting to the darkness with every step they took.

Ferdinand stopped. "Look behind. The door is still open."

They turned their heads and looked once more into the interior. There was a steady glow ahead.

Kai and Koiku walked forward. "We will go first. Stay here—and we will report." The two men walked slowly down the sandy tunnel. When they reached a curve, they stopped and looked back.

"It's brighter ahead," Kai shouted.

The men gathered their courage and started to join them.

"It's brighter ahead." They heard the sentence three times in quick succession—each with decreasing volume.

Kai froze.

"How did you do that?" Koiku said.

"It wasn't me," Kai said. All the words repeated.

"It is all right!" Ferdinand said. "It is all right! Quiet please," Ferdinand said softly. The echoes stopped. "There must be a large chamber up ahead," he whispered. "I have heard this before. It is called an echo. Our voices come back to us in an echo. It's all right."

They were all shaking. They had never heard echoes.

"I have good feelings about this," Ferdinand whispered. They couldn't see his smile, but they felt it.

With new confidence, the men walked toward the glow. The tunnel continued into the curve, but a tunnel to the left intrigued them. The light was coming from it.

They stopped at the intersection and felt a sensation. The short tunnel ended in a room that was carved out with a perfectly flat bridge to its center. The wall and ceiling appeared to be carved together in a dome. There was an aperture at the top of the dome and another on the platform. A single beam shone brightly between them. The room had no decorations or symbols. There was nothing but the single beam of light. The room was dry and warm. The dark walls and extreme glare were too much. The walls continued in a curve down below the platform.

They returned to the tunnel.

For a moment, Ferdinand stopped at the intersection and looked back into the room.

Dust particles reached the vertical beam of light and sparkled in the heat. They burned.

A faint odor filled the tunnel, and they retreated to the entrance.

The door was open.

A brisk breeze accompanied their orderly exit. They smelled the jungle canopy. They reached the trail just as the breeze halted. It reversed, and they heard a broad thump. The wind had caught the rock door and closed it.

They turned around in a start. The experience was stunning; they were speechless. There was nothing to see but the branches returning to their natural positions. The breeze stopped.

The men knew instinctively that is was time to go and walked silently back to their encampment on the beach, the total still mesmerizing with the blue.

As the day was coming to a close, they began to prepare the evening meal. They cooked and finished it quickly.

After the meal, Pohii worried about how they were going to tell anyone at home what they had discovered. He had to tell them about his experience in the judgment room, but what about the rest of it? He saw it as Ferdinand had shown them, but what would he say? What *could* he say? They wouldn't believe most of it. They couldn't.

Ferdinand listened to Pohii's concerns and waited for the other volunteers to express their views. The men talked about their families and friends and expressed their concerns. They had no idea how to tell the story—or if it was even possible.

Ferdinand knew there was a way, but had retreated from the idea of interfering. He felt that it would best be resolved among the volunteers and their society. An outsider's solution would be too much and too easy to reject.

The solution had always been there: an expression, a tool, a belief. Perhaps it was time for history to repeat itself—even if it was only a small part of history.

The blue lulled them to sleep.

Chapter 24

The next morning, a swell of emotions on both sides of the channel was evident.

The men ate the remainder of the food and began to move the canoes to the shoreline. The waves were inviting, calming, and reassuring. A signal fire was lit, dried leaves from the jungle floor were added, and a column of smoke rose. The ceremony lasted just under half an hour. The fire was extinguished. The canoes were ready.

"Majesty, a prayer," Ferdinand asked. He moved several feet away from the shoreline and took one last look at the mountain. He returned and faced them. "Dear God, please guide us safely as we go to Condonte. Thank you, God, for showing us your grace."

"Please be the first in my canoe," Pohii said to Ferdinand.

Ferdinand stepped into the canoe and patted his satchel.

The men and Ferdinand knew it was right, and they entered the channel.

The slight breeze and morning sun over Condonte was more than they could have hoped for. The easy rowing created a bond the volunteers would always remember.

Halfway across the channel, they could make out the assembly of citizens on the western beach of Condonte. Two grand fires burned near the landing space. They could see many canoes waiting to escort them.

As they passed God's Finger, they felt humbling reverence. They heard voices, yelling, and crowds singing. Their families were announcing their return. Many canoes joined them in the final moments before reaching the shore. They congratulated them with shouts of joy and enthusiastic waving.

Ho'uolo and the elders—along with Iliakahani, Ihilani, and seven women in duty to the family—stood in the center of the beach.

Kai's wife and children stood next to them. Koiku's family was to the south. All of the volunteers' families had been briefed and placed by Ho'uolo. The palace guards stood to either side as the canoes came to rest on the sand.

When the citizens saw the stranger, they gasped.

Ferdinand smiled at his new family, his new people. His new life was about to begin.

Iliakahani walked to him with arms outstretched.

"Ferdinand, welcome home!" she said softly with a smile.

Ihilani beamed. She knew it was very good.

Ho'uolo was happy but reserved in the welcome. He knew what was to come. He knew they would have to move quickly. Their beloved leader and the volunteers would have to get to the palace. He motioned to the palace guards.

Iliakahani finished her moments with her son and her husband, and they began the walk back to the palace. She had a sinking feeling that the majority of citizens would not be included in the meeting. They would remain uninformed.

The volunteers, elders, and others entered the palace. The guards took their place at the entrances.

The citizens had been briefed about the need for the leaders and volunteers to talk in the ancestral council room, but they were surprised when it happened so quickly. Their leader had triumphantly waved and smiled at the crowds as he left the beach, but they wanted more.

Ho'uolo knew the process in the council room would challenge them all, but it had to be done there. His vision of the long-range outcome was a measured truth. Some would say it was a partial truth.

Iliakahani would raise questions and concerns about the decisions they all had to make.

They were seated around the oval table in the council room, and the palace guards performed the swearing-in protocols.

Olohu, the senior among the palace guards, asked for quiet in the room. Ho'uolo had asked him to brief them about an important, very old, rarely used protocol. He began with his distinctive voice, which could pierce any nerve and command attention without the slightest intention on his part. "Please stand. Those at the table, place your hands on the table. Everyone in this room, those who can hear me, the palace guards included, must come to a decision. All faces in this room must agree. Those seated at the table are responsible for deciding. All who can hear me must agree—you may not leave the palace without agreement."

They had been sequestered. Some had never heard of it, but there was no objections.

"We will be cared for during our duties here in the council," he said. "We will be silent when others are present. When food is brought to this table—when we leave and return—we may not speak outside this room. When we sleep at night, it will be on the third floor. When we are not in this council room, we will pray, but we must keep our thoughts and not share them with each other. We must talk here, in this room, together, until we decide. The most important decisions will guide us from today and into our tomorrows. That is the wish of the elders." He looked into the eyes of all those present.

Many had never been in the ancestral council room. For some, the tremendous gravity had only begun to mount.

"Now it is your duty, your decision. You will hear the elders and then you will hear our leader. There will be questions." Olohu looked around the room. "You will listen, you will talk, and you will decide."

The room was silent. It would be a historical event.

Iliakahani counted the individuals in the room and those seated at the table. She wondered what the outcome would be. Even though she felt parts of the astonishing total, the humility, the love, the new duty, were primary to her. There were thirty souls. She knew it was good, and her moderate smile returned.

They all felt the rise in the blue. The symphony of good feelings warmed them.

Ho'uolo rose from his seat. "Welcome. Thank you, all of you. Thank you, my leader, for your visit to Mokiki. We will hear what the volunteers found, what they saw, and what they know. We will hear of new things, of a new place. Now we will hear from our leader, Pohii, all the volunteers, and our new citizen, Ferdinand. They will tell us what they saw and what they know. They will tell us what we do not know. They will tell us of our ancestors."

For a moment, an empty silence invaded the room.

Iliakahani and Ho'uolo were looking forward to the revelations. The volunteers knew what to do.

"Pohii, may we hear from you please?" Ho'uolo said.

The blue was streaming the feelings of a centered good. Iliakahani and all others felt the rise in the blue. The mission had more than been fulfilled, and now they would hear about it.

The volunteers and Pohii talked about their experiences.

"Is that what you saw, Ferdinand?" Ho'uolo asked.

Ferdinand felt the rise in tension. His thoughts raced. Diplomacy seemed the only way.

"That is what I saw. Yes. I saw it. That is what I can say." He spoke in his new language. He suddenly realized had not made a mistake.

Olohu entered. "We will have food now."

Those around the table and the palace guards were silent as the women in duty to the family brought in the midday meal on this first day of fasting. The "chasing moon" was a revered three-day event with two moons in a month—one at night and the second during daylight. It was a tradition that reminded all of the famine in the past.

The announcement of the meal had come at the right time. The blue had shown all of them patience.

Ho'uolo had asked each of the volunteers to speak about the time they spent on Mokiki. He knew they had come to a conclusion before leaving Mokiki. They had already decided what they would say. He knew they had talked about what they would say. He knew they had weighed the information with great care, respect, and dignity. He knew that Pohii and Ferdinand had voiced the concerns on Mokiki. He had watched it all happen in the blue.

His revelation had a new, wider concern. The testimony was too narrow and polished. They had not used all three days on one experience. He knew their reasons for divulging only a fraction of the total. The rest of the population was counting on the original mission's goal. Their decision had included Ferdinand's guidance.

He had convinced them that certain things must be kept private and silent. He was impressed by Ferdinand's reasoning, but something had to be done to guarantee that the singular tale they agreed to share would remain singular.

The blue entered with calm. The images were coming slowly. A progression in the images told him that the population would understand when mixed with the urgency for self-preservation.

Ho'uolo knew what Mokiki was—apart from legend. He knew the total. He had earned it. He worried that the population would fear it once more. He worried that a total reveal would be too much.

Iliakahani was shown that Ho'uolo had been seeing the blue for years. She knew that he was the person in the room who knew the most about Mokiki. She knew that each testimony in the council room was decided upon well before they landed the canoes. It had to have been decided on the beach before they crossed the channel. She knew it.

She had talked to Ho'uolo about her concerns for the chasing moon ritual. The decree from the elders long ago was fasting to celebrate the chasing moon. It reminded the people of their commitment to all others of the island nation through dedication and hard work. They would make sure everyone was fed. She had almost forgotten about it.

She turned to Ho'uolo for advice about how to handle the return of the explorers. She knew they would be hungry. Ho'uolo had graciously said they would be cared for and included in the ritual. *Of course, they would.*

She looked at Ferdinand—the one man she knew who could tell them a little more about what they saw. He could tell them with reason, with love, and without fear.

Ferdinand had a new image from the blue. He saw another chosen place in the palace and individuals overseeing the process of educating them. There was new schooling with closely held curricula, timing, and incredible information. Ferdinand began to feel the intensity, the gravity, and the epic goal. The enormous scale of the images had him close to despair.

The blue began to flow with a narrow focus. He saw himself receiving frustrating instruction and then teaching. He saw a select few at first as he instructed—and then a careful expansion of duty, truth, and love.

Most of his knowledge of Mokiki and the ancestors was theoretical. He wondered if more excursions would be necessary. As the first meeting progressed, he thought about how the ancestors had done it—the construction efforts, the thought processes, and the reasoning.

He wondered about the relationship between the ancestors and the spiritual feel of Mokiki and its iconic mountain. Was it possible that they discovered something more than elevated rock?

The ancestors had discovered ways to enhance their own perception of the mountain and the awesome feelings it generated. Through inspired experimentation, they had intensified it with remarkable engineering.

They were also aware of the good and the bad. For the ancestors, the balance was the perfection they had wanted and then abandoned. Each advance in the discoveries and the monuments they built had its place. They knew the advantages of each one. The timing was critical. The blue had provided balance, patience, and peace. The ancestors knew that Mokiki was the perfect place for their experiment. Their achievements were safe again. All the islanders had known was isolation, distance, mystery, and deception without a definition—until now.

Ho'uolo decided that everyone in the room could absorb the facts. The explorers had rescued Ferdinand from death, and their leader had fulfilled his mission to thank God personally. Those two things could be believed. One was unexpected with humble relief, and the other was full of glory.

"We must end today with the knowledge that Ferdinand has come to us—and that our leader did what he said he would do. He personally thanked God for us all. This is the message we can give all citizens today. This meeting has ended. We will return to this room at sunrise." Ho'uolo covered his mouth and looked into the eyes of each person in the room. His message was clear.

He lowered his hand and nodded to Pohii and the palace guards.

Chapter 25

The "keep it simple" commitment that Pohii and Ferdinand had come to on Mokiki's beach just before they entered the canoes was becoming more important than ever.

The difficult announcement would raise many questions. How could it be done with any credibility? They had searched for the words that told the truth—just enough but not too much. They worried about a frenzied desire to speak to God in person and many more excursions to Mokiki. It would indeed test the diplomacy in the truth and reassure the citizens that they needn't go on their own or in groups. The risks were too great.

Pohii asked Olohu to tell the citizens about the meeting's progress. Olohu had seen the audience to the north of the palace grounds. He walked to the crowds below the palace grounds.

"Pohii sends his greetings and his thanks!" Olohu began. "There is work still to be done! The first meeting has taken place! It was a good meeting!" Olohu knew the next thing he had to say would be the most difficult of his life. "Our leader's mission was good. Our leader gave thanks on Mokiki, and it is good!" He breathed a sigh of relief, no misspoken words. "The elders need more time! They will talk tomorrow and the next day! They like what they have heard! They know there is more! That it is good! As you sleep tonight, you can know that we will ask for celebration after the fifth day. It is good."

The crowds applauded. They had not been forgotten, and they knew they would celebrate after the fasting in the chasing moon.

Olohu smiled, waved, and waited. The crowd was slowly returning to their homes. The announcement had worked without so much as a pout from anyone. He was stunned by the ease, simplicity, and calm.

He turned once more and returned to the palace. He wondered what they were talking about in the meeting. He was starting to believe something he had never accepted—his balance, his life, and his love were in jeopardy—and he was trying to reject it.

The elders excused the others in the council room for the evening. They would remain for an important session.

Ho'uolo asked the elders to move to a chapel on the second floor. The room had a door to the corridor and an inner door to the sanctuary. The north side had a double door to the balcony.

Two aisles separated the benches; the first row was reserved for the elders. The tradition of opening the north doors to add light to the room, especially during morning prayer, was suspended. The nine elders entered and sat in the first row benches.

Ho'uolo walked to the two torches, lit them, and paused in prayer. He reminded the elders that they would decide what to tell the citizens. The tradition of the torches was used only when the highest of all decisions among the elders was taking place.

Ho'uolo stood and said, "What will we say to the people we love? What do they want to know? What should they know? What can they know? How much can they know?" Ho'uolo paused as the elders pondered his questions. Indeed, how much could they say? "These are the questions. We must think of the answers—and then we must think of how our loved ones will take the information. What will they believe?"

The debate began with innocence, love, knowledge, confidence, and experience. Each of the elders had faced many dilemmas in their careers. Each one had experienced trauma, joy, wonder, glory, triumph, and sadness. The doctrine of their faith—and the power it had—was a remedy that had always been revered.

They agreed that the population knew Pohii had returned from Mokiki—and they knew it was good. Pohii and Ferdinand posed a problem.

How would the people get word that Ferdinand had survived on Mokiki, guided the exploratory mission, and returned to live with them? They had seen him arrive with the explorers, but his return had been unexpected and unexplained.

That would be the first thing they would have to decide upon.

The blue entered the room with a calm centering. Ho'uolo was first to feel it. They fell into silence as the blue eased their tensions. Two of the elders felt it for the first time.

Koiku's father, Poalolo, had heard of it, but this was good. "So, this is the blue," he said softly. He had learned long ago to observe first, think second, and speak as the last option. His soft words were heard by all others in the room. He was feeling it with only a slight visual. When the moment came for him, he accepted.

The visuals were coming in a soft, lulling white.

He wondered why they called it the blue. He had heard whispers about it for some time. He had heard that it evolved over time. A visual came that he had not expected: an image of sea foam at the shore, the hypnotic relaxing of the back and forth, and the gentle movement of the lapping waves. He stared at the uncompromising image, and he couldn't stop. He snapped out of it when he realized the singular focus had frozen him.

Poalolo was thinking how he could talk about what he and the other elders had heard from Pohii in the council room. The overall feeling was that there was a general incompleteness in the details.

The second-to-last building had piqued his interest, especially the archive room. The tablets made him wonder why no one had brought one back. He knew he wanted them and saw an urgent need to protect Mokiki and its untold wealth of information from the ancestors. He would steadfastly disagree with any attempt to revisit Mokiki or reveal it to the citizens as a whole. Until the council understood it, they would have to carefully reveal only certain things on the island. Caution was an absolute necessity. It could require years of painstaking diplomacy before the population could hear about it.

He didn't like it at all. They would have to resort to secrecy—for the good of all the citizens. The planning could take a long time, and that had him worried. He remembered what Kai had said about the mysterious sickness on the island. His mind began to race. The sickness was the answer to protecting the island from further exploration. The sickness was the key to protecting the island. He would add it to the list of things he would say.

But what about Ferdinand? Would he agree? They had only talked on one other occasion. Before Pohii announced his decision to the captain, he had asked Ferdinand about his background. He had heard Pohii's praise, but he had not asked about his education and his devotion to God and his queen.

His respect had not yet been earned in Poalolo's mind—and he had not been born on the islands.

The blue increased, revealing just enough, with a warm feeling of reassurance. The elders felt the glow together. Ho'uolo, in particular, felt the rise in the blue: caring, protection, and love. They fell silent for a moment. They knew.

Ho'uolo had been waiting for a knock on the door. He knew he would come. He had felt it, wished it, and knew it. He opened the inner and outer doors to the corridor.

Chapter 26

"Thank you for coming," Ho'uolo said. "I had hoped you would come,"

Ferdinand entered the chapel without saying a word.

The elders turned to see him enter. They smiled. They knew.

Ferdinand had all the feelings—the good, the duty, and the fears of the future he was about to be thrust into. He returned their smiles. He knew he would be called upon for his perspective as a priest. The facts he knew from his time on Mokiki would be questioned. His way of thinking and his previous way of life would all play out in this solemn chamber. His previously unknown equals were in the room with him.

They introduced themselves. Ferdinand smiled at each one and bowed his head as was his own learned tradition. His humility was well established with the nine others in the room. He feared his knowledge of their language was not going to be enough, but he was wrong. He hadn't counted on the blue to help him.

The rhythm of his native Catalan language was so different from the Polynesian language he had heard among the explorers and the elders, and it was still a barrier. He thought he knew almost two hundred words and phrases, but this was far from fluency in his mind. He would translate in his mind, use guesswork via hand gestures, and look for other clues in context. But the total immersion was something he had secretly wrestled with from the first day he was tied to the trees.

He was sure his capture would end in his demise, but it had turned into near blinding luck. The blue hit him between the eyes with such abandon, and the entire experience was just now returning to normalcy.

His rescue came in the presence of the blue. He would come to call it his "new calm being." In the canoe upon returning to Condonte, he wept at his good fortune, his dramatic rescue, and the welcoming into the population.

He had not forgotten "the painful first step." He knew of the arduous tasks ahead with the men in the room—and wanted their inspirations and to learn more of their doctrines.

The elders knew that he possessed something more than perspective and experience. He knew of the outside world. That was the key to their survival with the inevitable return of those who had invaded just a month ago. They had very little time left. They could feel it.

The elders knew they would have to decide what news to reveal to their citizens. What things could be revealed? What would the citizens believe? The elders knew it was too much, too disruptive, and too unbelievable. They knew the islands very well.

To the citizens, there were only a handful of emotions: love, trust, and patience. But also disbelief and rage. Transitioning between sides was either very easy or next to impossible. There was very little middle ground.

The elders would listen to the conversation between Ho'uolo and Ferdinand.

Besides Ho'uolo and Poalolo, the elders had never heard Ferdinand speak in their language. It was hard to understand what he was trying to say. They wanted to listen to him, and they wanted to understand him.

Ferdinand graciously accepted the endless corrections in the language. He was learning fast. The blue was helping all of them at full speed.

Ho'uolo realized he had to limit the conversation to one or two topics at a time. It wasn't possible to talk about the overall grand scheme of his experiences on Mokiki.

Ferdinand talked about the captain during their departure and how he swam to shore. His choice to change his path was the most important metaphor that evening. His decision intrigued them and inspired them.

The first glimmer of admiration entered the room. They loved what they were hearing.

The blue slowly presented the best option.

Ho'uolo felt it. He knew the correct course of tomorrow: an introduction, a new beginning, a new commitment. He was shaken by how easy it was. Ferdinand had not yet been introduced to the population, and only a few had heard him speak. Most of the citizens didn't know who he was—even though hundreds had seen him arrive with Pohii. The rumors had been building for more than half a day—from the fearful and ominous to the delightful and spiritual.

"My friend, welcome. Please know we respect you. Please know that our people need to know you," Ho'uolo said.

Ferdinand's tears began to flow. His humility was driving the tears. "It is my honor to be among you all. It will be so as I meet and know all on these islands." His words were softly spoken and deeply felt.

The elders stood and smiled; not a single word was needed. They all knew it was good. Smiles were the only tradition the elders used in times of acceptance—not gestures or handshakes. Smiles were revered with the highest approval and welcome.

Ferdinand slowly felt the meaning build, and then he knew.

On the west balcony of the palace, Iliakahani was exuberant. She had felt the rise. The blue had come to her. She was alone on the balcony, and just for a brief moment, she wanted to tell someone about the event. She knew it was more important for the elders to introduce Ferdinand. The visuals came to her with a hint of the introduction in the morning.

The sun had set just. She walked into the bedroom and saw Pohii on the bed. He stood and smiled. She smiled, and they embraced. They fell asleep holding hands.

The palace guards awakened Ferdinand. He had chosen to stay the night in the chapel.

"Thank you," he said.

"Are you hungry, sir? We have food ready for all in the council room."

"Yes. Thank you. I will follow you."

The guards had been given special instructions by Ho'uolo to be sure Ferdinand was awakened first. Ferdinand would be allowed to eat as much as he wanted even though it was the second day of the chasing moon. He alone would be allowed it. He looked as though he was starving. He knew Ferdinand might refuse to respect their tradition, but he insisted that the guards tell him to eat at the request of the lead elder.

The women in duty to the family were excused when the guards brought Ferdinand to the council room.

Ferdinand walked up to the table, but before he took a seat, the guards motioned him to another seat at the table. "Please sit here. This is your seat now—the ten seat."

Ho'uolo and Pohii had chosen him as the tenth honorary elder. The decree was final.

"Yes, please sit at the ten," Pohii said as he entered the room with Ho'uolo. Their smiles were obvious and hit Ferdinand with a forceful and commanding love. *Ah, the painful first step.* Ferdinand's selfless humility and secret shyness had been trounced. He accepted. He had just been elevated in rank. He knew it was good, and his automatic humility slowly returned. His new duties were yet to be announced, but he knew it was the right time and the right place.

Iliakahani had followed her husband into the room. She was beaming. She loved it. She had heard it during a brief conversation with her husband as they walked to the council room.

The blue entered from all directions. Ferdinand as a new elder was an unprecedented event. The promotion to Elder for Ferdinand was spectacular. She was speechless. She watched her husband and Ho'uolo smiling at Ferdinand.

She knew the two most respected men among all men had just done the astonishing. It was the right thing. They had announced their acceptance of Ferdinand. She fought the urge to hug him and congratulate him. She stood silently as Ferdinand grasped what had happened.

For a moment, his chin dropped, and his mouth opened. When his composure returned, his gratitude was evident. The revelation in honor was unmistakable.

One of the palace guards whispered in Pohii's ear.

Pohii said, "Please eat with us now before the thirty come."

They watched him eat. They offered him more. Ferdinand did not refuse the food—he couldn't. He knew the acceptance was more important. He ate his fill.

His revelation from within the blue told him it was more than an elevation in rank, a reward, or acknowledgment. It was well beyond fraternal bonding. He felt the new love that comes from trust. They knew, and they felt it from him as they observed their own protocol of fasting in the chasing moon.

The decision was more than perfect. Ferdinand was the new elder.

Chapter 27

Ho'uolo raised his hand and waited. The conversations ended quietly, and he stood. "There is news that we must reveal today. We must tell everyone we have a new elder. We must tell them why. We must tell them it is good. That is what we must do." He motioned to a guard and whispered in his ear.

The guard exited.

"I have asked him to invite those who can come to the ceremonial grounds after the midday meal. I asked him to do this so we can introduce our new elder."

Pohii nodded. The elders nodded. Iliakahani beamed her smile.

The meeting ended an hour later. The elders were convinced.

As the council room was emptied, the smiles were unanimous. Pohii and Iliakahani walked to the west balcony to reflect on the meeting and the pending introduction. They asked Ferdinand to come with them.

The cloudless sky offered a view of Mokiki and a return of the blue. The three of them waited. The blue entered with a moderate glow. They all saw it at the same time. It was the start of something that even Pohii couldn't have foreseen: the acceptance of all those going to the ceremonial grounds.

For the first time, Iliakahani realized the blue was showing her the introduction and her desire to see the good for every soul on the island. The blue was showing them the good as it had always done. It was not a reinforcement. It was a confirmation.

"This is an important step in the next days," Pohii said with a smile. "I see you helping us, teaching us, and guiding us."

Iliakahani knew he was right.

"I hope I can live up to the requirement," Ferdinand said with a humble smile. He had seen the blue, but the staggering weight of their needs and education went well beyond his thoughts and imagination. The next few months were going to require preparation in epic proportions. The fact that paper and pen were absent from this society was his first worry.

The education he had received in Europe was in his memory, but now it mattered how each step had been organized. He had been trusted with teaching them about the outside world. The world was unknown to them; those now living there had never been beyond the islands. The blue had shown them. Their revelations had never been explained, and that was Ferdinand's new duty.

A palace guard announced that the ceremonial grounds were filling with many citizens.

"Yes, of course. It is time," Pohii said.

They followed the guard to the palace courtyard. They all had the best feelings.

The audience was more than anyone could have hoped for with such short notice.

Poalolo walked quietly to the podium and waited for silence.

"Citizens! Here is something good. We are about to hear about someone new among us. I now call upon our leader who will tell you of him." Poalolo turned to Pohii and bowed gracefully.

All eyes shifted to Pohii. He went to the podium and waited. He raised his hands and smiled. "I am honored to announce and introduce our new citizen. I know he is good.

I trusted him from the first time I met him. He is our newest citizen. He is Ferdinand. Please welcome him. He is our new tenth elder." Pohii began the applause with a broad smile.

Ferdinand smiled and waved, but he had not been asked to speak.

The audience smiled and applauded. They all felt included, and Ferdinand made eye contact with each of them. He walked among them and softly offered his hands. They needed a humble man, guided by faith, honesty, and integrity. He was beaming, and they knew it was good.

Iliakahani watched his body language, the citizens' reactions, and his elevated love. He was providing validation without the slightest hesitation. The elders accepted him—and so did the citizens.

The citizens felt it. This new man was every bit an elder—and something more. He knew more, and they knew it. They had the expectation of great things from him, but they had absolutely no idea what was in store for them. Time was inching forward, but it would accelerate to a colossal speed.

On the morning of the fourth day of fasting, Ferdinand woke up before daybreak. His stomach was growling. His mind was racing. He dressed and quietly made his way to the chapel. Something from the blue had called him. It was sweet and nurturing.

He knelt on the floor in the front row and began his morning prayers— the Lord's Prayer, Hail Mary, a blessing from the Holy Trinity. He prayed to Saint Mark, Saint Matthew, and the twelve apostles. He recited from Genesis. The blue slowly rose to accompany his prayers during the temptation of the tree of good and evil. It was a turning point for mankind. The innocence of human existence before temptation put his mind in a quandary.

The blue was rising with a mild intensity—a reassuring, loving, caring intensity.

"Oh, God. That's what it is!" Ferdinand mumbled. The innocence of his new flock was being shown to him. It was the starting point and the essence of his new nation. They had the will and conviction, but the schooling would have to be very careful. He knew it.

Ho'uolo entered the chapel quietly. Ferdinand knew who it was before he saw him. The glow in the blue told him.

"Please join me," Ferdinand said.

Ho'uolo knelt down.

Ferdinand said, "Who should we send?"

Ho'uolo paused. He wanted to absorb the question.

"It is Kai. It is you. And it is six of the volunteers," Ho'uolo said. "The eight of you must go to Mokiki once more. You and the others must bring back the twenty-four tablets."

Ferdinand knew he was right. But he hadn't seen the tablets Ho'uolo was talking about. He knew of the thousands of tablets. *The* twenty-four?

"The twenty-four I talk about are the only ones our ancestors made copies of. There are three of each one, and they are identical. To help us teach, we need to bring back one of each of the twenty-four." Ho'uolo had seen them in the blue, but he had never revealed his secret or the secrets on the tablets to anyone. It was time. They had to know.

Ferdinand was at a loss. "But there are so many of them." He had vowed to return and learn the contents of each tablet. And how could he find the twenty-four? The correct ones?

"You haven't seen the twenty-four," Ho'uolo said. "They are not in the library."

Ferdinand looked into Ho'uolo's eyes. Had he been to Mokiki? Had he seen the tablets they needed?

Ho'uolo smiled softly. "Ferdinand, you and Kai and six others must return to Mokiki on the second day after the last day of the fasting. I will tell you where and what to look for on the day you leave."

He was right. The eight of them would not believe him and would question him endlessly about them if he really knew where they were and had seen them—especially if he had seen them. Why would they venture again if someone already knew the contents of the twenty-four tablets? Why had he kept it secret for so many years?

Chapter 28

Ho'uolo was born just after the fifth immigration to the islands. His lifelong experiences in struggle, pain, and famine were eclipsed by his incredibly open mind. Fear was so easily replaced by willpower, and it often evolved into questioning fear. Why it manifested in others—and rarely in his own emotions—was something he had pondered. He had absolute ignorance of fear, fearful emotions, fearful events, and fearful things. It was a mild mystery and concern to him in his observations of all things and citizens.

His early childhood was anything but eventful. At seven years old, his parents sat him down and asked him what he saw in life at his age as they saw in theirs.

He wanted to talk to them about things he didn't understand. His praise for them was severely challenged when he innocently asked them about the strongest emotions: love, hate, fear, and famine. Of the four, fear was the one that evoked the most careful explanation. They told him that it was completely natural to fear something you had not experienced before. It could even cause a person to run away from it.

The wisdom in their words, the soft tones, and the care they used while defining fear and the other emotions had more of an impact than they had suspected. The calm, the caring, and the experiences his parents shared with him were etched in his mind.

At seven years old, Ho'uolo found that observing and listening before speaking was powerful. That one open, honest conversation was the foundation his mind had unconsciously built upon. From that day forward, his love, honesty, and caring built his life and his vocation.

It had not prepared him for the slow and honest opening of his mind. His mind's capabilities were opened and magnified—slowly at first.

Ho'uolo had witnessed the blue at the tender age of fifteen. He knew he had attempted to suppress it, but something told him to wonder about it and investigate it. With only a handful of experiences, he started to love it. When he accepted it, the expansion entered. The wonder, new feelings, and information flowed.

His parents were aware of his secret in the blue, but they waited for him to tell them. For that, he was eternally grateful. When he told them, it was as if the gates to a vast garden had been unlocked and opened. They calmly welcomed it for him. They secretly rejoiced that he had shared it with them. They were proud, but they were careful about acknowledging it too much. Their delicate words were just right for that moment. They didn't need to say more. They knew it was good for him. The look on his face was enough for them. They felt it.

At that moment, he knew they had seen the blue too. He wept openly and freely. The fear of incompetence vanished. The flow of visuals started. The silent thank you from his face was all that was needed. They knew. They waited. At just the right moment, they smiled at him.

Ho'uolo grew to the staggering height of six foot five. He was a foot taller than anyone in his bloodline. His mind consumed information with unheard of ease and capacity.

Over time, he began to trust his mind. He ran with the feelings that encouraged the right path and the long distances—and every one of them offered to him. Knowledge was central to his existence as he grew stronger. It was equal to his determination to love, honor, and obey.

He could instantly freeze information in his mind—in harmony with all other information he witnessed. His unstoppable memory and freakish ability to recall with infinite detail were overshadowed by his mind's vision.

No one had told him about his ability to completely and instantly recall anything from memory. It came naturally to him. At nineteen, he finally heard he had been called upon by his father and his father's three brothers to make a commitment to the spirits and submit to elder training.

The decision was clear, but he chose not to announce it for several weeks. The two-year training regimen was long and arduous, but that wasn't what concerned him. A mid-level leadership role in their society so early in his life was unprecedented. The instant fame and honor—along with the watchful eye of every citizen of every rank and responsibility—placed a heavy burden on him. He didn't know that he had witnessed the same emotions all others felt when elevated in rank. If they confidently wanted a promotion for whatever reason—with good intentions or not—they felt it too.

He talked about it with his father even though he knew what his father would advise. His father's kind and gentle words—with purity, honesty, and incredible honor—were all he ever expected. When he finally heard the words in private, he knew he had made the right decision. He would become the youngest elder by twelve years.

Since the day of final blessings in the graduation to elder, Ho'uolo had been the most honored elder of any island. He rarely offered any opinion until asked to do so. Such was his humble, caring, and soft-spoken self and heritage.

Each of the islands had its own ritual training requirements for elders, but it was remarkable how similar they were with the isolation of the islands. The same God and the same spirits.

The differences were minuscule, but they developed over time and reinforced their individuality and distrustful feelings between island factions. Pohii had done well to bring all the people together, but maintaining it took constant effort. Freely communicating between islands was the new normal.

As Ho'uolo prepared to give instructions to Kai, Ferdinand, and the others, he thought carefully about the very words he would use. He would tell them what to look for and where they were. Would it reveal too much, too fast, or too soon? Would it compromise their future, their past, and their primitive existence on the islands?

Were the tablets really all that important—or were they better off where they are, hidden forever on Mokiki? Would the ancestors have wanted them to be discovered again?

Although Ho'uolo had advanced in the blue beyond what anyone else had seen, he kept tabs on those who had begun their own acceptance. He knew the blue so well that he began a mental review of his fellow citizens and the timing of their encounters in the blue. Each one mattered. The jump after they became comfortable with its existence was important to him.

He had become aware of an increase in the number of those who had seen the blue and knew the day would come when it would be necessary to announce it to the entire population. He wasn't the only elder with this opinion. Three others had the same thoughts and varying degrees of concern.

The reveal could have infinite implications for a society whose main objectives were so tightly organized around survival and family. A quantum jump into the sixteenth century with other far-off nations could bring chaos, rumors, distrust, or internal strife.

The blue had not shown him any such events.

He had watched from a distance as Iliakahani began her love for the blue. He had watched the information come to her and how she had responded. Then it happened for her daughter. It had been the same for him fifty years ago. He had watched Pohii and knew he had seen it even before he knew what it was. Ferdinand had surprised him. This man from a far-off land had seen it on Mokiki Island before his rescue. He had watched him during the overnight interviews before the final meal on the day they were asked to leave the islands.

Even then, he knew Ferdinand had been exposed to it.

The quick transition in the blue, Ho'uolo was convinced, was a testament to Ferdinand's character.

Ho'uolo was the only one who had seen the events as the ships left the islands. He was the only Islander who saw Ferdinand jump into the channel and swim to shore. He had watched him as he took every step on

Mokiki. As Ferdinand marveled at the foot of each monument and entered them, Ho'uolo had seen it up close. He had seen the explorers meeting Ferdinand for the first time on Mokiki.

He felt each one's emotions as they explored the good, the bad, and everything in between. He saw more than they had seen. He had not wished for it. It had come in the blue with a purpose, duty, and vision he could not have expected.

The transition of knowledge had been waiting for him—and for them.

Ho'uolo thought about how he would tell them where to find the twenty-four tablets, which he knew were the most important. They were the foundation of learning, society, life, and progress. He worried about them being recovered and brought back to this island and how it would affect his sons and daughters. Would they believe, would they learn, or would the secrets have no effect? Should they go to Mokiki without an announcement to the population?

He knew it was time. He would tell those who would ask and would tell them the new mission was to recover artifacts. He knew the mission would arouse speculation, but he would calmly reassure them that it was good and nothing more.

On the fifth day of the casing moon, the anticipation brought an element of relief that starvation and famine had been overcome. At times, grueling hard work had its rewards. The population rejoiced in celebration of their community. Their commitments would survive the test of this ritual and any challenges.

Pohii and his family enjoyed the events and the meal. They enjoyed smiles, giggling, laughter, singing, and drums. They enjoyed hugs, naps, and happiness. They enjoyed the mingling of good thoughts and strengthened friendships.

Ferdinand knew he had made the right choice, but he had never imagined it would be so good. It evolved very quickly. The tension disappeared completely. He started to realize the depth of the love the people had for each other. It was the very definition of innocence and love. He wondered if they had a word in their own language for respect.

The word was used sparingly, but it was evident upon the first landing of the invaders and raids between islands. Respect had been tested many times. With the passing of time, however, the word retreated.

At sunrise on the sixth day, Ferdinand was the first to enter the council room. He wondered about the return to Mokiki, those who had been chosen to make the journey, the instructions for the volunteers, and what they would bring back.

Ho'uolo sat at the far right of the oval table.

Pohii, Iliakahani, Ihilani, and Kai sat at the far end of the table. Ferdinand sat next to Ho'uolo for the first time. Four elders sat to the right, and four sat to the left.

The smiles around the room were complete, and the energy was high. The blue had come with them, and they knew it. They could see it on the two women in the room. Iliakahani couldn't disguise it.

The palace guards swore them in.

Ho'uolo stood. "It is good to see you. It is good that you know the mission." He knew they had all seen it in the blue before coming. He had seen the blue coming to each individual in the room. "The mission is important. It is time. It is good."

For three individuals in the room, the validation came with skepticism and a nervous fear. They had not fully accepted the blue or its effects on them. They had only a partial exposure, and for them, it had not yet elevated to love the blue. They hadn't tried.

They were learning, but the revelation that he knew they had seen the mission was a bit too personal. Ho'uolo knew how it evolved and how the three would react to the blue. It was shocking to them.

Ferdinand raised his right hand. "My friends, what we have seen and heard is good. Yes, we have all seen it together. But what we haven't yet seen is more important. Yes, we all had our own ways of seeing it, but it's good—and we all know it. There is much more that we will see, together, as friends. If there is only one thing we do on this mission, what we do together as friends when we get back is more important. It is more important than the mission. It is more important than what we bring back." He slowly sat down in his chair.

The silence in the room lasted for three minutes.

His experienced words were sinking in. His passionate words had flattened all objections and vanity.

The truth was in the blue. Now they all knew. They all had accepted it together.

Ferdinand had not had to translate. He had said it all in his new language. Without a slip, he had not had to think about it—for the first time.

His position as an elder had jumped.

Chapter 29

The day had come. Ho'uolo felt the first glimpse of the sunrise. He dressed, ate, and confidently walked to the western beach. He knew he would be the first one there. He enjoyed the calm, the warm temperature, and the soft waves on the shore. The volunteers would be returning to Mokiki.

He watched the island across the channel, and he was consumed by joyous feelings. He inhaled deeply and exhaled slowly. He wanted the moment to last. He enjoyed watching the iconic peak on Mokiki at dawn. It was if it floated in midair until the entire island was revealed by the power of the sun. Even at a distance, he loved to watch it.

He watched as the cloudless skies offered a moment of reverence and high spirits.

He heard a light breeze from the east that flowed through the palms. It reached the beach.

The blue rose for him. He welcomed its mild entry.

Iliakahani walked out onto the balcony, and the blue found her. She knew Ho'uolo had found the blue on the beach. She couldn't see him, but she moved instinctively to join him there.

A few moments later, Ho'uolo felt her movement on the trail in the palms near the beach. He knew she would come, but his eyes remained looking at Mokiki.

Ihilani had glimpsed her as she turned at the bottom of the stairs and exited the west entrance of the palace.

Ferdinand was saying the morning prayers in the chapel when the blue reached him.

Kai woke with a start. The morning light entered his room for the first time that season.

Koiku had gone to the beach. The other volunteers who had never been to Mokiki had arrived.

The volunteers had been treated to a good meal last night in the council room. During the meal, Ho'uolo affirmed that he would tell them where to look and what to look for. They had all walked to the beach, individually, with purpose.

The eight volunteers joined Ho'uolo on the beach. Among the hundred or so who followed them were Iliakahani, her daughter, Pohii, and a contingent of palace guards.

The beach was quiet, warm, and perfect. The light breeze was calming.

When the last of the families had arrived, Ho'uolo smiled. "My sons and daughters, this is a good morning. This morning, the eight will return to Mokiki. They will bring back some things we will need from this day on."

His audience wasn't sure what he was talking about until his eyes met Iliakahani's. She smiled, and her eyes showed her love for him. They watched as he looked at her for a few moments.

A large flock of birds flew over the channel and moved in a gentle arc toward the northern cliffs of Mokiki. The annual migration had begun. *The timing is perfect,* Ho'uolo thought. "The eight. Please come with me to the canoes." He walked slowly to the shoreline.

The eight of them gathered at the canoes.

With a thin branch, Ho'uolo drew a symbol in the wet sand. He only needed to tell them once. The blue, always present, had embedded the instructions with precision in the minds of the volunteers.

Ho'uolo paused for a moment and waited for the blue. "You will find them in the orange monument in two rooms. You must go to the barracks room from the entrance to find the first twenty. They will be found through the right-hand door at the back of the room. They will be on a high shelf on the back wall. The first twenty are stacked together, centered on the shelf. They are in stacks of three each." Ho'uolo knew they could do it. They would be careful with each one. They had just seen it in the blue.

The blue embedded the instructions.

"The last four are in the large meeting room to the right. The tablets are in four frames on the left wall next to the two tables at the back of the room."

"Ferdinand, when you see the four, you must move them slowly and carefully." He knew the last four were protected for posterity.

For the new volunteers, the last instruction was ominous. They looked like they had seen a monster coming toward them, but the wind picked up and calmed them. The feminine had arrived just in time.

Iliakahani couldn't be more proud of her son and the other volunteers. She smiled broadly as she observed them all. Pohii felt it from her.

The women in duty to the family had prepared food for three days and placed it in the three canoes at the shoreline. Wainani and the other women stood behind the others on the beach. Wainani was focusing her attention on a new feeling. She felt a tiny kick in her abdomen. It was the first one. She was two months along.

"When you move the baskets down to the shore and the canoes. Be careful not to drop them." Then the instructions were complete, and his whispering ended.

The eight, with help from the palace guards, pushed into the channel. They turned to see their families praying for a safe crossing and waving their hands.

They began the paddling to Mokiki with the wind at their backs. For Ferdinand, the stamina was his first challenge. It was a test of his physical endurance and mental strength.

It was just before noon when the canoes touched the sands of the beach. The iconic mountain and all its splendor loomed above the cliffs.

Ferdinand noticed an elevated energy. It was just enough to exit the canoes, bring them ashore, and prepare the camp on the beach.

A signal fire was prepared and set alight. It burned for an hour as the men prepared the midday meal and repaired the shelters.

The time they spent was relatively short. Like a fully trained regiment, they knew precisely what to do. The volunteers worked together; there was very little direction needed to accomplish all the preparations for survival on the island.

The blue had entered Ferdinand without a visual, and it had guided them. The feeling of guidance and reverence overcame him. He likened it to his morning prayers. He wondered if they all had felt it.

While they were resting after the meal, the blue increased to the point of visuals. For the new volunteers, the intense clarity caught them by surprise. Kai, Koiku, and Ferdinand knew it well. They knew the emotional feel of the arrival would lead to the visuals, and they looked at the others. They reacted to the experience with jaw-dropping wonder and awe. The blue was focusing on the mission and its progression with intimate detail.

Ferdinand noticed that the visuals had a slight blue tint in the background. He saw the detail in natural colors. His awe turned to fear when he noticed that the visuals had almost completely replaced his normal vision. He shook his head. The return to reality relieved him.

He knew that the blue was more than an emotional experience; it was a physical one as well. He wondered if the power of the Blue had a new definition or a new, unknown dimension.

Ferdinand's experiences in the blue had been mostly positive. He searched in his mind for anything that could represent a negative, but nothing came to mind. The neutrals and the good were there, but he couldn't remember any bad visuals.

He knew that the blue was present even at the peak of fear, but visuals had never been a part of that emotion when he was aboard the captain's ship. He separated the good within the blue versus the intensity of any bad experiences in memory. There were only the neutral and the good in his thoughts from the blue. His other recollections of anything bad were fading, and at last, he knew it.

The new volunteers fell in deeply. The calm, centered neutral—and the increase in energy—enveloped them in the total absence of fear.

They loved it.

Iliakahani knew they were safe. She had seen the smoke signal from the fire. She also saw the blue come to them. Pohii knew, and Ho'uolo knew. The crowds diminished, but the families wanted to stay until they had seen the signal. The palace guards remained with them.

"Yes, they are safe," Pohii proclaimed.

Ihilani and Iliakahani stood together on the beach as the others returned to their individual tasks. The two reflected on the mission. It was new, but the wind on the beach gave them the feeling that they would return with something more than extraordinary. They had no idea what the tablets would reveal. Their isolation from the outside world had been penetrated only two months ago, but the gates were opening. Her mood changed from good to neutral as she thought about it. She worried about the future and what it might bring. The answers weren't coming.

She reached for her daughter's hand, and they talked about it as they walked back to the palace. Iliakahani was worried about the explorers. She had watched as the newest explorers as they accepted the blue, and even Kai felt a new elevation in the blue. She couldn't have felt more joy for him as the tears came.

Ihilani knew what the tears were for. No conversation was needed. She placed her right arm around her mother's back, her hand resting on her mother's shoulder. They silently cried together.

Kai had felt the unquestioned love with the blue, the calm, and the centered neutral. For him, it wasn't just the love—it was the absence of fear—that had him by both ankles. There was no escaping it; he now felt the total good. He knew that he *had* accepted.

The men talked about the blue while Ferdinand listened. He wanted to hear their revelations, how they would interpret the blue, and what it meant to them on an individual basis.

The blue slowly crept in.

Ferdinand noticed the smile on Kai's face. He was instantly aware that he had joined the others in the blue. Ferdinand's eyes opened wide in the knowledge that Kai had let go of the skepticism that had always ruled his personality. He knew the expansion would take time, and his priorities would find a new point. Kai had shown the first steps in a leadership role on the earlier mission—even with his father among them.

Ferdinand felt respect and admiration for Kai. He was proud of him.

Pohii walked into the garden and joined his wife and daughter.

Iliakahani smiled and said, "My husband."

He reached for them. "My wife and daughter," he said as they embraced.

They silently enjoyed the moment, breathing together.

"We will see them in three days. They will bring our future," Pohii said. He knew it was true. He waited for them to take his hands, and they walked into the palace for the midday meal. They would talk, and they would listen. They had invited an elder from each island to join them.

"They are resting. They will eat again, and then they will sleep. Tomorrow, they will be working for us," Iliakahani said.

Pohii had seen a long presentation in the blue, although its hue was a mixture of blue and white. He had witnessed a climb and the entrance to the triangle before it ended. He wondered why the images were coming in that color. He had seen the centered blue while on Mokiki.

He had so many questions, but he couldn't decide who might offer the best answers. His wife had talked about her experiences with such unbelievable clarity. Was it something he could answer for himself? Was it Ho'uolo, his best adviser? Was it Ferdinand and his extensive experience? The possibilities were circling in his mind.

The women in duty to the family left the room as Pohii entered the council room. The guards performed the swearing-in protocols and paid special attention to Ihilani.

She had thought about not going to this meeting even after her father insisted she attend. She had only looked into the room from the courtyard. She had never received an invitation or sat at one of the seats. Her nerves were on high alert as she answered the oath in the affirmative.

Her shaking hands reached the table, and she sat in her assigned seat. She could conceal her tension, but the others in the room knew.

Poholuku, the elder from the north island of Halau, sat to her right. Her mother sat to her left, and Pohii sat to her left. Ihilani felt that she was going to have to participate in the meeting, and she felt tremendous emotions. She felt as if she would not be able to speak.

Ihilani knew from earlier conversations with her mother that Poholuku had voiced concerns about her father when he announced he would go to Mokiki to thank God. She didn't really know him, but she knew of him. He was a dedicated and solemn personality. He was not close to anyone in her family, even Kai. His spoken words—and the words of the spirits—told her more than anything.

She did not fully trust him. They had never had any conversations. The occasion had never presented itself.

When all of them were seated, her father spoke first. "We now know the eight are safe. We know what they will do. Now we will talk about what we know, what we have seen, and what we saw today. We will talk about the eight. We will talk about the blue."

A shiver ran through every nerve and vein in the room. It was out in the open.

Iliakahani smiled broadly—and so did most of the others.

Pohii said. "From this day on, we can talk about the blue—the blue we have all felt and some of us have seen." He made eye contact with each of them.

The smiles began to recede.

"We have all felt it, and that is important." He paused. "Some have felt it for a short time. Some have felt it for a long time." He had a brief conference with Ho'uolo and Poholuku before he had gone to the garden to greet his wife and daughter. The two elders had seen the blue for years— Ho'uolo far more than Poholuku. They had advised him that one person would offer the best answers. The answers were what they needed for the meeting. One person had seen the blue in an innocent way.

He had worried about what he saw as his duty to this nation versus placing this person on the spot. It could bring a chill or outright refusal. The blue had shown him love in the outcome.

"Ihilani, please take a moment, as long as you need, and then tell us what you know from the blue. Start with your Gran-mama." Pohii smiled as he introduced her.

Iliakahani could see the shock in her daughter's core. She put her arm around her. The reassurance entered very slowly. The smiles and warmth in their eyes convinced her. She gathered her thoughts, took several deep breaths, and the blue came to her in soft tones.

The feelings were placing her in the centered neutral. She recounted what see had seen in a visual that she had only shared with her mother. Her grandparents had talked to her about the blue and how it was protecting her, everyone, and the islands. She was no closer to understanding it other than the explanations offered by her mother about the emotion of love. She missed and loved her grandparents.

Iliakahani said they absolutely adored her.

"That is what we talk about—our future," Pohii said as Ihilani dried her tears. "That is what the eight will bring with them. It will take time and God's guidance to understand our new nation." Pohii sat down.

The others had not understood the remotest possibility of a long-range future. The elders always predicted the crops but not much else. There had never been a need for planning for more than a month or two at a time. They often focused on spiritual events. The maintenance of the present was all they thought they could do. To the best of their memories, planning a dwelling and placing it somewhere on the island was a common and well-practiced event. It was the pinnacle of planning. Building just one was a community event. Many worked on it until it was complete and the island's elders had blessed it. The elders governed this highly revered segment of their society.

That was what the elders feared most. They were responsible for permitting any new construction on the islands. The blue was showing them that they would have to change the ritual for something other than new houses.

The new information streamed in, and the unknowns seemed to endlessly present themselves. The visuals were present for every single person in the room.

The expressions on the elders' faces began to soften.

They knew, together, that there was a future for them and the islands. A passionate, loving, and glorious future awaited them.

Chapter 30

On the eighth day at sea, the lookout on the mainmast of the captain's ship shouted, "Land, dead ahead! Land, dead ahead!"

The maps had not failed him. His first mate had reported just last night that there were only enough provisions for one more day at sea before the dreaded rations would have to be imposed. The relief was balanced by the fact that this port of Stone Town, Zanzibar, had been ruled by the Portuguese for at least a decade. This was the one port where his maps had no date reference at all. He scribbled a note in his journal for an update upon arriving in homeport.

The captain knew that their claim to the island was fragile at best, and by some miracle, it was made profitable in the coveted spice trade. The lingering poverty in its population and routes to and from East Africa had allowed the flourishing slave trade to balloon to epic proportions.

He hoped that provisioning the fleet for the next sailing around the southern tip of Africa would not amount to more than an overnight at anchor. His personal view was an abhorrence of slavery even though he had seen it at the naval academy and his parents had briefly owned some in his childhood. Some of the wealthiest citizens in his homeport had been to the auctions.

But duty and demand for profits for Her Royal Highness had to come before his personal opinions.

He noted upon docking that the harbormaster's fee was a pittance compared to his surprise in Singapore. His respect for his opponents was always tempered by his loyalty to his queen, but his knowledge and opinions could not escape from what he knew beyond the borders of her realm. He had formed an early opinion that Spain was gaining much faster than Portugal could. Even with the lucrative spice trade was booming for them. *Such a shame,* he thought.

He had many friends who lived in Portugal. With the pope's decree that divided the world for the two countries, he thought Portugal—who, with Spain, had accepted the findings in dispute of the unknown—was nearly incapable of the financing required of the distant lands they would find. Their discoveries and those of Spain took years to organize, yet he saw the blundering on each side. The competition wasn't even close in his opinion.

He knew they had discovered Brazil, but the questions about what they would bring to Portugal were still unanswered as he sailed around South America and into the Pacific.

"Captain, what are your orders, sir?

"Provisions for two months—see to it."

The first mate swiftly closed the door behind him and began the dubious chore of rounding up the shore party, finding them, waking them, and finding what he could in the bazaar in port. *This most disorganized of outposts,* he thought. He was used to cutthroat bartering, but this port was incomplete without the constant threat of unrest at every corner. The attitude of all the shopkeepers was intensely harsh, yet he was able to find as much as he was ordered to and returned to the ship while only experiencing a knife at his throat on three out of the eight stops he made. He considered himself lucky to return with about a third of the gold he had been given to pay for it—and he felt lucky to be alive.

Deckhands were posted to watch the dock and harbor at night as the provisions were hoisted aboard the ships. The deckhands had been given hand cannons for the night since the captain was wary of thieves stalking the dark harbor.

At sunrise, the captain was relieved that his fears had not evolved to ordering the deck cannons. The fleet had exited the harbor without incident, but he posted a lookout to watch the harbor until it was out of sight.

The longest part of the voyage home was before them. The sails were filled, but the coldest part of the journey was at the halfway point. A bone of contention among the crew who would have to huddle around the stew pots for the meager heat available during winter at those latitudes. Someone would have to be assigned to mind the pots all night during the two weeks before they returned to a more temperate climate.

As normal, seniority or lack of it would rule. For safety reasons, a small fire in a separate pot was always monitored while underway at sea, especially at night. It could not be overemphasized. They heard the procedure every day. The pots were extinguished altogether during heavy seas.

His concerns about safety were overturned when he realized he would be rounding the Cape in December. He felt like such a fool.

It would be the middle of summer, not winter. The cape had cooler temperatures with its Mediterranean-like climate, but the winds were legendary. Known for a little more than a century, the northwesterly winds were a challenge to all navigators.

The unpredictable gales and high seas required extraordinary skill for anyone who had to chart that route home. He had navigated the much more treacherous path around the tip of South America seven months earlier.

The captain knew to keep his distance from the shore at all cost. He had plotted several ports under the control of European nations along the way, just in case. He wanted to complete the route around the southern tip of Africa without having to dock at any of them. He plotted a course that would take two additional days but seeing the coastline of Africa added the menace of pirates of the kind he knew from many a northern nation. He would sail at least eighty miles out to sea. He knew it would take constant monitoring with all the skill he could muster.

He sighed in relief when the fleet crossed twenty degrees longitude. The Cape of Needles was the southernmost point on the African continent. He knew he had to follow the sun for the next hour and couldn't rely on his compass alone. It varied from moment to moment until it returned to normal. He was glad it had occurred in the midday sun. He planned to avoid the rocky coastline—and the pirates.

The weather and normal seas were an invitation to a skirmish with the opportunists of ill repute. He had ordered lookouts to watch for any other vessels and had the men ready at a moment's notice.

A single vessel posed almost no threat unless it was scouting. Two foreign vessels made him nervous if they were the same size as the smallest in his own fleet.

In the Atlantic currents, his anxiety eased when the lookouts saw high landmarks on the continent. His route took him thirty miles out at sea for most of the rest of the journey to São Tomé.

After provisioning once again, he would sail west for three days before turning north for three weeks. After a brief stop at Las Palmas in the Canary Islands, they would head home through the Strait of Gibraltar.

Chapter 31

Ferdinand was just finishing morning prayers in the shelter when the blue slowly entered. He noticed its welcome feeling. *Ah, the blue*, he thought.

The others were preparing a fire for the morning meal, the most important meal.

The sun had been up for an hour. Kai and Koiku were talking quietly when Ferdinand emerged from his shelter. The others were stone-faced within the presence of the blue. They were silent as Ferdinand joined them for the meal.

As he helped in the preparations, the others quizzed him on a multitude of topics.

"What is to do today?" Kenokeku asked. This nineteen-year-old unmarried man from the northern island had volunteered only after his grandfather Ho'uolo had reassured him. His experience in the blue was just at the beginning. He almost stuttered the words. His fears were not at all addressed.

Ferdinand chose to begin carefully. He said that the feeling on the island would be so new as to terrify and so old as to nurture, but it would calm and energize at the same time. It would take time, but they would get used to it. The explanations were coming in the blue as he spoke.

Kai and Koiku felt that the blue was synchronizing Ferdinand's words with the feelings coming from the blue. They all stopped for a moment, but the blue kept coming.

As the first images came, a sound came from somewhere up the valley. It was building and racing down toward the ocean. The eight turned to the southwest as a huge spray of water found the lowest precipice. The ground shook. A cascade some sixty feet wide roared into the ocean. The volume of water reached its peak, began to taper off, and then stopped. It lasted for only two minutes, but the size of the flow and its near predatory sound had them aching for an explanation.

The splash over the rocks created a momentary mist that reached one hundred feet into the morning breezes. It carried the cloud southwest and out to sea.

The silence in the light morning wind returned.

He loved the calming of the light breezes. *So, this is the feminine I heard of!* Ferdinand had heard about their belief in placing a female gender on the wind. The most significant event had been the wind—and not the cascade of fear. Had the blue tested him once more? He wondered.

For the others, the fear remained. It took a lot more time for the centering to unravel their nerves.

When they finally returned to center, they looked at Ferdinand. He had purposefully watched as they released the fear of the waterfall and all its power. "Shall we go?" he said with a grin. They fastened the baskets to their backs with straps. They would collect leaves before entering the triangle.

The eight men began the slow climb up to the Escarpment. The shadows from the overhanging trees eased the slow burn of energy as they carefully raised themselves up the trail.

They felt encouraged by the blue and the instructions from Ho'uolo. The visuals of the mission repeated in their minds as they climbed.

At the intersection of paths, they rested for half an hour. The leaves moved in the trees behind them and on the bushes and other flora on the slopes of the high mountain.

The blue restored their energy.

Ferdinand noticed a slow but steady increase in the images and an increase in clarity.

They all knew what to do. The men had heard Ho'uolo's instructions, but now the images were shown to them: the places where the tablets would be found, the care and safety required to move them from the shelves into the baskets. Then the baskets lifted onto their backs for the return to the beach, and the slow descent to the beach. It was all there; they were convinced. They stood with Ferdinand's lead.

"We go. This way." Ferdinand spoke the first words in two hours. Their energy was renewed, and the positives were elevated. Ferdinand was suddenly aware that there was something different this time. Perhaps it was the contrast between now and nearly starving the first time. He went through the full spectrum of his memories from the first time. Something was different. The miserable humidity was absent. It was cooler than he remembered. There were no clouds in the sky.

They walked past the other monuments and stood at the final intersection—the orange triangle—and filled the baskets with broad leaves.

Ferdinand said, "For the new men, this is the entrance we need. I will tell you what you need to know before we can enter." Ferdinand cleared his throat. "The walkway you see is guarded by a bad feeling. Your stomach will ache. It can't be helped. We must walk through it to that door. It will take some time to recover, but we will gather together inside—after the door."

"Let me go first!" Koiku knew he could do it. He remembered the other times he had walked through the sickness. His volunteer mindset was working as hard as ever.

"All right. Please show us," Ferdinand said with a smile.

Koiku sprinted into the shadows as the sickness rose in him. It was a little more intense than he remembered. He grasped the door handle, flung it open, and entered the lobby. His instinct to forcibly breathe in recovery was more elevated this time. He waited.

Kai entered with his hand over his mouth. The nausea was subsiding more slowly than before.

The others entered one by one.

Ferdinand knew the sickness was greater this time, but the recovery was more important than any questions its difference might have imposed. "Breathe. Take several more breaths." He paused. "Take more breaths. It will end as you breathe." He was fighting the sickness too.

After several minutes, they felt much better.

"Let's move to the door we need first," Ferdinand said.

They went to the door of the barracks room.

Ferdinand waited for them to stop next to him. He had to determine whether the sickness had ended. "Breathe," he said. They would have to carry the tablets in the sickness. He worried that they could not run with the added weight on their backs. "This door is first."

They walked to the single door together, and the sickness ended.

Kenokeku gathered his thoughts and remained silent. Something told him that the room had more than just a special meaning to the ancestors. He had listened intently to Ferdinand. He had seen the visuals in white as they turned to light blue. His inquisitive nature took over. "You said that this room is where they lived, but the blue didn't say who they were?"

"That is true," Ferdinand said. "I still don't know how long ago they were here—or who they were. I think they were just like us, but they left a long time ago."

Kenokeku had heard this thought several times, but being there amplified the meaning for him. He was enthralled. He didn't understand it, but he liked what he saw. The fact that someone other than God himself had built any of it was racing in his mind. *Someone just like us*, he thought.

Ferdinand reached for the door handle, grasped it firmly, and pushed. The door opened easily and remained open. He realized his energy and strength had returned to normal. He would have to adjust his movements. He was first to enter, and they all followed him.

The blue only showed them images—and Ho'uolo had shown them the work to be done—but he had to find the right ones. Ferdinand hoped and prayed they were the only ones to be found. "I think it is at the back of this room ... through a door on the right."

The men nodded and walked with him to the back of the room. Past the baths and the beds, he saw the door and stopped. An electric current ran up his back and his neck.

There were *two* doors on either side at the back of the room.

He searched his memory and that of the blue but found nothing.

Chapter 32

He knew it was on the right and moved toward it. He reached for the handle and pulled, but it didn't budge. He moved to the left door and pulled. It moved open and revealed a putrid smell. A round hole in the floor indicated its use. A chamber pot was wide and long enough to accommodate the hole in the floor. He quickly closed it. *As if the sickness outside wasn't enough, now this?*

"Let's try this other door again," Kai said. He was thinking about returning to the lobby.

They all pushed the door, and there was an initial inward movement. It stopped with a thud as if colliding with something on the other side. It opened just enough for them to see the left interior wall but not the obstruction. The light in the room hadn't reached its peak.

A dank smell filled the room, somewhat reminiscent of cedar. One of the shelves behind the door had rotted and fallen behind the door.

"Get a stick," Kenokeku said. "Something is behind the door."

Kai found a wooden slat from the end of one of the bed frames. "Here, try this!" he said.

Kenokeku wrestled with it and moved several things from behind the door. He reached in and moved things—despite the splinters—and the door swung open.

Ferdinand entered the room and inspected the damage. One shelf had collapsed, but it had not held any objects at all. The tablets had been stacked on two shelves in the back of the room.

The men removed the baskets from their backs and placed them on the floor.

Ferdinand couldn't believe it. He found eighty-four tablets. "We must look at each one to be sure we take the right ones. Can someone return to the rooms and bring back a chair or a bench—something to stand on?"

Koiku and Kenokeku ran out of the room and returned with two chairs. Their eyes were watering from the smell.

"Thank you." Ferdinand climbed onto a chair and began to inspect the tablets. The power of discovery and a feeling of great adventure filled him. *There is the first tablet,* he thought as the blue rose to the maximum.

A layer of thick dust was everywhere on the top of the tablets. He decided not to blow it off and stepped down from the chair. *Why was dust in this room, and none in any of the other ones? I must find something to clean them with first.* Ferdinand went to the kitchen and opened the cupboards. He found a clean dish of ceramic origin, a partially soiled brush, a spoon, and a small fork. There was also a blade with a handle. He placed them in the square dish and walked back to the small room.

The other men were taking in the fresh air of the main room.

"We should let it air out," Koiku said. He was fanning the air into the room in a futile attempt to exchange the air. The wood maintained the fragrance despite his attempts. That one room had none of the low-level sick feelings that the other rooms had.

Ferdinand said, "We must go into the room and get the tablets."

The lighting took several minutes to cycle down to darkness, and then it slowly returned. They talked while they waited, reminding themselves about their instructions.

In the room, the discomfort in their eyes diminished. Their fears were absent.

Ferdinand stood on the chair and raised the dish to just below the first tablet. He delicately brushed away the dust. The tablet was riddled with intricately carved symbols, but he left the interpretation for the return to Condonte.

The symbol that told them it was what they were looking for appeared on top of the first tablet. It was centered in the first and second rows of the symbols, and the written sentences continued on either side.

"We have the first," Ferdinand said. His smile and sheer delight in the discovery was balanced with caution. He focused on removing and packing the tablets. "Koiku, please stand with me on this chair." He placed the dusty dish aside.

The tablets would have to be turned before they could hand them down to the other men.

Ferdinand turned the top tablet ninety degrees and was surprised that it was only a little more than two inches thick. It weighed less than he had expected. They picked up the tablet with little effort. They didn't know if it was fragile as they handed it down to Kai and Kenokeku.

Two other men had arranged the leaves in two piles and placed them next to each other. The first pile was taller than the second. The tablets would be placed in the second pile and leaves from the first were used to wrap them.

As the tablets were arranged on the floor, Ferdinand inspected them to be sure each one was different. He checked for the all-important symbol on the first row. He had noticed duplicates on the shelves that didn't have the correct symbol.

Ferdinand watched the men wrap and lower the first tablet into the basket. They made sure it was centered in the basket. They put three tablets in each basket, and more leaves were stuffed into the basket so the historic cargo wouldn't move while they carried it to the beach.

They moved the heavy baskets out into the lobby and lowered them to the lobby floor without incident.

Ferdinand knew he would have to gather the courage to find the last four tablets. He saw the images in the blue. He reviewed Ho'uolo's instructions and knew the challenge was in the meeting room.

Iliakahani saw the blue as it came to her on the west balcony. The outcome would be the most transforming and glorious time for all the islands.

The next few moments for the eight were more than just a new beginning. The last four tablets would defy even the most heroic of choices among men. She could hear the ringing in her ears already. She saw the astounding brilliance of the lighting and the fall to near darkness. She shook as the Blue presented the images, but it wasn't showing any of the eight men.

The blue changed course, and the images became foreign. She heard rumbling from the west—well beyond her knowledge and her world. The images appeared in no apparent order. There were ships and other men— good and bad, with noble intent and otherwise. Some were disciplined, organized, and powerful. Others were disorganized, desperate, and stumbling among the waves. She didn't see the captain—the only one she knew. Some of the ships were clean and glistening, but most were dirty and in need of repair.

She noticed the absence of people in the images. They just showed seascapes dotted with vessels. She wondered where Ho'uolo was. She had many questions for him. She was on edge. Her daughter and the women in duty to the family stood beside her, frozen in the moment.

She saw Ferdinand enter the next room with conviction. She was aware of Kai as he entered with the others. The women's focus was fixed westward for the next few minutes.

Ferdinand and Kai gripped the door and pulled. The doors flung open with ease, which neither had expected. The room light began to slowly rise.

The eight men confidently walked to the back of the room and waited for Ferdinand.

They thought of Ho'uolo's instruction from the beach. He wanted the blue to replay.

Ferdinand said, "Please stand over here." He gestured to the rows of seats opposite the lectern.

The men stood together and watched Ferdinand with unblinking eyes.

Ferdinand moved slowly and deliberately toward the horizontal surface he had inspected before. He passed through the opening between the large tables at the back of the room and looked for the two stones from Ho'uolo's instructions.

He stopped. "There they are."

Chapter 33

Ferdinand found two round stones, a four-pointed star, and a square one. Both symbols had detailed carvings. Intricate inlays of multiple colors in each made them unique. The four-pointed star had varying shades of red, yellow, and white. Each of the details had been polished to the point of mirror perfection. *The four-point star symbol turns on the light—or does it?*

He withdrew his hand as the doubt entered. The ambient light in the room had reached optimum brightness. He remembered that the last four tablets were framed on the wall. Which wall? He looked around the room. The white walls didn't have any frames that he could see.

The cabinetry and other furnishings were the only things with any sort of decoration. The floors were polished stone. The ceiling only had one adornment, other than the colossal artwork: a sphere that hung from a short column. The wall behind him was white.

Ferdinand looked at the other men and reviewed Ho'uolo's instructions.

The blue began a slow rise. They could feel it.

Ferdinand started to look at the wall to his right. Ho'uolo said it contained the frames that held the last four tablets. He stared at the seemingly unadorned wall and the white surface.

The Blue advanced to a moderate level.

He gazed between the cabinetry on the left and the tabletop on the right. The image of four frames began to reveal itself, ever so slightly, as if guidance from the blue had shown it. He momentarily looked away, and the images were gone. They slowly returned, and he wondered if the blue was teaching him again. Perhaps he needed to focus on the task at hand.

The images in the blue were of a confident and loving commitment to the task—even in the face of dread, fear, and shock. The two round stones with their distinctive symbols arrived in the images.

The bottom of the frames was as high as his shoulders. The images were barely defined in the blue, but he knew they were there. They were disguised to merge with the white wall surface.

The commitment to his mission helped him overcome the tension he felt from the blue. He moved behind the table and placed his right hand on the stone with the four-point star. He pressed down on it, but it wouldn't move.

Then it came to him.

He would have to turn it before he could press down on it.

He turned it to the right until it stopped. He waited, watched, and listened. He took a breath. Nothing.

He pushed down on the stone, and it stopped after an inch. Again, he waited. Nothing.

Ferdinand was now making an effort to avoid frustration as he watched and listened. Calmly and deliberately, he moved the stone once more.

He heard a sound like a rock moved over another rock from above and stopped. He removed his hand instinctively and turned his gaze to the sound. The globe above them was moving counterclockwise, and it began to open slowly. It hissed and projected light against the wall within the hidden framework. The light was getting stronger and brighter. The glare intensified and heated the entire room.

The men shielded their eyes as they witnessed the buildup of light. They smelled something smoldering, melting, and burning. They couldn't see any smoke. The wall was melting.

Just below the frames, the beam of light diminished. The globe began to close, and then it returned to its original position. It had burned away three inches of the wall and clearly showed the frame's positions. The frame had slithered in its molten state to within an inch of the floor before it cooled and congealed.

Ferdinand had never seen anything like it, and neither had the other men. They were frozen, and their nerves were on fire.

It came to Ferdinand in the blue: the stone with the square. He recovered as his own fears were overcome by duty. He returned slowly and quietly. He reached for the square, but the blue intensified and brought him images of a retreat. "Come here with me for this next step."

The men turned to him and followed his orders quickly. The men ran behind the tables.

Ferdinand said, "When I push this next stone, we will have to be ready. Go under this table and cover your ears. Do not look at the wall." Ferdinand took a breath, turned the stone to the right, and pushed it down an inch.

Nothing.

The men retreated below the table, covered their ears, and waited.

A cracking noise started for a moment and stopped. A faint hissing increased to a whistle and elevated to a shrill, unbearable noise. With a final blast, the vault doors within the frames flew out into the room and crashed to the floor. Dust went sailing throughout the room.

The vault doors disintegrated when they landed on the floor.

The men huddled below the table, covered their mouths, and wiped their eyes. Ferdinand likened the event of hearing heavy cannons as they fired a broadside in unison. He knew that the blue had protected them. He felt love and a new respect for the blue. With God's guidance, they were all safe.

They heard another faint noise. The two stones had returned to their original positions.

The blue showed him one more image. Time was of the essence. "It is safe now. Let us get the tablets, go to the beach, and head home tomorrow."

They clambered out of their hiding place and stood for a moment. The last remnants of dust were floating to the floor as Ferdinand stopped in the passage between the tables. "Move your feet carefully over the floor. Drag your feet on the floor. Do not lift your feet. The shards of stone from the blast are sharp."

They shuffled along the floor to the new openings in the wall. Four perfectly square holes were surrounded by frames. The frames were just above their heads, but they couldn't see into them.

"Koiku, please bring over one of the benches. Kai, please bring the last basket. Slowly."

Koiku pulled and pushed the bench into a position below the open frames.

"Koiku, please sit here on the bench." Ferdinand knew the bench wouldn't move if Koiku sat on one of its legs.

Ferdinand stood on the bench and looked into the frames. Each one had a single tablet on the floor within the frames. The floor was four inches below the framework. The tablets had been carefully and precisely placed in the vaults.

The wall showed no evidence of melting. But his skin felt the remaining heat from the frames.

They felt a mild vibration. The wall was restoring itself to its original design. The ancient architects must have never been satisfied with inventing ways to avoid labor-intensive maintenance.

Ferdinand reached into the first vault and lifted the tablet with unexpected ease. He delicately removed it and handed it down to Koiku.

Koiku handed it to Kai for wrapping and placement in the last basket. It was going like clockwork. Ferdinand repeated the process with the second tablet.

Ferdinand stepped down off the bench and inspected the progress. "Koiku, sit on the other end of the bench while I take the last two." Ferdinand thought the process had been too easy. He felt a modest rise in air temperature from his left, and a mild urgency entered his back and abdomen.

Ferdinand climbed back up and focused on the third tablet.

One of the men gasped.

The first frame's fascia was being restored with a slow and molten flow. It moved from the top of the first frame to the bottom, sealing it once more. Then the flow began in the second frame.

Ferdinand handed the third tablet to Koiku and quickly reached into the fourth vault. The stench was overpowering as he grasped the final tablet. The fourth frame's restoration began as he withdrew the final tablet. He took a long breath and handed the last tablet to Koiku. The fourth frame was a third of the way closed as Ferdinand stepped down from the bench.

The first frame was cooling as the fourth finally closed. The molten state concluded with the reduction of the odor, but it lingered in the room.

The men wrapped the final four tablets in leaves and placed them in the basket. They shuffled across the room. Kai and Ferdinand opened the doors, and they quickly exited to the lobby. The doors behind them closed on their own.

They felt and heard a rumble in the floor—and then silence. The ancestor's monument and all its grand purposes had returned to its neutral, pristine state with complete restoration and cleaning in the meeting room they could no longer see.

Ferdinand knew they needed to pause after leaving the room, especially since they would have to exit through the sickness again.

They lifted the baskets onto their backs and placed the straps over their shoulders. When they were ready, Ferdinand walked to the interior door and said, "I will go first. I will move quickly. I won't run. I will see you on the trail." The exterior door opened easily.

Ferdinand stepped outside into the bright sunshine, walked briskly to the intersection, and stopped. As the men gathered together, they realized that the sickness was minimal.

Ferdinand wondered if the immersion in the blue was causing the sickness to wane upon their exit. "We must go down to the beach. I will go first. I will walk slowly. We must walk the path calmly and carefully. Watch me take ten steps and then follow—each of you ten steps apart." He made sure the basket was balanced on his back before he took his first step.

The walk down to the beach was slow. They would load the canoes in the morning.

Thirty minutes later, they arrived on the sand without incident. They carefully lowered the baskets and began to prepare the meal.

An hour before sunset, they ate and talked. They longed for the sunset, their well-deserved sleep, and the return to Condonte.

As they retired into their shelters for the evening, the blue elevated.

Ferdinand was first to feel its approach. With his eyes closed, he saw the colors begin—a soft swirling of different shades of blue. The occasional soft red and violet mingled with the blue. It was a clear signal that the blue was coming.

Ferdinand fell asleep, lulled in the blue.

Chapter 34

Iliakahani could feel the blue coming as she returned to the palace from the west garden. It was time for sleep after a long day. She needed the rest. She climbed the stairs to the bedroom, and her beloved husband was reclining on the bed. She knew his somber mood as she stepped quietly into the room.

"Hani," he greeted her. Using her pet name was a clear signal that he had something on his mind. He patted the bed with his left hand. "I want to tell you how much I love you. I know, in my heart, that there is nothing more important than this. You are my reason. You are my purpose. There is something I saw today. I think it is the blue. It will come tonight ... as we sleep."

"Yes," she said softly. Tears of joy went down her cheeks as she embraced him. It was a perfect moment. She knew the blue had elevated in him. It was so good to hear it from him.

"It will come to me as it comes to you," he said. "I know we will not be alone when it comes. There are many who will see it and dream it."

Was this the effect of the blue? The absolute honesty?

The comfort he felt in their relationship was renewed. Their marriage was solid, loving, and genuine. "I love you," he said. It felt so easy, calming, and true.

She knew his deeply held feelings, the rush of emotions, and vulnerability. She loved to hear it from his lips, his heart, and his soul. She returned the sentiment with a kiss on his forehead and then his lips. She embraced him, and they looked into each other's eyes for a long time.

His feelings were so honest and absolute. Thinking about her often brought him close to tears.

The blue was coming in their dream.

Never before had they known what they would dream—and they had never shared the same dream. As they closed their eyes, the colors started.

They loved it. They fell into a deep sleep on their backs, holding hands.

Chapter 35

Ferdinand was awake in the darkness. The sun would rise in an hour. Nestled in the shelter, he said his morning prayers. To him, the Lord's Prayer and the Hail Mary were the most important prayers.

He recited his favorites from John, Matthew, Mark, and Job—the passages about catching fish, making bread, and drinking wine in the celebration of Mass.

It occurred to him that he would have to teach them and make them believe. He had not yet started to translate the tablets.

He had written something down from the earlier mission when Pohii was with him. The words were found in a room they had left from the first mission. It came to him again in the dream. He wasn't sure if the blue had jogged his memory. The words were prominent in the room with the fireplace, the worktables, and benches, and the cabinetry. The workroom— between the library and the last room—he had the words he had written down, carved on the wall.

From his dream, he remembered the moment when he had written it down on a scrap of wood. The blue had reminded him of it. He thought it could be a key to unlocking the tablets. The blue had shown it to him with the feeling of law, warning, and command. It repeated, several times, and he had written it down. The dream showed him the carving. *Do it right. Do it safely. Was it the most important message he had found?* Time would tell. Today, they would return home with the truth that was discovered long ago by the ancestors.

The stillness and quiet had him wondering. He stood and walked out of the shelter. The moon was especially bright. He could see its shimmer on the waves down at the shoreline. He noticed the breeze coming from the east and slightly south. The calm of the early hour was a true inspiration. He continued his morning prayers.

The earliest beams of sunlight began to fill the distant horizon, and he watched the progression as the light mingled with the clouds. The earliest beams touched the high cloud layer majestically. The violet, red, orange, yellow, and white sunrise was perfect.

A rustling in some of the other shelters indicated that the others were awakening. He calmly waited.

Kai was first out of his shelter—with duty foremost on his mind. A whispered greeting and a smile returned as he inhaled deeply. He exhaled, stretched a bit, and set out to light a fire.

Soon, all of them were assembling the morning meal—the last one they would have before setting off for home.

Ferdinand's mind was racing. All the things in his future were calling for his attention. He feared the changes the future would most certainly bring.

The men inspected the canoes, outriggers, and oars.

Koiku steadied each canoe as the others loaded the important cargo. They cast off for Condonte with light winds. The waves in the channel were small, and they made the first mile with ease.

Ferdinand focused on the long effort ahead of him; the width of the channel was the least of his worries. He saw the beach as they moved past God's Finger.

He thanked his Lord and Savior with every push and pivot of the paddle. He realized his metaphor for the future in the duty, purpose, and teamwork. He knew that God's guidance would be his foundation.

All the others in the canoes were thinking about their loved ones and how they missed them. They knew they could make the twelve-mile crossing, but they longed for their embraces. As their muscles burned, they were filled with the joy of accomplishment—the decreed goal fulfilled.

As the canoes came to rest on the sands of Condonte, they heard cheers and screams of joy from the women.

Iliakahani ran to him as Kai he stepped out of the canoe. "I am glad you are back, my son." She wrapped her arms around him.

Kai's wife knew it was best to wait. Alaina had seen this return from the blue and didn't want to change a thing. She smiled in relief.

Kai's five-year-old daughter ran to join her father and grandmother in the embrace. Her tears took Kai by surprise.

"It's all right now. I'm back. I'm here." Kai picked her up and carried her back to the beach.

Alaina graciously waited as Kai put her down for a moment and dusted off his hands. He stretched out his arms for Alaina, and they softly embraced. There had been no doubts for either of them. They knew this outcome. His daughter returned for more.

Ho'uolo watched silently as the men stepped out of the canoes. Each one had been welcomed. Pohii had watched Ferdinand as they rowed the last half a mile. He felt the concern, the mountain of expectations, the duty, and the dread.

Ho'uolo saw fearless duty and revelation. He had seen the tablets in the blue, but the new language was not speaking to him. *Were the tablets just a capsule of their positive achievements? Why was there no record of their failures?*

He now thought about his late father, it had been a long time ago. He had so many questions.

Chapter 36

The captain navigated the southwest African coast and knew it was time to head into port. The lookout shouted the sight of land dead ahead. São Tomé Island, to the west of Gabéo, was the second-to-last Portuguese outpost on the voyage home.

This island had a mountain that the residents called Pico cão Grande. It was rounded at the top but only about half the height he expected. Seeing it for the first time brought back certain events from Condonte with unexpected clarity.

The familiar image of the vertical shear peak on Mokiki Island returned to memory. He had dismissed his brief exposure to the blue. In the channel between Condonte and Mokiki, he had felt it and rejected it. He had been rejecting the truth. The blue had anonymously entered and had never left.

The fleeting images were intense as the harbor appeared. He saw smoke in the harbor. Through the precious glass, he saw three ships in the harbor.

He signaled the fleet to come to arms in case there was a raid in progress.

They could hear gunfire and cannons. He searched for an insignia on the vessels. He knew that none of the vessels were docked or had dropped anchor. He knew his own fleet had not yet been seen. The advantage was clearly in his favor.

There was no doubt that a raid of some kind was in progress.

He ordered a turn to port. The fleet would hug the coastline of the island. The fleet moved north along the coast, out of sight of the hostilities in the harbor.

The captain had always confirmed things with his own eyes, but the images were casting doubt on his confidence from the naval academy and schooling. An unusual swirling of the winds caught the sails with a singular and unique ferocity.

The blue entered without resistance.

As the fleet neared the place where their approach would no longer be hidden, the blue showed the captain the insignia. The British flag below the black flag. In the desperate battle ahead, the ships were clearly not acting on behalf of the Crown.

The captain, on his lead ship, knew his own fleet was more than capable. His vessel was no match for his opponents. It was almost unfair. His vessel was twice their size, better armed, and his sailors were better trained. He watched the range of his opponents' cannons as they moved in. He ordered the position of his ships just inside the range of his own cannons.

He ordered the fleet to concentrate on the vessel to starboard. "Open fire," he said calmly to the executive officer who coordinated the assault. The first volley from his frigate announced their presence just outside the harbor entrance.

The cannonballs sailed toward the starboard vessel. Fifteen of the twenty-four hit the vessel, and chaos erupted. The citizens onshore were surprised again.

"Fire," the executive officer shouted. In the second round, eleven hit the vessel—and six sailed through the rigging and hit the pilings of the dock. The citizens ran in all directions.

"Fire." Two of the heated ballistics hit the gunpowder stores below deck, and the vessel exploded. The debris fell on the center ship and parts of the dock.

The fist of superior seamanship was clearly validated as the starboard ship sank.

The captain smiled as black smoke filled the harbor. His opponent's sails were shredded, and their masts crashed on the deck.

He watched the finely tuned synchronization of his crew, the gunpowder roared as the broadside shots were fired from each of his five vessels, and the cursing, sweaty crewmen as they ran from the cannon recoil. They returned to reload the cannons. *Clockwork at its finest*, he thought.

The assault was ordered on the center vessel.

"Fire!" The fleet moved closer, the volleys continued, and they blocked the harbor entrance.

There was no chance to escape.

Cannon fire from both hostile vessels fell short of the target. The center vessel was hit, and its foremast fell.

The captain ordered a split in the concentration. Two ships in his fleet targeted the center vessel, and the three others targeted the remaining port vessel. The gun battery on shore finally entered the exchange and targeted both remaining vessels.

A fire erupted on the center vessel. The vessel to the port side was undaunted and ordered cannon fire. None reached the captain's fleet. The shore battery reduced it to splinters, and it sank with no survivors.

Seamen from the center vessel were given the order to abandon ship as the flames engulfed it. The survivors swam to shore in terror, and the brief battle ended.

The captain knew the victory would have grave consequences for any survivors and his own fleet. He ordered the cease-fire as the shore battery went silent. He dropped anchor.

He waited. He knew those on shore would hunt for survivors of the dastardly ships, and punishment would be swift. He listened carefully and quietly. He heard two gunshots and then silence.

He waited for a sign that order had been restored. When a Portuguese flag was raised, he knew. A small boat rowed out from the dock with a white flag.

The captain had not expected the citizens to surrender to him. Why were they surrendering to him?

He brought out the glass once more. He saw the two men rowing. The man facing forward was a priest or a bishop. He wore the traditional garments of High Mass. He appeared to be praying.

The captain lowered the glass and squinted in the sunshine. When the small craft reached the halfway point, he noticed the citizens beginning to line the harbor.

A sequence of images came to him as if through a window of lightly frosted glass. The priest would offer his humble thanks for the defense of the island. As a reward, he would surrender to him if the citizens were spared.

The captain's thoughts ran through many emotions—a mere mental complication. Duty to the mission and to Her Royal Highness had always been his focus. Whatever they found had to be returned to Spain. Secondarily, he needed to make arrangements to stock the fleet with nonperishable food for the trip to the next port.

The priest saw the Catalonian flag on one of the masts and the coat of arms flag on the lead ship. His native Portuguese gave way to Spanish. He had not heard Catalan in a long time and felt he had lost it over time. The small boat arrived in the shadow of the captain's ship.

"Permission to come aboard, sir?" the priest said with a hopeful smile.

The captain saw his smile and shuddered for a moment. He saw images of Iliakahani, Ferdinand, Pohii, and Ho'uolo.

The priest was smiling.

"Granted," the captain said without even thinking about it. It became obvious to the captain that this priest needed to be hoisted aboard. He gave the order and ropes were cast overboard.

The priest was equal in weight to two men. Four crewmen fastened the ropes through a block-and-tackle on a port halyard and found the effort required to hoist the man aboard. The priest grabbed the handholds and ladder.

The captain was secretly amused while watching the priest negotiate the four-foot railing with all his strength. The priest's garments amplified the difficulty. The gasping and harsh sounds of his breathing weren't helping him either. The priest was sweating buckets when he finally stood upright on the deck.

The captain asked his lieutenant on deck to approach him. He thought that the time given in protocol might be enough for the priest to recover.

The captain didn't have a feeling about the conversation he was about to hear. As he was thinking about it, he momentarily parted his lips and moistened them with his tongue. He tilted his head slightly to the left and gazed at the priest, assessing him.

The priest withdrew a hand cloth from a pocket beneath his garments and quickly wiped the perspiration from his face and neck. He adjusted his garments, raised his head, returned his hands and arms to his sides, and took a stride to meet the victorious captain. His own duty and that of his flock on shore denied him even the hint of a smile or relief that hostilities had ended. He was on deck for one reason. "Thank you, sir! You and your fleet saved us from the dread of pillaging from those you have so handily defeated. Our citizens are in your debt. We want you to know our history is thin with support from the Crown in Lisbon, and we wish to surrender to you."

The images had been right. The captain couldn't help but pause to absorb it. The images showed him the surrender. It was a warning of sorts. He felt the shock in revelation for the first time and astonishment that there was something to the mystique of Condonte. He had seen it in the retreat from Condonte, but he had convinced himself that there was nothing to it. It was nothing but complete balderdash—an emotion that had no place in his career in the armada.

It was definitely not a manly emotion. He had dismissed it and disallowed it to reach further in—until now.

The captain's exposure within the blue had not been discarded after all. He had tried with confidence to put it out of his mind, but he realized the feeling for it didn't go away. His mind was wrestling with powerful emotions that were ordinarily under the strictest control. His fear questioned his own extraordinary confidence in everything. It was the reason he had been chosen to lead the fleet.

The weeks of interviews at the naval academy and with the Crown's own counsel were now being tested to the maximum. His superiors' choice of him as the head of the fleet was nothing like the shock when the blue presented him with a whisper of the events as they unfolded.

He knew this priest wasn't just asking him to accept his surrender on behalf of his flock. He was offering the surrender of the entire population.

"I could not allow your surrender to the bloodthirsty pirates, and you may not surrender to me. The request is denied," the captain said bluntly.

The priest was frozen and speechless. He had not expected the captain to say anything of the sort.

The sailors on deck were stunned. The first mate watched the captain and knew the man was doing the right thing. but he didn't know the words to describe what he had witnessed.

"We have come to purchase goods for our journey home. Please return and allow me to follow you to the dock for that is why we have come— nothing more." The captain had dodged the unknown. There was the possible political reversal of fortune for his homeland.

He knew he couldn't risk claiming these islands for the Crown. It had not been a part of the charter of his mission. After all, a war in the homeland was neither wise nor prudent. To create an enemy of Portugal—even with the obvious weaknesses they had in a nearly bankrupt treasury—was not up to him to decide.

The captain waited as the priest was hoisted back down to the boat. The captain had no intention of governing an island for his queen. He was much more interested in purchasing goods for his final leg home. The captain felt confident that this man of God was honest and forthright. The docks were the goal, but extraordinary care would be required to avoid the wreckage in the harbor.

He could see the centered and port vessels' masts as their hulls rested on the bottom. The smoldering of the centered vessel was still evident. Nothing was left of the starboard vessel.

He raised anchor as the Portuguese flag on the high pole was lowered and raised. It was the signal he was waiting for. The masses appeared along the docks. They cheered as the ships slowly entered the harbor.

The captain had ordered the four other vessels enter the harbor first. There wasn't room for more. The dock had no berths, but the dock sidings were wide and long enough for his entire fleet and then some. He had no intention of docking. He would avoid the risky navigation required and allow maneuvering in case the three vessels he had just defeated had been part of a larger fleet. A sailor was ordered to the center topgallant mast as a lookout—just in case.

Chapter 37

Ho'uolo and Iliakahani stood next to each other on the west balcony at sunset. It was such a beautiful time. They watched the clouds move north beyond Mokiki and Thorn Mountain. They felt peace and comfort.

The blue arrived slowly and softly.

They watched vivid images of faraway events. The fleet they had known for just a short time approached an island. They felt like it was someone they had known for a short time. It was a man they had talked to before. They had watched his every move and mood. At the stone table, they saw his commitment to his country. Iliakahani loved the way he handled himself in times of extreme dread and unpredictably.

Ho'uolo had respected him, his confidence, and successes. He had not always agreed with his vision of things or the initial appearance of arrogance. He admired the man's presence and persistent demand for excellence from those he led. The harshness of his rhetoric sometimes proved painful to hear. He knew what had to be said and when it had to be said. That sharp focus was the most astonishing component of the captain's personality.

They watched as he entered the harbor. Iliakahani knew the captain was in the blue. She felt a swelling of the good along with a powerful bad. For a moment, she looked at Ho'uolo's eyes. He was staring within the blue. She felt his path was different than her own. She felt the breeze on her skin, and she knew the outcome would be better than she had ever dreamed.

She saw the brief clash of brutality. She felt the terrifying loss of lives unknown. She knew these islands had been spared by the captain. He had no choice in a distant land. He had been in the blue, and it had started for him in the north garden.

Ho'uolo was perplexed by the blue. He questioned the centered neutral, the love for all others, and the ignorance of an unknown foe. Did his exposure to the blue have limits?

He wondered about the unknown. Could it be explained? Could the choices revealed in the blue be the challenge of his life? Could love be the highest and most final of all emotions, decisions, and directions? He needed more time. Discovery was looming, and he had seen it before.

Up to that moment, a decision had not been necessary—but it too was coming.

The captain's orders for the first mate were to get provisions.

The boats were dispatched to the docks. Each ship sent rowboats instead of docking since the wreckage and damage to the docks had yet to be assessed. A battle-ready stance was ordered, and the cannons were returned to readiness.

The captain would remain in port overnight. When the first boats returned from the docks, wine was lifted aboard. The captain had a feeling that the quantity was well above the budget. The priest had gifted it to them as a reward for saving the island from anarchy. The captain would postpone his own celebration.

At sunset, two-thirds of the provisions had been brought aboard. The captain ordered the remaining supply brought aboard in the first light of day.

From the smallest ship in the fleet, James Cristo ordered the last of the cargo to his ship before dawn. He had spent the night talking to the bishop. The wise bishop confided that some of the ornate Orthodox religious decorations had been stolen from the office and might be at the bottom of the harbor.

The bishop was relieved that the cross on the wall behind his desk hadn't been touched. It held much more artifacts of his faith within its dimensions and placement on the wall. The bishop knew the furniture in his office didn't belong along the same wall as the cross. He had always been careful with the cross. He had always dusted it with gloves on, very respectfully.

It was always spotlessly clean. The east wall windows always shined. The curtains and three-hundred-year-old armor had been severely damaged during the raid. A door was dangling by a thread, and its drawers were strewn on the floor. His vestments had been thrown everywhere.

The prized staff cross—or crosier—decorated with bronze and glass was missing. He had only used it during High Mass during Christmas and Easter weeks. It had been gifted by his superior, one of twenty-four cardinals, some years ago. It had been a part of the office of the bishop and wasn't really his possession, but he ached. *Such a painful loss*, he thought.

A sapphire measuring eight inches across and weighing six pounds had been gifted to the bishop from a traveler familiar with mining in Southeast Asia. Rumors of its existence had swelled among royalty throughout the known world. It was coveted in India, Asia, and Europe. The bishop knew it was only a matter of time before the enormous stone brought suffering to his island. He had been waiting to gift it to the Vatican, and this hero to the island flock was his best option.

He feared that it was the real reason the Pirates had come. He knew his island flock would no longer face the rumor or possibility of its discovery and violent outcome if he put the matter to rest once and for all. Giving it away was his best option. His heart felt so much better knowing it would end up in a royal court in Europe—even though he wanted it to go to Rome.

The pirates were always motivated by unknown opportunities. They risked everything for treasure and glory. In their midnight raid, they had walked over the carpeted hiding place of the magnificent blue sapphire. The cleverly built-in notched piece of hardwood floor in the bishop's office was covered by a horsehair rug and his massive oak desk.

At midnight, he and the bishop had come to an agreement that only the two of them would know about it until the fleet docked in Barcelona. James told the bishop about the mission's discoveries and failures. His yearlong commitment to the Crown was winding down. He worried that Her Majesty would be disappointed with the mission.

The bishop had insisted that he accept a gift as a reward for defending the island. The bishop knew that James was facing considerable risk in accepting the gift in the eyes of the captain, and he had sweetened it with grace, dignity, and personal sacrifice.

The sapphire would go with the captain's fleet—and so would other gifts. James agreed with the bishop and secretly accepted the gifts. They were loaded aboard his vessel two hours before sunrise and locked below deck. The captain wasn't told.

James had given his two most trusted crewmen strict orders to secrecy. He told them it would be welcomed by the queen and the captain.

The high humidity at dawn brought a morning fog.

Now, in early January 1529, the last of the provisions were brought aboard. A light breeze from the east brushed the fog aside.

The captain could see a calm group of citizens with the bishop on the west end of the dock. The bishop had learned the captain's name, rank, and mission. He knew his rescue was more than fitting in legend—and he had nothing more than duty on his mind. It was an elegant and unexpected outcome—even with the battle fresh on his mind and the wreckage in the harbor to clean up.

The bishop was in awe of the captain and his fleet. He offered the traditional morning prayers for all to hear. He added a prayer of fond farewell at the top of his lungs. He wanted everyone to hear it.

The captain gave the orders, and the fully stocked fleet departed. *Ten days—at most—to the Canaries and then home.*

Chapter 38

Iliakahani had known the image she wanted most from the blue for some time. It had come in a random shocking experience in the visuals. She knew that her daughter would also see it, but she had waited for the perfect time. "My daughter," she whispered. "Let us go and talk."

Ihilani knew it was very important. Her heartbeat shot up. Her soul was guarding her, protecting her, and allowing her to reject any attempt at revealing her internal truth and deepest secrets. Her mother had seen it in her eyes. Dread and the fear held Ihilani by the throat.

Iliakahani knew, but it was important to tell her daughter what she knew. She loved it. She wanted to share what she knew.

Ihilani was terrified. Her mother offered her hand as they reached the palace. Externally she was grateful, but internally, the anxious feelings had not subsided. She imagined all sorts of topics—each with a dark outcome.

The two of them reached the west balcony.

Iliakahani pointed to the bench while Ihilani obediently sat down. She saw an expression of concern on her daughter's face. Slowly, a smile crept in. Then she beamed.

She sat next to her daughter and grasped her hands.

Ihilani was unable to speak.

"I know, my daughter," Iliakahani whispered. "The blue showed me."

Ihilani could hardly breathe. She didn't know what to think. Her face returned to shock.

"The blue showed me, and the blue has shown you. I have seen him," Iliakahani said.

Torrents of tears broke loose for her daughter, and she needed a moment to recover.

"Yes. He is the one, my daughter."

Her mother's confidence shocked her the most. She had seen him in the blue, and now her mother was talking about him.

"He is one year older, my daughter. He is an unmarried man," her mother said with a broad smile.

Then Ihilani burst. "Oh, Mother! Tell me!" She embraced her mother and looked at Mokiki Island over her mother's shoulder.

A soft breeze from the east touched them. It was the feminine. Like a soft blanket, it comforted them.

"We have known his name," her mother said. Iliakahani and Pohii knew him since he was an infant.

Ihilani withdrew from the embrace and looked into her mother's eyes. She wanted to hear what she already knew but had not yet admitted even in her own mind.

"We watched him with Ferdinand on Mokiki," she said. "We watched his face as he helped them on the island. He has an honest face, a caring face, a loving face. We watched him smile. We watched him laugh." His innocence in duty and grace had been revealed in the blue to both of them. His guarded humility to love had convinced them that it was time for him as well.

Ihilani wanted to hear his name—even though she knew it.

"I have asked for him to come here tomorrow for the midday meal with his parents and sisters."

Ihilani was not ready for it to happen so soon. "Oh, Mother. Please say his name!"

"He is ... Kenokeku is the one, my daughter."

Thousands of questions were racing through her mind. The fear was replaced by shyness and embarrassment. She didn't know where to begin.

"He is right for you, my daughter," her mother said. The wheels had been set in motion for the long-standing tradition of marriage.

Ihilani was worried. The commitments had been made for her. Kenokeku's family had selected her and already loved her from afar. She didn't even know. She thought it had not been shown to her in the blue, but she had dismissed it when the blue brought her his images.

Iliakahani knew that her daughter had been in the first level of the blue for some time. She wanted her to experience the next level, and she knew it would come. She knew her daughter was still rejecting things not associated with her close family and friends. She was learning the blue herself. The first step in the blue, beyond her daughter's own comfort boundary, was warming her heart. She found herself resisting tears. She knew her daughter had tested the boundary. Her secret feelings had revealed the truth and her future.

"My daughter." Pohii had followed them back to the palace. He knew where they were. He knew it had to be his wife who would tell her.

"Father!" she said and ran to him. She embraced him. He had come at just the right time. He kissed her forehead.

She rested her right cheek on him and heard his powerful heartbeat, which she had always done in times of anguish or loving. It was so important to her.

"You will soon love him as your mother and I do," Pohii said. It was an absolute. He could trust the young man with his precious daughter.

Ihilani's fears were melting away, and the tension in her bones disappeared. Her parents approved! She felt faint, but her father held her in his strong arms. Ihilani openly and loudly wept with the revelation. He knew it was good for her. He smiled as he held her.

Ihilani felt the winds swirling around her. She knew the tradition very well, yet she was still uncomfortable with it. She felt the love from her parents and the traditional pact they had made for her. She felt a new love for her future husband. *How can you love without comparison and without redefining love each time?*

The blue arrived. The three of them felt it building. Her parents knew it was for her. It was the moment they had wished for. Their daughter could see it, feel it, and begin to accept it.

Kenokeku, Ho'uolo's grandson.

Early the next morning, the quarter moon seemed especially bright. Iliakahani was consumed with joy as she quietly left her bedroom. She stopped for a moment in the second-floor corridor. Her hands momentarily rested on the railing. She took a breath through her nose.

Her eyes moved from the night sky above the courtyard to survey the three corridors along the north, west, and south.

She reflected on what she knew, and she reminisced.

She wanted it all. For most of her recent life, things were very good. Her future and that of her daughter were foremost in her thoughts.

She had checked on her sleeping daughter.

She walked down the stairs, and she turned.

She stopped for a moment.

She heard whispers.

The aromas of roasting vegetables smelled so good, and the kitchen called her.

The five of them were preparing a feast. The women in duty to the family had begun less than an hour ago.

For a moment, she wondered if she should go in and help. *Yes, of course.* Iliakahani smiled as she entered the kitchen.

"Good new day. Are you hungry?" she said softly. She knew them all.

Kahania, the wife of one of the late elders from the north island, had been in full exposure of the blue for many years before the captain and James had departed. She was older, wiser, sweeter, and infinitely loving. She had started the fire under the rock counter and checked on the ventilation. She opened the cabinet and selected the perfect pan, and the perfect knife. She was supervising the food preparation. She was well known for her abilities in the kitchen. Kahania had been put in charge of the meals during the first and last conversation with the captain.

Today, Kahania would plan the meal for this special occasion. His family was coming today!

Iliakahani smiled and watched the women working together. Kahania led the others. She treated each of the other women with respect. They had always called her "Mother." It was one of the society's traditions for addressing seniors. It was unanimous. They loved her.

They especially enjoyed sampling and checking the meal as it progressed. Each step in the preparation was done with pride, and they enjoyed every minute of it. The flavors and aromas were perfect for her daughter's special day.

"Oh, Iliakahani. I am so happy you are here. May I get you something please?" Kahania said.

"It is just a little early. Tell me where to help," Iliakahani said.

"Please eat and enjoy the day. Sit."

"Yes. Thank you," Iliakahani said as she relaxed for a moment. She had no words to describe her friend. Her heart knew. Kahania had a mountain of class and limitless love, but her wisdom among women was historic. She never wanted to be anything more than a woman, a mother, and a friend. The purity of her soul made her stand alone.

Kahania was always organized, but she felt that she had started the preparations too late.

"Iliakahani, please see that the table is ready and decorated. Thank you so much," Kahania said with her grand smile.

Iliakahani beamed. She felt the unquestioned trust in her words.

Ihilani was out of bed. She worried about today—her life-changing day. Even though she knew more about her future, she had countless questions. She had seen him from afar many times. She felt as though she had always been shrouded in her family's protection and comforted in her fears.

She stood in silence as her mind tried to sort it all out. She had waited for him for so long. She felt the full range of her emotions. She felt anxious desire and longed for the love she saw in her parents' relationship. She wanted it. Would he be the one? She wanted it so desperately. Was she ready? Did she love him?

She felt like screaming out loud. Then she heard footsteps. She gasped.

"It is me, my daughter."

"Oh, Mother!" She turned to the voice.

She couldn't see her. She turned frantically, searching.

"I am here," Iliakahani said.

"There you are," Ihilani said as she reached the top of the stairs.

Iliakahani waited.

Suddenly, they both felt a tremendous rush of the blue. They both paused. Ihilani was shaking. She was wowed by the images, the warmth, the love, and the innocence. They were convincing and powerful. The bright blue arrived with balance and truth. The ultimate detail was in the reverence above all else.

Her daughter had not yet seen the forecast of love between the two. But she knew they would feel love at close range, love at first sight, and total comfort with each other. It was the ultimate truth.

Iliakahani saw a more important image. Her daughter was destined for marriage to a wonderful man. She saw it, she knew it, and she loved it.

Although she had never had the opportunity to talk to him, she knew she loved him. She knew they would absolutely love each other.

She felt tears, prayers, and joy. She knew. Ihilani almost ran down the stairs. She wrapped her arms around her mother.

Ihilani knew the blue, but this was near its maximum. The filling of her heart was not yet complete, but she was feeling the warm images. Her fears of the unknown were being rendered useless with each new image. For the first time, she knew the broad horizon of acceptance. The answers to her longing were slowly fading. She loved it. She was losing the firm grip on her doubts. The constant questioning seemed less important. Her goal was near, and she knew it for the first time.

Then she realized what her mother had felt yesterday, and the tears burst forth. She felt her mother's joy in their embrace.

"Oh, Mother. Thank you. I know, Mother. I know!"

She wept with joy. A new confidence began. Her mother was confirming it, and the blue showed it. The feelings and images were telling her the same thing. *He is the one!* Her emotions were changing. The doubt was leaving. She entered the calm, the centered neutral. Everything felt right. It was right for her.

The breezes from the courtyard confirmed it. The welcome feeling from the feminine wind came just in time. The blue slowly retreated as the sun appeared over the eastern horizon.

It would be mid-morning before *he* would arrive.

Kenokeku had been given the ritual bathing at the sacred waterfall and its pond this morning. The elders in attendance made sure that the strictest of marriage rituals for the husband were carried out to the letter. He was clean. He was ready. He was blessed in the prayers with the high expectations required of all new husbands: respect for the woman, respect for the community, and respect for oneself. He responded quite easily with grace and humility. His father was his witness. He was dressed in traditional new clothes for this occasion, and they began the walk to the palace garden.

One of the palace guards was dispatched to escort the guests to the north gardens and its formal stone table.

The perfect preparations were ready. In the traditional way, Kenokeku was seated after his father and his mother. His two younger sisters were placed on the south side of the table. Kenokeku was at the far left. He couldn't wait to see her up close.

Pohii's family was notified of their arrival. The moment had come.

Pohii waited in the central courtyard of the palace. At any time, his wife and precious daughter would come down to be escorted into the gardens. He patiently waited for them. His smile and anticipation grew.

The palace guard entered the courtyard and stood silently behind him.

Ferdinand appeared first. He had said his morning prayers in the chapel. A small visit from the Blue told him of today's events, but he had known all along.

Pohii welcomed him with a smile as he watched him walk down the stairs. The innocence of his broadening smile was infectious as Ferdinand took his place next to the palace guard.

Iliakahani and Ihilani, hand in hand, appeared at the top of the stairs. They were both wearing flowers in their hair. White flowers for the daughter had been selected by her mother and at least one elder. Yellow and pink had been hand selected for the mother, a long-held tradition. The women started to descend the stairs in the sunlight.

Ihilani couldn't wait. She wanted this day so much.

Ferdinand knew Ihilani would see him the instant they walked out of the palace to the north garden. He heard singing and drumming and knew it was time.

Ihilani and her mother stopped at the bottom of the stairs.

Pohii hugged and kissed them. He stood next to her and grasped her hand. They took a moment and simply breathed together. It was the start of something new.

A single white bird flew north overhead. Iliakahani couldn't believe the perfect timing. She knew the omen was a signal that it was meant to be. She turned to her daughter. "The wind is coming. Now we go," she whispered.

Ihilani was anxious. Her dreams were coming true. She already loved her new man.

Iliakahani was visited by the warmest feelings she had ever felt. She smiled.

Pohii walked proudly with the utmost confidence that it was right.

Ferdinand had some of the same feelings as he walked close behind. He wanted to learn the ritual and see how the blessings were spoken.

They stopped at the east end of the table. The palace guard escorted them to their place settings. The placement of each guest was among the most important features of the ceremony.

The ritual procession was conducted in silence. The table was elaborately decorated with flowers. It was subdued compared to a marriage ceremony, yet the introduction and its solemn meaning were just as important among the elders. It was always conducted with reverence and grace. The community would accept them as a couple before marriage. It was the proper introduction before God and the spirits.

As the guard escorted Ihilani to her seat, she looked across the table.

Kenokeku was beaming that sincere, humble smile that she quickly adored about him. Emotions were slowly building in her soul. She knew without question that he was the one. Her mother and father were right.

And the final doubt slipped away. The light breeze in the garden confirmed it.

Ho'uolo was in the upstairs chapel. He had wanted to attend, but tradition said there could only be two generations in attendance. He would be there, witnessing in the blue, even if he weren't sitting at the table with them. His grandson was being introduced today, and he knew they would get married.

The blue was coming. He knew this was important. The blue was coming.

The blue entered with kindness and caring.

Ho'uolo shifted his focus and concentrated on the blue. He felt something new and something old: his childhood, his marriage, and his recent past. He ached for the love he had for this society, his parents, his wife, and his children. He would visit Loulu Island again. He knew he needed to go.

The next morning, the preparations for Ihilani and Kenokeku were being announced. Their special day was three weeks away.

Ho'uolo congratulated them, took a step, and quietly exited the gardens. He had asked two of the palace guards to take him to Loulu Island. He told the guards it would be a short trip of a single day. He had not said a word to anyone else. He made an effort to think about nothing else but the walk to the beach to disguise his powerful memory and hide it. He was walking with his son, Keku, father of Kenokeku. Ho'uolo's wife and two daughters were visiting with Wainani. They wanted to go after hearing her news. Identical twin boys was a very rare event among islanders.

Keku had watched his father, but he was not going with him. His own duty on Condonte was not yet concluded.

Keku knew he wanted to see someone on Loulu. He bid him a safe journey as he watched him enter the canoe.

Iliakahani felt like something was wrong. She felt it in the absence of him—and her love for him. She knew he was leaving, but she didn't know anything more. A shiver of her nerves told her so. The absence and loss stretched from her neck to her toes. She hadn't felt that fear in a long time.

Finally, the blue came to her. The feeling of duty surrounded the images. It was Ho'uolo's duty. It was his mission. The blue showed her an image of Ho'uolo as he climbed into the canoe.

For Iliakahani, it wasn't enough. She tried to resist the questions, but they kept coming. Why was he going now?

She accepted that it was his mission. She knew it would come in revelation. She knew it would come in revelation. For the first time she knew it would come. He would return.

Chapter 40

"Las Palmas," the sailor shouted from high on the mainmast. "Las Palmas, dead ahead!"

The first mate rejoiced in the news. It had been nine days at sea. He wanted to get ashore. He ran to the captain's cabin and briskly used the knocker.

"Yes?" the captain shouted. He had just closed his eyes for a nap.

"Las Palmas, sir!" the first mate shouted.

"Yes. Thank you. Dismissed!" So, his maps were correct. He could once again trust the illustrations of the currents. The currents along the coast of Africa, before the turn north, were west to east. As he made the turn north, he faced the north-to-south flow.

He went out on deck with his glass and looked carefully at the east coast of Gran Canaria Island. He saw no other vessels. He turned his focus northward along the coast.

There was Las Palmas and its landmark Montaña de Vigia. Geologically, the dormant volcano jutted out to the northeast with a narrow isthmus between it and the rest of the island. The harbor was positioned on the east side of the isthmus.

He had docked there many times. It was one of his favorites. He saw the Castilian flag in port from seven miles away.

He wanted to stay there for as long as duty was permitted. Two days were plenty. He could celebrate better at home in Barcelona. He knew his crew wanted shore leave, especially here in friendly territory, but the duty and purchase of provisions came first.

As he approached, he was aware that the blue was coming once more. The visuals were not masked by any calm. This time, it was blunt history. The first was in a conflict, the second was in relief, and the third was in glory.

He could see the two new dock cranes. One was tending to a Dutch merchant vessel, and the other appeared to be idle. Two more ships were tied down on the dock.

He noticed the land crew working on the breakwater pier. It was an enormous task. When he entered the harbor, he knew something was wrong.

The ordinary transfer of goods was about half the normal pace. The carpenters and painters were busy at their work. The restoration was clearly the focus.

He saw a familiar face walking along the dock toward the south end. Commander Rojas was gesturing for them to throw the ropes. His crew secured the fleet. The smallest vessel would wait at anchor.

As the captain walked down the plank, he said, "Comandante, my friend!" The captain knew him from the academy.

"I thought you would have been killed by now!" the commander said with a smirk.

"It *has* been a long time," the captain said. He smiled. "It's been too long, sir."

"I wish you had been here ten days ago, my friend," the commander said.

"What happened here?" the captain said.

"Those evil pirates from the north came here to burn us down. We were fortunate to run them off before they set more fires," the commander said.

"What pirates?" the captain asked.

"The bearded one from England—with two other ships," the commander said.

"They had been seen from Vigia just before sunset. They came into the harbor and started blasting in the dark," Commander Rojas said.

"I'm glad you sent them back to the sea, my friend," the captain said. The news sent a shudder up his spine.

"His Majesty sent us two shore guns, and they were ready three days before the pirates came."

"*His* Majesty?" the captain said.

"Of course, you wouldn't know. I must apologize, my friend."

"What happened to her?"

"Her Majesty is incarcerated in Castillo de Aragón, and the Royal Court confirmed it publicly within a week. You see, she is mad. His majesty's coronation was soon after that." He cleared his throat. "One of my friends at the academy said he doesn't expect him to go very long without marrying."

The captain felt a mixture of relief and dread. He knew the Queen had been suffering before he left. He would have to get accustomed to a new king. "Who is the new king?"

"He is Charles I, emperor of the Holy Roman Empire," the commander said.

It was stinging. Barcelona was silent as the transition progressed. The majority in the city that he called home had a begrudged respect for Castilian royalty. They fondly remembered their own royalty. The captain tried to absorb it.

The maps of Europe had been redrawn several times in the past two decades. Sardinia and parts of the Italian peninsula were ruled by the Spanish Crown—and so was the vast New World to the west. The queen had been responsible for the consolidation of New Spain, which was now under the rule of the young King.

He knew about the construction of the palace at Alhambra, high on a hill in southern Spain. The captain thought of it as a statement that the dreaded Moors were banished for good, but he secretly loved their architecture.

He knew he had time on his final leg to rearrange his opinion and his loyalty. It was required, but he wasn't happy about it. He decided they would stay in port for two days and then continue home.

Early in the morning, the captain awoke in his cabin. The brief voyage home would bring relief and a new challenge in a new world with the young king. Commander Rojas had briefed him of his own perspective of the king's personality, but the introduction and meager offerings of the captain's mission were coursing dread through his veins.

He had known about the secretive prince before his mission had started, and now the young king was free from the shadow of the queen. That freedom presented an unknown that the captain worried about the most.

Just after the midday meal, the fleet raised anchor and set sail for Gibraltar.

He had learned that the king had sent the newest Spanish flag to be flown on each of the Canary Islands. The ship carrying the new flags would probably reach Las Palmas the day after the captain's fleet departed for Spain.

Favorable winds offered the fleet a feeling of anxious relief as the sails were filled, and their sighs captured the ocean air.

The captain knew this route well. He ordered two degrees east of true north. The island of Madeira and its low population, high cliffs, and mountainous terrain had been low on his list of ports. Even with its striking beauty, he thought it was a stop of last resort.

He was close to home, and he dismissed it. They passed twenty miles east of Madeira.

He ordered the fleet toward Faro, Portugal. Twenty miles from shore, he would turn east toward Cádiz, Spain. He would avoid the coast of Morocco, its rarely trusted ports, and the strongholds of pirates. He was always alert for the English armadas and the less-than-reputable outcasts in the area. He wanted to avoid conflict with any vessels.

In two days—with favorable winds—they would reach Gibraltar. He was most anxious to get home.

He made the turn east an hour before sundown. Half an hour later, he spotted an empty cove and turned toward it. Just beyond the border with Portugal and forty miles from Cádiz, he dropped anchor for the night. Being near the Spanish coast felt good, but it was hardly the time for a celebration. He ordered a watch for the night. All was calm.

He saw no torches at the shoreline. He was out of the normal shipping lanes, but he ordered minimal lighting. Only those that could not be seen from outside were allowed.

When darkness fell over the scene, the captain was finally able to relax. He retired to his cabin, drew the curtains, and lit a single candle on his desk. He reclined on his bunk and stretched his hands behind his head. The slight draft in the room caused the flame to gently flicker. He liked it that way. The shadows in the room lulled him.

He was used to the noise on the ship. The men below deck were falling asleep. When he was finally able to hear the soft waves on the shoreline, the calming sound seduced him to sleep.

His eyes opened wide when the sun was just below the horizon. He wrestled the blanket and sheet and cast them aside. He was very hungry. He put on his trousers, boots, and jacket.

He lit two candles on the table and reached for the breadbox. He opened it and took a huge bite of the bread. He reached for the small knife, drew some butter from the glass dish, and smeared a generous amount on the second slice. He added marmalade. He longed for a sip of tea. This just discovered beverage from the Orient had been brought aboard in Singapore. Just before leaving port, he had six large bales of tea leaves and the precious seeds stowed in the center hold. He had purchased them with his own gold.

His first mate had been given instructions for how to brew it and pour it. The agony of the time needed to brew was rewarded by the first sampling of the new, must-have drink. He absolutely loved it. He couldn't wait to share it with those he knew in Barcelona.

There was a knock at the door.

He pulled the latch open, and the door swung in.

"I have boiling water for you, sir." The stone-faced first mate knew how to gauge the captain's mood.

"Please come in," the captain said. In a rare moment, he put aside his rank. "Please pour it for me ... and for yourself."

Chapter 41

Ho'uolo stepped out of the canoe on the beach on Loulu. For him, Loulu Island was always welcoming and calm. It was such a loving and wondrous island. *Ah, it is good to be here once more,* he thought.

There was one person he had returned to talk to. Lokoihu was a man of few words, honest to a fault, caring, and loving. The dedicated holy man was eleven years older than Ho'uolo. He had taught him the ways of the elders for two years before he was elected and elevated to elder on Loulu. Ho'uolo really never got over how much he looked up to him in the spiritual sense—even though he was much shorter.

He saw Lokoihu tending to the fish harvest on the beach. Ho'uolo felt a little guilty as he watched Lokoihu struggle to reach the smoking rack. That was how he had always done it. He had accepted the struggle. The rewards were always more important.

He watched him inspect the fish in his intricately designed fish pen. His care and maintenance of his fish pen were legendary. Among the countless fish pens throughout the islands, he had tended this one only. He carefully tended to each stone and replaced each bamboo gate numerous times each month. Ho'uolo saw Lokoihu's dedication.

He carefully took down the best fish and smelled it. The fire had done the job. He laid it on the pulled leaves on the bamboo rack and wrapped it. His job was complete.

He began the short walk to his modest dwelling where his much younger sister would prepare the meal. He handed the fillets to her. The outdoor cooking would take only minutes among the stones.

Ho'uolo knew that he was welcome and that Lokoihu had seen him. He began the walk to meet him at his home.

For Lokoihu, the blue was a constant. He had accepted it early in his life. It was easy. He had chosen the simple things, the good things. He did not just know *about* them. Like a loving companion, the blue was always guiding him. Each of his spiritual beliefs—a very long list—was held with a separation. Each belief was much more than relevant. The total of his spirit was simply the total absence of doubt. His devout love for God and his love for the blue and its centering never presented the slightest conflict. He held no regrets or longing—only loving memories. He had a special place for the blue and the doctrine of the spirits and God. They were never compared in his mind; they were just simply welcome.

Ho'uolo's shadow stopped ten feet shy of the entrance.

Lokoihu waited, nodded to his sister, and turned his head.

"You come to decide," he said softly. His smile meant to acknowledge and welcome his friend.

The honest welcome felt like a stone to the head, but his friend had said the words in such a kind, compassionate, innocent way. He had come to him for his knowledge of the blue. His occasionally blunt wisdom of all things was eclipsed by his unbelievable intuition.

He hugged his sister, and she continued the preparations for the meal.

"Please sit," he said as he pointed out a bench at the table. Lokoihu sat across from him, calmly placed his hands on the table, and looked at Ho'uolo. He would listen first.

"I am so glad to see you," Ho'uolo said. "I have come to you about the blue."

Lokoihu knew. He knew the secrets, the total, and the discoveries. He knew that Ho'uolo was wrestling with the absolute, the transitions, and his mountain of concerns. Lokoihu smiled broadly, taking in the moment. "You love the blue—and you love God more. We all love the blue when we know it. We have always known and loved God."

For a moment, Ho'uolo felt like he was a mile away. There was so much comfort in his friend's words. The stunning revelation took him by surprise. His mind's eye was looking at the image of his own father. He knew his father would have said the very same thing. That was it. Comfort was the issue. It would have to be.

There was a long pause as they looked into each other's eyes.

"So you have your decision," Lokoihu said with a warm smile and a glint in his eyes.

His sister placed the meal on the table. They prayed.

"Shall we eat?" she said politely.

They ate the meal in silence. The food wasn't the only thing Ho'uolo was digesting. He smiled.

"You will know," Lokoihu said.

"What will I know?" Ho'uolo swallowed the last bite.

"What you know of Mokiki and of Condonte," Lokoihu said. "You will have a greater understanding when it comes. I see it for you. I feel it, but you must see it before I can tell you. I see what our ancestors wanted." He paused for a moment. "You must discover it for yourself. I know that you will discover it. Be patient, my friend. It will come after you return to Condonte." Lokoihu finished with a broad, loving smile. He *knew* it.

"Thank you, my friend. I must go." Ho'uolo felt like his gratitude had not been enough, especially with the forecast of discovery. He knew that Lokoihu expected him to ponder the conversation without further questioning. The questions mounted with every breath.

The blue eased in. It was calming and centering. The blue elevated to allow him to think about what he had learned. For a moment, he knew he would discover it. He smiled and beamed.

Lokoihu reminded him of the tradition, and they offered the prayer. The prayers before and after the meal were exclusive among elders. The food had come from God's harvest, and they thanked him for it. They thanked Lokoihu's sister for her excellent cooking.

Ho'uolo walked back to the canoe. Two guards darted out from the shade. It had been just over an hour. Ho'uolo had brought them a meal from Lokoihu's sister. The guards gratefully inhaled the meal. They brought the canoe back out to knee-deep water and steadied it as Ho'uolo hoisted himself into the seat. They dug firmly into the water with the oars.

Not a lot to think about. Ho'uolo would offer the words as the next few days revealed.

Ho'uolo took a breath, held it, then let it out. He felt comfort, compassion, and peace. He couldn't believe the simple emotion of comfort. It was the absence of conflict in all forms. It was where everyone felt safe, cared for, and loved. He knew it was to be his guidance from then on. It had been there all along, and Lokoihu had shown it to him without saying the words.

The wind at their backs helped them return to Condonte without incident.

Chapter 42

Ferdinand had settled in, but he was frustrated by the progress in translating the tablets.

There was no milestone yet. He had become more confident in speaking his new language, although he had been kidded about his accent. He was working on that too. His mind was working overtime on the tablets, guidance from his Savior, and his new family.

He talked about his slow progress with everyone in the palace. He had talked to Ho'uolo, heard his impressions, and he found encouragement. There was something about Ho'uolo and his slow approach—until the day he talked about the blue.

He had the feeling that the blue was so important to Ho'uolo that there was only one thing greater to him. He knew it, and he felt the honesty, integrity, high ethical standards, and honor.

Two days later, Ferdinand's emotions swelled. He had finally deciphered a portion of the alphabet on the tablets. He had a feeling that the alphabet he was studying was different than Romance or Germanic languages. Something about the alphabet intrigued him. He had determined there were twenty-one letters. There were similarities to Arabic and Romance languages, but the letters looked more like Greek or Oriental ones.

One looked like a crude drawing of a house. It had two small vertical lines on either side of what appeared to be a roof. It stayed with him because of its obvious lack of embellishment and style. He wondered if it was really part of the alphabet at all. Perhaps it was a sort of marker at the beginning of a paragraph. It was rarely used in the written form. Perhaps it was a letter *and* a word. He remembered the phrase he had written on the wood in the workroom.

As he walked back out into the third floor corridor, the blue was rising. He felt the need to slow his pace. And then a clue came.

Oh, God! The roofed letter means house or home. That's it! He wanted to test his theory. He went to the small conference room to continue his research. As he closed the door behind him, he was suddenly aware of someone else in the room.

"Oh, it's you, sir!" Ferdinand gasped the words. Ho'uolo waited a moment. "Please tell me what you know," Ho'uolo said softly. Ho'uolo knew of the event and its timing, and he wanted to be there for the revelation. He could see the clarity coming. The visuals of the tablets had never been enough for him. The translation was the most important part.

The word had been revealed in the blue. The symbolic house was a marker in the written form of the ancestors' language, but the blue revealed much more in that one symbol.

Ferdinand said, "I think that this symbol is the letter for *house*. One letter has one meaning, but it seems as though it has the shortest history behind it. I think it is the newest letter in the ancestors' alphabet. I say this because it is slightly different on each tablet where it appears. An informal feel to it has become apparent. The design of the letter or symbol has an infancy feel to it. It's almost as if they had not come to a formal decision about its concept. I think it finally means *new house* or *our home*."

Ho'uolo was aware that Ferdinand was approaching a breakthrough. He worried about the ancestors' secrets and the ultimate reveal. The grand scale of it all was unbelievable. It was more than anyone could come close to comprehending.

Ho'uolo knew the next few days would be shocking to his friend. A mountain of new information was written in stone. His assumptions and interpretations were about to be validated. He was terrified and hopeful at the same time.

The blue was coming and building quickly.

Ho'uolo turned to his right and saw it coming. *Unusual,* he thought. It surrounded him, and he felt a rush of sound he had never witnessed before. The deep, low sound had the feel of authority. The sound captured his attention as it rolled in with the blue. The power focused on him. The images flew in: instruction, history, and commitment. He had seen the man in the blue—but never in the foreground. The tall, old man had shoulder-length white hair and a beard, which was rare among islanders. The man said, "The Cahbrean goal." He had pronounced it "cha-bree-an."

Ho'uolo was instantly aware that the image was only a single line from a speech the man had given centuries ago. It was only the second or third time he'd heard the *B* sound. He knew this man was the leader of the ancestors. He had heard ambient sounds in the blue on many occasions, but it was the first time he had heard an ancestor's voice.

He worried about the sounds he had heard in the new words. The letter *B* was not present in the islanders' language, but Ferdinand knew it.

Ho'uolo was reminded of the elder Poalolo's warning in the council chamber. He would choose to protect the discoveries with the sickness on Mokiki until the council members were absolutely convinced that the time was right for the reveal—or any part of it. He knew that he had been correct.

Ferdinand investigated the tablets for several more weeks. He knew that the sounds of each letter were important to the scope of the language. There was a definite feel to it—perhaps an origin in India, Persia, or somewhere in the Orient. He was careful not to move with any conclusions so early in the translations.

Each tablet started with a theme or a question that would be answered in the text. At this point, it was just a feeling without any further breakthrough. The first tablet was clearly the ultimate challenge. He decided he should start with the four retrieved from the meeting room. He had heard the Cahbrean ancestors were driven by duty, but he was not yet convinced.

The first tablet had a large first letter like he had found on many documents in the past.

The letter B was the first letter on the tablet. It had an elaborate design and singular beauty. It was dominant, artistic, classic, and troubling. His new flock had never used the sound. Only a handful of citizens had ever heard it. It was the ancestors' alphabet.

Pronunciation was the real barrier to telling his new loved ones about its true feel and scope. He wanted to unlock the first tablet, and its first character would be the door.

He had counted the words, and there was an average of four hundred on each one. Certain words were repeatedly used. The real breakthroughs came when he used his new language as a reference. The Germanic, Norse, and Romance languages had a minimal influence from that point on.

He felt it creeping in. The blue was coming. He felt a need to look westward. He was drawn to the family room and the balcony.

The blue gently began with a history of the Cahbrean goal. The ancestors' experimentation had discovered the full range of emotions and the physical elements that supplemented each emotion. The side effects of each one of them had been carefully studied.

Ferdinand was taken aback as the blue swiftly changed into a commanding authority. The intensity had a firm grip on his soul. He stood frozen.

Chapter 43

The images were coming slowly. Ferdinand remembered the words he wrote down on the piece of wood for the translation effort.

The blue exited.

To him, it was equal to having the blue grasp him by his shoulders and shake him.

He had thought about it twice before. He had seen the words in the workroom. He had a fleeting thought that it might be a key to the translations. He paused and tried to absorb it.

He turned away from the railing, calmly walked back into the palace corridor, and turned left. He knew it was in his bedroom.

He found his satchel on the chest at the foot of the bed. He opened it and removed the wood with its ash markings. He returned to his workstation and placed the wood on his desk.

The three words were different lengths. He felt he had seen them together in the same order on the fourth tablet. He walked over to the long table where the tablets had been carefully placed.

Yes. There it is. Oh dear God! They are talking about safety! He saw the troubling B on the fourth tablet. The words on the fourth were talking about safety.

Once he knew how to begin, his energy flowed. His smile elevated in the first breakthrough.

Ferdinand's excitement was building. He reached for the door knob and opened it. He shuddered as Kahania withdrew her hand and looked into his eyes.

"I have brought you a way of remembering," Kahania said softly.

"You scared me," Ferdinand said.

"I brought you some tools," Kahania said with a warm smile. "Here is some bamboo and some dye." She offered the cloth-wrapped implements and two small containers. The cloth was dense but supple, perfect for writing on, but there were only three cloths.

"I know you need them. I can get you more," she said with an innocence that he found endearing.

Ferdinand accepted the offering from her in silence. He was stunned. How did she know? He thought they didn't exist on these islands. It was just what he needed.

Oh God!

She had been *offered* the solution. Among the countless others who had prepared for war, she had inadvertently stumbled on it herself—in the blue.

She was sharpening darts and injured her finger. She recoiled from the injury, sighed in relief that the darts had not been dipped, and put the offending dart back on the cloth. She felt a sudden increase in the blue as she watched the dart release her blood onto the cloth.

She had placed the stain firmly in her memory. It had always been just a stain before, but now she knew it was a marking.

She had known of dye from adding color to clothing. This cloth was used for cleaning. It could easily be rinsed clean as the day it was made. It was a long process to boil and press bamboo root fibers.

Ferdinand didn't know what to say. There was much about her he didn't know.

How had she done it? There was something about her that he instantly respected. She was twice his age.

And then he knew. *Of course!* She had lived in the blue for a lot longer than he had. *There is no doubt. In her long life, her heart was in it at all times,* Ferdinand thought.

"I know you know how to use them," she said. "I will leave you now … for your work."

Ferdinand was feeling like he was standing in a hurricane. The images were coming so fast. Her smile was all it took. He almost melted.

Kahania calmly stepped away, turned, and walked back downstairs.

Ferdinand couldn't let go of the moment. It had a permanent place in his memory.

He walked back to his workroom. He thought that there must be more to the blue than he had imagined. Then the blue elevated.

A current ran through his shoulders and the back of his neck.

It was the third word of the phrase. The blue brought him to the second.

Duty was the image—but why?

The first word came in the visuals. It was too vague—perhaps a phrase rather than a single word.

It was coming. Softly, it revealed: *Progress in honor, duty, safety.*

Of course! It's a slogan! He instantly knew it had to be more. It had a history. It had more meaning than the concise phrase itself. He was energized. He knew the rest would come, but he thought about the phrase. *Their commitment, their architecture, their vision of a grand experiment?*

The energy in him was building with each word he now knew.

In a week, he had fully translated the first four tablets. While working on the fifth, he wondered about the ancestors and their goals.

Ho'uolo decided to remain in the palace while Ferdinand worked. He knew that the translation of the last few tablets was a forewarning of catastrophe. The experiments had nearly gone wrong. He knew about the concern the ancestors had in proceeding with the unpredictable outcome of the system they had built. He also knew where the mysteries of Mokiki had originated.

Ho'uolo felt that the conflict in his mind about whether or not to go ahead with the mission was irrelevant. The epic reveal had to happen even with knowing the deadly dangers the ancestors had grappled with and ultimately contained. The citizens deserved to know it. They innocently deserved the nurturing protection. They deserved the one thing that kept them all together: love.

Ferdinand was spending his days translating and learning. He was exhausted.

The last five tablets were unbelievable. The connections were engineered into the entire complex. There was the dam, its intended schedule in the neutral sustaining role, its manual options and settings, and the power routed to the other monuments, including the dam. Before building it, the ancestors had experimented with electricity. They routed it to each building and realized its dangers.

He had not seen the six floors of catacombs below the triangle building. He knew the triangle building was their headquarters—and the aboveground floor had been built last. The structure below the room of columns, which he had just translated, intrigued him the most. It was developed as the central nerve system of the complex. It was capable of receiving and simultaneously transmitting in a wide range of frequencies. The ancestors had recorded it on the tablets as *harmonies*. Ferdinand had initially thought they were referring to music—like in an orchestra or church choir or both—but they had discovered the full range of frequency.

It ranged from sound to light and well beyond. They deduced that each kind of frequency had a speed they could document. They also found that frequencies could have powerful effects on the human body.

At times, the low end of the frequencies had a unique effect on hearing. It made them sick, and it matched certain unique dimensions within the human inner ear. It could cause varying degrees of nausea and imbalance. They knew the range of each and narrowed it down to the concise range and volume intensity for each side effect.

Perhaps the most terrifying side effects in the hearing range were the long-term effects. There was permanent ringing in the ears or total loss of hearing. The most sinister of all was the short-term effect of exposure to nausea: dehydration or death. The *sickness* had been engineered.

Their stumbling experiments were the turning point in the entire complex. They knew that each narrow range of frequencies could be focused and manipulated, but they used the word *compliment* in its various forms to hide the real consequences of their experiments. He knew it.

At that moment in the ancestors' history, there was a sudden shift in their overall approach. They knew they were on a precipice. The breakthrough had to be hidden.

The fifth-to-last tablet was the most shocking. It covered the harmonies of the mind.

The full range of emotions was described regarding individual frequencies, and the true ability and unlimited capabilities of the human mind were forces to be reckoned with. They could be trained, influenced, and recalled. They controlled independent thought and the doctrine of the masses. They had stored the parameters of each and every one into the design of the columns room. Thousands of them covered their dreams, achievements, and history. There was no mention of disasters or calamities of any size.

The complexity of the countless settings for the harmonies was staggering. The experiments revealed how much power each of them required, and they had tested them with varying degrees of intensity. They had discovered the neutral for each one.

Their best achievement was debating policy. The policy balanced the harmonies. Their discoveries were far more powerful and grand than they could have imagined or planned for. Their experiments had blindly evolved to dangerous and catastrophic levels many times. Their withdrawal from the unforeseen was the one thing they had forecast, but was that the reason they had vanished?

Ferdinand had not yet discovered how long it had taken to build and engineer all things on Mokiki, but he had a feel for it. There was no mention of the time the ancestors had begun or when they had departed. He had a feeling it had taken at least one hundred years of absolute secrecy.

When he was on Mokiki Island, it never occurred to him to look for evidence of construction methods or building details. In his memory, there were no visible signs of patterns, grids, cranes, or ramps. Perhaps they had cleaned up any evidence of construction as they went.

The most spectacular and unbelievable description he found on the third-to-last tablet was for the weather. The ancestors had placed near-biblical effort on this subject. Their intent was to bring a harmony to it. They could not control it, but they could use it.

They discovered that static electricity was a key to certain weather phenomenon, including static buildup in storms. Lightning had a very narrow frequency range. They found it intriguing.

They had experimented with eels when cloud formations were nowhere in the sky. They knew which two organs in the eel generated the shock of electricity. They knew how the eel used it with no danger to itself.

Ferdinand remembered the time monument. He was shocked to read that the ancestors believed that the Earth was in orbit around the sun. Indeed, another scholar in Europe had yet to announce his heliocentric theory. The Vatican College of Cardinals—and the pope—would strongly object to that blasphemy.

The tablets were revealing far more than Ferdinand could absorb. He knew they were way ahead of any other society in science and astronomy. He had an ominous feeling that they were also ahead of themselves—even though they were obviously in the category of genius in mathematics, architecture, and engineering.

It was time for sleep. His mind had worked overtime, and he felt exhausted. Everyone else in the palace was asleep. He went to his bedroom and started his evening prayers. The pressure in his chest began to ease. The muscles in his upper body slowly responded to the need for sleep as he relaxed.

Chapter 44

Iliakahani spent some time in the afternoon sitting on her favorite bench in the north garden.

So many good things had happened in the past few months. Her daughter had been introduced to a wonderful man, and with the blessing of both families, they had wed in a traditional open-air ceremony in the palace garden.

She had watched them constantly smile at one another. She knew it was perfect for them. It filled her with joy that was not unlike her memories of Kai's wedding to Alahina.

The blue approached and took her by the throat. She could feel the welling of emotions as it filled her. There were no visuals, but there were many sounds for the first time.

She knew that her newest son, as she thought of him, was deeply in love. He glowed as he embraced his new wife. She knew her daughter was experiencing the best aching of all in her heart. Ihilani had not been herself lately. She had little energy, and her conversations were limited. She wasn't feeling well. She had been refusing certain foods and demanding other ones.

Oh God! She's pregnant! She smiled, and her hands automatically covered her cheeks and lips. When her smile faded, she realized this one would be difficult. She didn't even have to think about it. Her daughter needed her in more than a spiritual sense. She would need the loving attendance and care throughout it all. In her mind, she deserved it.

The blue had shown her the sounds of chaos: infant sounds, childhood sounds, loving sounds, demanding cries, and giggling. She saw children laughing, tickling, and playing.

She knew it. She felt it. She felt the breeze at her back. She didn't know how many weeks along her daughter was, but the thought of a new grandchild—a new member of the family to love—was all it took. She cried joyful tears. She wasn't the only one.

Pohii had been watching her and admiring her as she rejoiced. He was listening, waiting, and smiling. He watched her tears as the blue came to her. He saw the special moment, and he knew. He walked out of the shadows, and she felt his presence.

As he walked toward her, he looked up at the afternoon sky. The blue was coming. He knew it. He knew there would be an unknown. It was a feeling now, but the experience would test him. He felt the dread of duty.

She was waiting for him. He knew she would help him decide. She was more than his woman; she was his lover and his partner for life. She had always been his best friend. She raised her arms as he approached. She saw the full range of emotions on his face as she gently embraced him. The kiss and hug lasted for several minutes. Raw emotions coursed through their nerves.

The Blue was sending visuals. They both saw a pending invasion. The enemy was over the horizon, and they knew they were coming. There was something new about it. It was terrifying. They shuddered—knowing they would face it together.

The blue was not showing them an onshore arrival. It had always shown them events in the proper sequence. The timing of the visuals had convinced them about the truth.

They returned to the palace, convinced that the events would come from the east of Ohluku Island. Pohii thought about his duty as leader of all the islands. He contemplated sending a contingent of palace guards and many canoes full of warriors to Ohluku, but he didn't know if the enemy would land there.

Pohii had begun the planning and the analysis of the pending threat. His thoughts had to move to a strategy. He only had one day to think it through.

Iliakahani gently flexed her grip on his hand. He was surprised to see her smile. "Hani, what have you seen?"

"There were two," she said. Her expression changed in an instant. "Our family will know, but many more will not." *How would she tell them? Could she find a way to tell them? Should she tell them?* She felt an odd isolation in the visuals. "They are coming, but I didn't see their feet on the beach."

She reflected on the first time someone from far way had visited them.

Pohii knew she had seen the same images! They would experience the unknown together. The ominous feelings entered.

They went upstairs to experience the sunset together. As the sun approached the horizon, they went to the balcony. They wanted to see the distant island and enjoy it.

As the sunset began, a cloud layer moved in. It enveloped the top two hundred feet of Thorn Mountain. The last few minutes of sunshine cast a shadow on the bottom of the cloud layer.

The shadow on the ceiling of clouds pointed to the east. After a few minutes, the sun slipped below the horizon. The moment felt like it was the grandest of all emotional experiences. They hadn't realized that it was a shadow until it slowly faded.

For Iliakahani, the dread entered. It was an omen.

A moment later, Pohii felt it too. The cloud shadow had pointed east. It had pointed to the eastern horizon.

Chapter 45

In the morning, Ho'uolo was compelled to go to the one spot on the northern shore of Condonte where he could see all the islands and the channels between them.

It was just an hour after sunrise, and the air was calm. He felt love for all the citizens of the islands.

He could feel two things moving. One was in a familiar mode, and the other had a sinister tone. A mild vibration moved through the rocks. He saw it ripple in the broad channel between Condonte and Halau. It was moving eastward in a perfect line as it advanced. Someone was coming from the east.

The geysers two miles to his left began bubbling. He turned to watch them. The random display, never quite predictable, started with a steady buildup. He had always watched it in wonder. The fish broke the surface to get away from the closely spaced vertical fountains. The geysers pulsed for two minutes. There was something very different about it. They were only half the normal height.

When he felt the heat, he realized it came from the steam. He remembered a similar display, months ago, after the lightning struck Mokiki's northern cliffs. Jets of steam extinguished the flames as they parted the clouds. He didn't like it at all.

There was a quick movement under his feet. The vibration was coursing through the northern beach of Condonte, and he felt nauseous. He saw the visuals, and he instantly knew all the colors were wrong. The feelings in orange were stunning and frightening. He felt the news was a mode of protection from Mokiki. It was alarming. He turned his attention to Thorn Mountain. The colors of the sunrise were on the peak.

Ho'uolo felt the horror as the event progressed. The powerful events were hidden beyond the horizon. He realized someone—or something—was suffering. No, it was many of them. He knew the savage event wouldn't be known for days. He cried.

The orange lasted for hours, but it felt like the full day had passed him by. He realized he had just witnessed the progression. He knew that his ancestor's planning and grueling debates had influenced the event. Their creation was in charge. *Why now? And why not during the skirmishes between the island factions?*

It began to fade back to blue.

The citizens would feel agony from swift defeat, slavery, unbearable decrees, dismissal of their culture, and foreign domination.

The power was allowed in the orange when the timing was right. When the enemy had the most sinister intent, the culture would plunge into darkness. The enemy would be stopped at just the right distance over the horizon.

Ho'uolo had never felt it before—and he didn't want to.

Defending the world this way was far worse than war with spears or darts. The shocking deaths from the unknown in broad daylight were shielded from view. He felt the anguish, but he was relieved he hadn't seen it in the blue.

He wondered if the images of the event would appear from the blue, and he dreaded it. He searched his memory for images that showed loss of life from the blue, but there were none. The only thing he saw were languishing memories of the losses of loved ones.

The blue showed him a brief image of Ferdinand.

Of course, he thought. *I must talk to Ferdinand.*

He turned away from the channel and started a brisk walk to the palace. The witnessing in the orange heightened his nerves. He never wanted to see the orange again. He was partly relieved that visuals weren't part of the orange. He knew the ancestors' decrees and debates had forbidden visuals in the orange. Perhaps the visuals were reserved solely from the blue.

The palace loomed as he drew nearer. *Why the blue and then the orange? Why those two? Were those the most important questions? What was the right question?* His confusion mounted. The anxious quandary was the only thing he could think about.

Halfway up the trail, he felt the approach of the blue. He stopped. The stunning visuals came to him with a halting truth at an extraordinary speed. There was an assembly at the palace. He knew it.

He saw critical and dire feelings in the visuals.

He shivered in fear. It had been a long time since he had felt it. The emotion had been suppressed in the bottom of his mind for years. For the final visual, he had to come to grips with the inevitable.

Kahania felt Ho'uolo first. Her experience in the blue and her very hard life had shown Ferdinand what he needed at just the right time. She was focused and intense. She was also the sweetest woman he had ever known. He admired her remarkable placement of her emotions. She was flawlessly correct and humble. She was bright, caring, and loving.

He knew she had provided Ferdinand with the bamboo and paper at just the right moment. She had a history in her core. Her marriage vows were absolute—even two years after his passing. The man she loved had made her feel complete. She still felt married to her one man. She had been with him for forty-eight years. He knew she would be grieving in secret for the rest of her life.

She had lived in plural for so long that she couldn't refer to herself in the singular. It wasn't possible. She had always thought of others first.

He knew Ferdinand had been struggling with the translations, but the timing of Kahania's offering was perfect. Ferdinand had noticeably accelerated his translations. It had been both wondrous and terrifying.

The findings would take some time to absorb. The citizens had never experienced the advances they were about to hear. The true challenge was deciding the course they would take.

Anything new was almost always hard to accept—if it was not outright rejected.

In a slow simmer, the blue elevated.

He walked to the community lodge to the north of the palace. The midday meal was being presented in the east room.

Wainani was feeding the twins. Her husband, Holouku, was in attendance, as always. They all felt it coming.

Ho'uolo looked at Wainani's face. Her lips parted as the first visuals arrived. He knew the tears were next for her since he felt the same way.

Only a few citizens beyond the palace saw the visuals. An alarm was felt throughout the community, but there was minimal panic. They had just recently finished preparing for war, and they knew what to do.

The blue hadn't shown them war. It had shown them suffering rather than conflict. It had shown them the approach and a warning. The feeling was overwhelming.

"My daughter, Wainani, stay here with your husband. You will be comfortable and safe here." Ho'uolo knew she felt the alarm as well. He knew he had to return to the palace.

He turned and walked briskly. Duty was now foremost on his mind.

Ho'uolo had seen it in the blue. The new power had capabilities on an enormous scale that could not be ignored. He thought he alone had felt the orange. He was reviewing the event and the serious emotions in the reveal.

Iliakahani and Pohii knew. Ferdinand knew. Kahania knew. They stood together in the palace courtyard. They knew he would come.

As the palace came into view, he reflected on its ideal location. It was hidden until the trail ended, the jungle abated, and the gardens began. It was like walking out of a small cave and into the sunshine. Its placement had always invoked awe in him. The familiar sight was always an intense surprise. He shuddered as he walked toward the palace.

Chapter 46

Ferdinand didn't know where to begin—much less what to believe. The tablets had documented the ancestors' mission, but he still didn't understand the scope of the complex on Mokiki.

He knew their discoveries during the development of the structures were important. Ferdinand turned his focus on the harmonies.

The ancestors discovered that when plurals were heard and felt, the sounds could range from soothing to terrible. The auditory volume in each category made a big difference.

They could enjoy or tolerate each sound. The full range was from no sound to beautiful, to unbearable. Every note—from octave to octave—had an influence. They had found something they called *undersound*. A year later, they had found what they called *oversound*, but they had focused on the range of human hearing.

The real breakthrough came when they found the range of vision. They knew the harmonies and the complete range from no vibration to millions. They discovered the colors they had associated with vision were also found much higher in the spectrum of vibrations.

They discovered the lethal range of vibrations and stopped the experiments when they saw a skeletal projection on the wall in the room of experiments. The accidental discovery forced the ancestors to stop and retreat from the room in terror. They were convinced they had created a ghost. They thought it had chased them. They never saw it again.

The leadership had ordered the shutdown of nearly all of what they had created.

The furious debates that followed concluded that the experiments must not proceed in any part of the building. A year later, they had decided, with tight restrictions, that they could proceed only if their experiments were very carefully and narrowly focused.

The grand experiments were idle for years. The ancestors observed the heartbreak of a major setback to the dream. Some of those involved in the trials were sick and getting sicker. Their medicine wasn't helping. The ancient arts were of very little help. Something new was affecting them in ways they had not foreseen.

The leadership came to the consensus that the mixing of vibrations was the cause—without knowing the effects. They had stumbled on the range that burned into the walls and melted it with contact. They didn't know that the mixture was perfectly answered in mathematics. They had added one vibration to another, but the effect was several times higher than the design architecture of the power they used to produce one high vibration. It was well beyond the range of human hearing and vision.

They had experimented beyond the range of vision and reached what they called "the second range" of red and violet and finally "the darkness."

Perhaps the most violent of all was the upper range in orange—just before the red. There, the ancestors had scaled back their experiments. The red could be controlled and used to great advantage, but it was irresistible. The peaceful uses in construction efforts were enough to justify it, but the range above red was beyond their stated goals.

They decided to forbid experiments above the red. It was too much— and the risks were too great.

The experiments in orange were limited, and each new effect was monitored and evaluated. The discovery that nausea was a side effect in the orange was explored very carefully. Years were spent while each change, step, and individual vibration in the orange was understood.

They investigated the floors, the walls, the ceilings, the doors, and the windows. They checked the insects, birds, and flora. The orange was a deterrent on most things that were alive.

They noticed an odd effect on the window glass. After long exposure, it would eventually turn brown and crumble. It was an acceleration of the natural process of glass. They knew they would have to replace glass for any number of reasons, but they had not expected the rapid disintegration when exposed to orange.

Normally, the glass would not need replacing for up to twenty years if it wasn't damaged. In the orange, it was reduced to ruins in a little more than a month. They were forced to cover over all the windows on Mokiki Island.

They had not discovered the answer of tempering with the ceramic ovens they had left dormant in the caves of Mokiki's other mountain: Guardian Mountain.

Long ago, the meeting room had been filled to capacity to debate the orange. The Cahbrean goal was about to find its final work.

The last tablet defined it. The orange was too powerful to abandon altogether. Its purpose and its uses were to find its own priorities and responses. The harmonies were overhauled. The final decree said that the orange would interact with all other harmonies. The protocols had a clear definition: "Respond to them. Act only when justified in policy."

The overall function of the Orange held a simple place in the protocols: "The orange shall be put in place to maintain. To broadly maintain, while sustaining and discovering, adding the new, replacing the old, all things in harmony."

They concluded that the final goal had been reached for the construction and all modifications. It was then necessary to tune the work, make the final adjustments, and refine the outcome.

Their plan had always included abandonment as the final act, and they knew it would come. They knew the systems would continue on their own for many years. They decided to return after several generations when the people had forgotten about it. The leaders knew the incredible potential they had designed. They had witnessed it for themselves. The delicate balance was the inspiration they had never thought possible—until the leaders knew it.

Ferdinand was totally overwhelmed by the size and scope of the ancestors' mandate. It was the true ultimate in his mind with purpose, conclusions, and vastness. He was shocked to think he could find a way to even come close to explaining it—or any part of it—to anyone.

Chapter 47

James Cristo was weighing the arrival in his homeport. They were, at last, coming home. He knew he had to deal with unloading his ship at port. He wanted it to be just after sunset—in the dark.

He knew about the huge cargo of tea in the captain's lead ship, but he had kept his own cargo a closely guarded secret. He had sailed at the back of the fleet for a reason. While in port at Zanzibar, he had a discussion with the captain and heard his views on the slave trade. By the time they docked in San Tome' weeks later, the tea would not be enough for the queen. The secret talks with the bishop and his desire to divest himself of the sapphire were just one of the things in the hold.

The captain in the lead vessel was worried about the Strait of Gibraltar. Just two hours ahead, he would be navigating the narrow part of the strait four hours after sunrise. At just seven and one-half nautical miles wide, he knew the fleet could be seen from either side. He was going to have to be lucky not to encounter anything other than Castilian vessels. His intent was to use the high winds to propel the fleet home with no sightings of vessels from any other country or direction.

He had decided to plot a course only a mile from the Spanish coast. The westerly tailwinds made the course into the Mediterranean possible. In the Tarifa Narrows, the currents would clash and form wave fronts. At five miles wide, the waves were the point of transition or psychological boundary between the Atlantic and the Mediterranean. The eastbound wind-driven waves of the Atlantic and the westbound currents from the Mediterranean were in a constant rhythmic battle. The mythical phenomenon was found nowhere else in the world. The waves sent a shiver up the captain's spine every time he crossed them.

The Rock of Gibraltar and the Ceuta Peninsula and its dominant hill on the north Mediterranean coast of Africa were widely thought of as the "Pillars of Hercules." Held by the Castilian Crown for mythic reasons, the captain knew it was really for strategic military reasons. Queen Isabella and King Charles had made the outpost a top priority. He wanted to avoid the Moroccan coast even though it was part of the empire.

The captain knew the route home very well.

The fleet was making good time. The Rock of Gibraltar flew by in the high winds. As his fleet passed Cabo de Palos just before midnight, he reflected on his voyage. The home harbor in Barcelona was his goal. He felt remorse at the loss of crew to disease and abandonment. He was thinking about his most recent events in Las Palmas, Cadiź, and Cartagena. Each one held fond memories. He would be forever grateful that none of his ships were lost.

At dawn, the captain gave the order. The fleet began the final approach into the harbor of Barcelona. Then he saw the horses. The cavalry? He took his glass and raised it slowly.

Something was happening.

The coincidence, the advantages, and the dread pulsed in his mind.

The timing couldn't have been coordinated with the return of the fleet. It was just unthinkable. Anyone on land with any family member in the armada was accustomed to the relief and complete surprise when they returned.

When he saw the coaches of the royal entourage, he knew they preceded the royal arrival from the capital. Then a feeling that it was a precursor to what would take place in the morning. Who was coming?

James was eager to enter the port. The fleet had dropped anchor two miles out from the harbor. An Egyptian trade vessel eased away from the dock and slowly moved out of the harbor.

The harbormaster finally signaled, and the fleet slowly began to move in just after first light. When they finally docked in the harbor, James knew he would have to hurry. His cargo needed to be secretly unloaded and put in a secure place onshore.

He knew the constable's office was nearby. He also knew a considerable bribe would stifle any questions he might have. Normally twenty gold pieces would do. It was his best option.

The captain rushed to see his wife. It was so good to see her in the home he had built for her on a slope overlooking the Llobregat River and the valley below. On the left side of the veranda, they could see Barcelona and the harbor.

Then captain and his wife returned to the plaza. The bells of the Cathedral of the Holy Cross and Santa Eulàlia announced Sunday Mass.

They heard six horses pulling a carriage into the plaza. King Charles's ornate carriage had elaborate gold and ivory decorations. It stopped in front of the cathedral. The bells rang a joyous welcome to His Royal Highness.

The captain of the royal guard stepped down from atop the carriage and opened the door.

The count and the bishop waited dutifully in front of the three-tiered stairs of the cathedral.

King Charles stepped out onto the plaza and surveyed his audience. He was impeccably dressed, with hand-stitched gold threading on his white shirt, light brown vest, and royal red jacket.

Captain Gregorio's wife absolutely loved his shoes. Catarina saw them shine—even in the shadows.

The king turned to his right, and James smiled. For a moment, he thought the King had seen him and had returned his smile. Had the king *felt* his mysterious smile?

The king whispered something to the captain of the royal guard and entered the cathedral.

The glorious Easter Mass featured its incense, pageantry, and the doctrine of the Lord and Savior. The inspiration, the passion, and heartfelt thanks to God had most of the congregation weeping.

The bells joined the gospel choir when the two-hour celebration concluded.

James watched as the king, and the faithful began their slow exit from the sanctuary. He wanted to be the first to follow the royal entourage out into the plaza.

King Charles had a scheduled luncheon meeting with the count. The royal guardsmen escorted them to the count's office. The captain of the guard surveyed the plaza and the avenue. He was looking for James. His summoning gesture sent a broad smile across James's face. James knew he must use a more discreet look. He was being summoned to meet the king of the empire! He chose his best military look.

The fact that it had all been done silently and secretly had a supreme effect on the captain of the guard. James approached him in the most dignified way he could muster.

"You have a message for His Royal Highness?" he whispered.

"Yes, sir. I bring gifts from our voyage," James said.

The captain of the guard was responsible for many other things. He was skilled at saying just enough to get to the heart of the matter and judging the responses to the questions of someone he had never met. As the head of security, he was always aware of the elaborate royal protocols.

"I will tell him after lunch." The captain of the guard was following a hunch that the return from the voyage was good news. He didn't know how the King would respond, but he felt James Cristo was going to surprise the king in a positive manner. "Wait here."

After an hour, the captain of the guard returned. "His Royal Highness will see you at three o'clock."

James's mind was racing. He would have to run. "Yes, sir. Thank you, sir." He walked calmly until he knew he was out of sight of the plaza and the lunch crowds. When he turned the corner, he ran the eight blocks to the constable's office. He brought an armed escort on horseback back to the count's office.

He had serious doubts, but he returned with the locked wooden chest a few minutes before three o'clock. James dismounted, and the captain of the royal guard walked out of the count's office. "His Royal Highness will see you now."

James was almost speechless.

"Come with me now."

They walked with a purpose.

Two of the men who had returned to the square with James carried the locked wooden chest.

Once the captain of the guard opened the door to the count's office, all of them entered the foyer. They stopped.

"I will announce you. Wait here," he said.

The silence in the room of dark wooden walls was shocking. It was as if they were standing in storage. The high windows cast an uneasy light on the opposing wall. There were no decorations apart from the modest reception desk and stark benches on the other side. It was hardly a welcome feeling for the magistrate in charge of the city. It was definitely not a place where nobility would wait for an audience with royalty. He knew it was the correct protocol for a secondary captain of the smallest ship in his uncle's fleet. The moment was very humbling, but he waited with enthusiasm.

He heard footsteps coming from the other side of the waiting room door.

Two royal guardsmen opened the heavy door slowly. "There is not much time. The king will see you now." The low tone of his voice had the feeling of a secret. "Your two men may also come in, but they may not speak. They will not be addressed by the king."

"One moment please," he said. He walked quickly to the front door and made sure it was locked. Since it was Sunday, the count's office was closed for the day.

"Follow me. His Royal Highness knows you bring a gift to him. Do not speak until he addresses you. Call him Your Royal Highness with each sentence. Be brief and cordial. Honor him, and he may honor you. You and your men will leave your weapons with two of my guardsmen here in this office." He opened the interior door and walked down the corridor.

James wondered where the bathroom was. *Oh dear, not now.* This once-in-a-lifetime meeting would be challenging. He decided to hold on for dear life. He was resolute and in control.

The captain of the guard said, "We must wait a moment, and then we may enter."

"Captain, sir, where is the chamber? Please?" James's expression revealed the urgency.

"Oh, of course." The captain of the guard pointed to the second door on the right, the only one without an inscription. "Quickly, please." He tried to hide his smirk.

James walked quickly and returned moments later with a sheepish smile.

"There you are—just in time. His Royal Highness will see you now. Follow me," the captain of the royal guard said.

Guardsmen began opening the heavy oak door inward.

"Please sit on the bench."

The captain of the guard motioned for the office doors to be closed. Silence.

The lock was turned on the door, and James realized there were others in the room. To his right sat the bishop and three others, whom he didn't know. On his left sat the count and his wife. Captain Gregorio Cristo and his wife were there too. James was stunned.

He went from shock to a smile in under a minute. He knew this would be a shared moment to remember for all of them, including his own guards.

"Please stand!" said the captain of the guard.

The king finally entered and broadly smiled. He said nothing.

The ceremony was formal and traditional. The captain of the guard said that the king would speak in formal Spanish, and he repeated the message in Catalan and French.

The king sat in the center chair, which was reserved for the highest-ranking official, usually the count himself. The count was awarded the traditional royal merit for keeping the peace and supporting the Crown—and so was the bishop.

The king graciously thanked them.

The captain of the guard called on Gregorio Cristo.

King Charles said, "I am glad you are here, Captain Cristo. I know your voyage was a success. I am grateful for your service and offerings to the Crown. You have honored the empire, and now I decree an honor upon you. For service to the Empire and the Crown, I bestow the title of Caballero Señor de Catania." The king offered a polished and bejeweled dagger on a red velvet pillow to signify the elevation in public rank.

It was the Spanish royal equivalent of knighthood. The coveted position came with, among other things, the elimination of taxation for life.

The captain of the guard called James Cristo.

The king was aware of the locked wooden chest.

"Captain James Cristo." The king motioned to the captain of the guard, and two of the guardsmen brought the wooden chest forward. James handed him the key.

"I know you brought a gift," the King said.

The wooden chest was unlocked and opened. The king asked the count's assessor to inspect it. The man reached in and whispered something to the captain of the guard with a pale look on his face.

It would take at least a week to thoroughly determine the value of the raw, uncut diamonds and rubies. There were other precious gems and gold coins of unknown origin. The raw, uncut sapphire impressed him the most. It alone, wrapped in linen, had him mesmerized.

He had never seen such a big sapphire. He knew it was unique for its record-setting size. It was a dream for any royal jeweler. He thought it had a priceless potential the instant he saw it. When he saw the linen had the embroidered words "Santo Pietro," he knew the most recent owners intended its final gifting to the Vatican. He asked the captain of the royal guard to transport it to the king's residence.

The captain of the royal guard whispered to the king.

"Thank you," the king said, knowing that he would have to be very discreet. He knew he would have to wait for the results of the final gemology before any additional rank could be bestowed on this deserving man. "James Cristo, your gift to the Crown is welcome indeed. I know of your dedication and service to the empire. I hereby decree the title of Señor de Catania. You and Gregorio Cristo are welcome at my residence. You both shall live here in Barcelona with my blessings and gratitude."

The ranking just below his uncle came with similar benefits, including the elimination of taxes for life, although the title was rarely transferred to the next generation without petitioning the Crown.

Those in attendance applauded the two heroes. They both smiled with pride.

The rewards ceremony concluded with dignity, grace, and honor. Their efforts had been recognized as worthy of the Empire and the Crown. James felt humbled. Elevation in public rank was a complete surprise.

As they exited the ceremony, James and his uncle reflected on their memories of Condonte Island. They were lucky that the islanders had chosen not to execute any of them. Captain Gregorio said, "I know it was over a year ago, but I can't shed my impressions of that island."

"Yes, I know," James said.

"It sounds impossible, but I'd return to Condonte someday."

"I would too, sir," James said.

"There is something about it that just stays with you. It just makes me want it more." For the first time since he proposed to his wife, he felt an emotional jump. "I don't see the backing from the Crown that would be needed, for the voyage that couldn't be explained. Maybe someday—but it would have to take banishment from Spain."

James said, "It would be a long and dangerous journey. Could we find it again?"

The captain's face froze. "We?" A smile swept across his face as they walked away from the plaza. The captain put his hand on James's shoulder and said, "Yes, it is a good dream."

Chapter 48

Forty-five miles to the east of Ohluku Island, the ever-present winds of the vast South Pacific were calming. The fleet was slowly coming to a halt. The temperature was rising. The humidity was rapidly elevating. The sun's rays from the cloudless sky wrought sunburn.

The inertia of the ships in the formation became a concern for the admiral. They would have to be vigilant at the helm. The sails and rudders were useless. The fleet halted.

The rippling in the open ocean went unnoticed.

The next weather front, far to the east-southeast, offered no hope. It was too late. The men were starting to feel the onslaught. The sickness was far worse than motion sickness while at sea, and the fleet wasn't moving. The orange was upon them.

There was a ferocious exodus of fish away from the scene.

The admiral was incapable of shouting orders. His sailors were running for the railings. Some didn't make it to the top deck in time. Two of the ships collided—and then a third and fourth collided too.

The orange increased. The rippling intensified. It was as if the ocean around them was boiling.

None of the men stopped with the first expelling of their guts over the side. The men were weakening quickly. Massive headaches and uncontrollable shivering arrived. Each breath became more impossible.

Some of the sailors cast themselves overboard in desperation. Others collapsed on deck.

It was pandemonium. There was nothing they could have done.

The casualties had fallen in the space of four hours.

Afterward, it was absolutely silent.

The fleet succumbed to the currents. It would be days before the first ship would be seen on the horizon.

One ship had begun the movement, and the others followed. The spacing between ships was random. The sails caught the slow breeze, and the ships drifted in the open ocean.

The orange retreated. The blue remained vigilant for several hours and then slowly subsided.

Chapter 49

Ho'uolo had just finished the morning meal with his family when the blue came to him. The very slow rise had him wondering what it would reveal. He stood, kissed his beloved wife on the cheek, and exited into the sunshine.

He was worried. The blue was elevating, but the slow pace was what garnered the concern. That morning, he had seen two palace guards running toward the palace. And now he knew.

The guards relayed important information. He didn't have to follow them. He knew the fleet was slowly approaching Ohluku. He knew the threat had been unmercifully stopped in the open ocean. And now this was proof, and he dreaded it.

The two guards arrived at the palace just before the meeting was to be announced. Pohii heard the news and took several breaths. One of the ships, a large one, had been seen east of Ohluku Island. Pohii ordered the alert.

Five hundred warriors with spears and darts were sent to Ohluku within the hour. It was certainly a precaution, but he had to be ready. He walked down to the northeast beach and entered his canoe. Four of the palace guards rowed the oars for him. Kai went with him in his own canoe. It was automatic for him.

Ferdinand raced down the path and climbed into one of the last canoes.

The large ship was still more than three hours offshore. Then three more ships appeared. Soon, the entire fleet was visible.

Ho'uolo said there would be no threat from the ships, but Pohii knew of the visuals from the blue. Ho'uolo had felt the devastation and told him of it. Pohii had to be sure. The warriors had carried six canoes across the Island to the easternmost tip of all the islands. Pohii knew the currents would bring them there. Ferdinand arrived on the beach to see for himself.

The first ship went aground on the offshore reefs. The sudden shudder of the sails and masts told them so. The stern of the ship slowly pivoted clockwise in the currents. The port side of the ship made contact with the reefs and began to take on water. At only a half mile offshore, the slow event had a churning sound. When the ship's hull succumbed to the reef, the ship listed to starboard slightly and stopped, completely entangled in the coral.

The waves were minimal, the current was constant. Two more ships found their final resting place farther north in the reefs. A fourth collided with the third and veered over the reef. Two ships appeared as though an earlier collision at sea had conjoined them. Even then, they struggled with each other in the waves. They passed well south of the reefs and moved on out to the open ocean—never to be seen again.

Each man on the beach was assessing the threat. Pohii was aware of the enemy's encounter with the orange, but he knew his warriors had to be ready.

Ferdinand had the most trouble with the approaching fleet. He knew something was very wrong. He felt a catastrophe of biblical proportions had befallen them. It had turned into a frenzy for the thousands of birds that descended on the scene. After only one day, the ships were completely stripped of the dead. The fleet had been at sea for four days after the orange. He couldn't believe it.

Ferdinand had talked briefly with Ho'uolo before leaving Condonte. He gently grabbed Pohii to turn him away from what he knew would be a grisly discovery. "There is one survivor," Ferdinand whispered. "Ask four of the guards to search the second ship. He is weak, armed, and terrified. He thinks he is next to die. He has locked himself in a room beneath the deck in the stern."

"You will go with them." Pohii knew that Ferdinand had the intellect and faith to bring the survivor back from the ship alive. Ferdinand was shocked. He stood with his mouth wide open. He was completely opposed to it.

The blue entered.

Ferdinand knew Pohii had been in the blue. He was certain of it, but his experience with his faith and his Savior helped him make the swift turn.

Pohii provided the shock.

His Savior had warmed him with a familiar, loving embrace. His fears were trounced. He knew it was the right thing to do. "Thank you, Majesty," he said softly as he turned to the canoe.

Ferdinand's fears were answered when he and the five guards stood on the deck. The stench was as unbearable. The remains of the dead were strewn on every possible railing and floor. They walked carefully to the ladder down to the hold and took the time to adjust before they descended into the dark interior.

When they reached the bottom step, they wiped their eyes and breathed through their mouths, which was just barely better than breathing through their noses.

Ferdinand's prayers accelerated with each step he took. *Oh, dear God, please let him be alive.* When he saw the door, he knew it was the one in an instant.

The guards drew closer as Ferdinand grasped the door handle. It creaked as it opened. There was someone in there. His head was down, and he was motionless.

The guards removed his dagger carefully. The man was barely breathing. His chin, neck, and clothing were covered in vomit. They grabbed him by his hands and feet, and he offered no resistance. As his head fell back, he momentarily opened and then closed his eyes. He was nearly comatose.

Moments later, the lone survivor was carefully lowered into the canoe.

Pohii turned to the women and ordered food.

The five guards vigorously rowed back to the beach. Ferdinand was paddling. The survivor slumped over in the center seat.

Pohii stood in the blue. He sensed this man was close to death. This poor soul—this enemy—was now a prisoner.

Pohii watched as the prisoner was lifted out of the canoe. There was nothing familiar about him from the blue.

The women had food ready.

The young man was incapable of walking, but he was still breathing. The anguish of near starvation and dehydration had overtaken him. His body had begun to shut down. Using voluntary muscles was impossible. Those on the beach felt it. The women offered him water. A garment was brought to him. They thought about unrolling it, but they offered it as a pillow while he rested in the shade of the palms.

His breathing began to soften ever so slightly. His eyes were closed. He had peeling skin and severe sunburn. His curly blond hair was the only topic of conversation between the women attending to him. They had only seen black, brown, and gray hair. They were intrigued. They touched it gently, and some giggled and withdrew their hands. They didn't know the singular experience this man was having. The nurturing touch was reviving him slowly. He was turned to his left side. The man was given a soft fruit, small pieces at a time. The first piece went down and expelled seconds later.

The women waited.

He was given another. He chewed it halfway and swallowed it instinctively. They waited, another, then another. He was given more water. Within an hour, his right arm moved. When his hand touched his mouth, the women felt relief. He was showing the very early signs of recovery.

The blue was rising slowly. Ferdinand felt it. Pohii and Kai knew it too.

"We will wait, and then we will take him to Condonte," Pohii said. He knew the women on the island were helping him. He also knew that the ships would have to be guarded, inspected, and secured. He ordered a trusted detail of forty-five warriors to remain with the vessels and see to the salvaging.

Late in the afternoon, the young man opened his eyes. He was too weak to struggle. "I surrender to you," he whispered.

Ferdinand was the only one to understand him. He knew the language from his religious training at Cathédrale Saint-Jean-Baptiste in Lyon.

"You have been rescued," Ferdinand said. He noticed a slight accent within the man's French; perhaps he was from northern France. It was something he would have to talk about with the ancestral council.

Two days later, Pohii knew it was time to go. The canoes began the short journey back to Condonte. The prisoner had not said a word since his surrender. Ferdinand was ready to hear him, but he knew the man's military training would keep him silent. He was still very weak while the symptoms of the orange subsided. The canoes were brought back to the western shore of Ohluku. Half of all the canoes were now rowing back to Condonte.

Pohii motioned for the palace guards, and the prisoner was brought to the next canoe to leave. His hand bindings were checked, and when he entered the canoe, the bindings were attached to his seat. The canoe was fitted with outriggers on both sides of the hull.

Pohii stepped out of his canoe and stood for a moment on the shore of Condonte. He had been away for days, and he couldn't wait to see her smile. For a moment, he looked back at Ohluku Island. The new unanswered questions were mounting. He worried. The meeting would have to be rescheduled soon.

As Pohii walked back to the palace, his mind was racing.

The blue was building quickly.

Each image from the meeting lasted for an instant, and they repeated over and over again. Pohii knew the conversation would affect everyone on the islands. The dread set in. He saw a foreshadowing of their lives in the future. The timing remained his worst fear. He walked up the trail to the community lodge, gathering his thoughts as he went.

When he reached the community lodge, he could smell it. It was his granddaughter's birthday. The meal preparation was almost complete. It was all there in his scenes. The smell of the cooking fire was relieving the dread—just when he needed it. He smelled cane, coconut, and cinnamon. His heart melted. He turned and entered the lodge.

"Gran-papa!" She ran to him with her charming smile. "I love you, Gran-papa. I love you. I love you. I love you!"

She knew he would come to her birthday party. She wrapped herself around his right leg. He reached down and picked her up. He hadn't forgotten her little kisses and hugs. It was always something he cherished—even when she had been naughty.

"Thank you, my little one. I love you too." He put her back down. Her eyes told him that she wanted something more. Her adorable little face with those big brown eyes focused on his.

"What is it, Ha'ani?" he said, but he was not ready for her answer. The blue was coming, but the timing felt different.

"Can he come too? Can he come here? Please?"

"Little one, who should we bring to the party?"

"The new one, the one with … the yellow hair! *Please?*" she said. The child sent a shock up his spine. He did not want to refuse her, but he was speechless.

Ferdinand, Ho'uolo, and Iliakahani had heard the request from across the room. Ferdinand's face showed his dismay. Iliakahani broadly smiled because she knew. The blue was building a loving and effortless surrounding. Ho'uolo beamed a smile that all could see and feel.

"I will think about it, little one." Pohii showed her an uneasy smile, but Iliakahani knew it was genuine.

The blond man's personality was still an unknown. They all knew he was still recovering. He was still weak, but he was able to stand. A short, unstable walk was now possible—even with his bindings.

Ferdinand had not heard a word out of the prisoner's mouth since the day he surrendered. *Had Pohii's granddaughter seen the prisoner in person—or had she only seen him in the blue?* He gasped. She had seen his image from the blue. The women who were attending to the prisoner and the four palace guards watched his every move. He had also been watching them.

The women smiled at the prisoner. Their comforting feelings were a welcome relief. The calm surrounded him. He slowly and humbly enjoyed each and every meal presented to him. He thanked them with a smile and a bashful nod each time. Had it not been for his peeling, sunburned face, they would have seen him blush. His blue eyes had the women mesmerized. He was so different.

On the west balcony, the afternoon breeze was perfect. Pohii and Iliakahani were joined by Ho'uolo, Ferdinand, Kahania, a very pregnant Ihilani, Kenokeku, and Lokoihu. The wise man rarely ventured to other islands in the group. Loulu Island was his home, and to him, it was the most important place on earth.

"It is good," Lokoihu said softly for Ho'uolo's ears only.

Ho'uolo's mouth opened, but no words came out. The question had not been presented, but the answer was so good and completely shocking.

Yes, the prisoner would be invited to her birthday party. Iliakahani smiled; she couldn't believe it. She looked into the eyes of all the others on the balcony. The breeze accelerated. She saw the very good in Lokoihu's normally reserved expression. She saw Ferdinand's admiration for the man he had never met. She saw her husband's acknowledgment of the correct course for his people. Kahania was beaming.

Ihilani walked slowly to the all-families room. She sat on the first bench and began to breathe heavily. Every woman on the balcony moved automatically and walked behind her without saying a word. They all knew it was time. She had not yet begun, but they knew they had to help her. A room downstairs would have to be prepared. The community lodge was too far way. Iliakahani fought off the tears. Her duties—and the timing of both events—had her by the neck.

Ha'ani's birthday party would be brought to the stone table in the north garden. Kahania went to the kitchen without even thinking about it.

The new prisoner was escorted to the north garden that afternoon. He had been bathed, his clothing had been cleaned, and his skin had been treated with thick coconut oil. His face shined in the sunlight.

The oil wasn't all that comfortable with the humidity, but it was relieving his sunburn. The peeling had abated on his face—but not on his neck or hands. He was seated on one of the benches when Ferdinand told him he would be attending Pohii's granddaughter's birthday party.

Ferdinand spoke quietly to the prisoner. He told him that she had asked for him to come, and the prisoner's expression changed. The relief in his smile was no disguise. He realized he would live out the rest of his life there among the truly gracious island population.

"J'adore l'ile," the prisoner said. It was the first words he had said after his surrender. Ferdinand knew he was in the blue.

The transforming was rapid, to say the least. Ferdinand knew this first conversation with the prisoner was a breakthrough in the making. They could learn from this outsider, this young man from Europe. The future conversations with him were going to help them all. He knew it. For now, the birthday party for Ha'ani was the most important event. Ferdinand knew he would finally be introduced at the party.

"Please. What is your name?" Ferdinand said.

"I am Arin of Bergen, my priest." He knew Ferdinand was a priest? Ferdinand's flawless formal French was more than a clue. So, he's from Norway? Ferdinand tried to mask his surprise. He paused and let it absorb. "How many languages to you speak?"

"Norwegian, Danish, English, and some German, but they are fading. I lived in Marseille for most of my life. Two years in Calais," he said in French. His honesty was obvious. There was no need to guard it any longer.

So, this is the accent of immigration? "English?" Ferdinand asked.

"In Calais," Arin said.

Of course, Ferdinand thought. The city had been under the British Crown for several decades after the war, but he thought of it as a truly French community.

"My family was constantly looking for work and an escape from famine. We crossed the border into France ... I was an orphan at sixteen ... I joined the navy at Marseilles. I told them I was nineteen. I've been with the navy for five years, almost six."

Ferdinand could see him withdrawing. The truth was buried in the pain of the loss of his parents. However sullen he might have been on this subject, Ferdinand knew the soldier was evolving in the blue. He could feel it and see it. He was allowing it, but he needed to accept it.

The food was brought to the table. Flowers adorned it.

Pohii and Iliakahani were seated at the east end of the table.

Two palace guards stood next to Arin. Arin watched every detail and every movement of those being seated at the table.

Iliakahani sat at her husband's left as was the custom. She was ready to return to her daughter's side.

Kai and Alaina sat with their two-year-old son to Iliakahani's left—the place where Ihilani would traditionally sit.

Ferdinand took his seat next to Pohii.

Lokoihu, Ho'uolo, and his wife were seated next with a seat left open for Kahania.

Two women in duty to the family brought Ha'ani to her seat next to her mother. Kai's son was staring at Arin. He was very good at staring. He couldn't help it. He stood on the bench; his arms and hands braced him at the table. He was leaning left to see around Ferdinand and across the table. Pohii smiled but kept himself from giggling. He knew his grandson very well. He gently grasped Iliakahani's hand. Her momentary focus on her staring grandson had relieved the anxious feeling of concern for Ihilani. She turned and smiled at her husband.

When Ha'ani saw him for the first time, she ran around the table to her grandfather, shrieking as she grabbed him by his left arm. "Gran-papa! Thank you! I love you! I love you!" She ran to Arin and plunged herself into his stunned arms. "You are here! You are here!" She ran back to her grandfather, hugged him, and kissed him again.

Everyone at the table giggled and enjoyed every second of it.

The palace guards stood frozen, embarrassed that they had done nothing to protect Pohii's granddaughter.

Lokoihu knew that the blue had protected her. The timing had been perfect. He also knew that their new citizen had just been accepted—even if he didn't know it yet. They had all watched his tenderness and disbelief as the child embraced him.

Her wish had come true.

For Arin, the moment softened. He was able to breathe again. The shock on his face changed to a blushing smile. It was the first time in a very long time that anyone had shown him even the slightest affection. He was embarrassed, humbled, and slightly relieved.

Ferdinand stood and smiled. The charming greeting had set the tone. "May I take a moment and introduce our new guest?"

The nods in the affirmative from all around the table were automatic and effortless. The only exception was Kai's two-year-old son. His mouth was still agape. He didn't know what was happening.

"We have a new citizen with us. His name is Arin," Ferdinand said.

Ha'ani whispered his name over and over.

"He comes from another land, another country. He speaks a different language. He is now among us as a citizen. We can learn from him. He is a young man. He is a good man. He said that he loves it here."

The silent smiles from everyone as they looked at Arin were the most powerful dream he could have imagined. He raised both hands and covered his face as the emotion peaked. He took a moment to regain his composure. He looked at them and beamed a smile that began his citizenship.

It was the calming relief in the first level of the blue.

"Arin, Arin, Arin!" Ha'ani shrieked. She loved him.

Arin finally joined the giggling. Iliakahani beamed her smile in tears.

The meal was started, and Arin's shackles were removed. They enjoyed the small flour cakes—a recipe from long before anyone lived on the islands. It's soft, flaky texture and sweet taste had Ha'ani begging for more. It was another highlight of the celebration for her.

Iliakahani wanted to be there with her. She moved around the table and kissed her granddaughter.

Ha'ani returned an effortless smile.

Then Iliakahani turned to the palace, the women were ready. They counted the timing between contractions. They were telling her to breathe. The second contraction came long after the first, and they knew it would be all night and into tomorrow before the birth. Just before sunset, she was carefully moved down the hill to the community lodge.

Ha'ani beamed. Her party was concluding. She hugged her brother. He gladly returned the hugs without really understanding the ritual. A party for his third birthday was four months away. He couldn't remember the first two.

She ran around the table and hugged everyone. Each person mattered to her. She loved each and every one of them. She couldn't help it—even with those she had never met. Finally, she climbed up on Pohii's lap and smiled at him.

He couldn't resist. He absolutely loved this moment with her.

A soft breeze caught the palms at just the right time. Everyone felt it. It was the perfect moment.

Pohii knew the meeting would be delayed. He took a deep breath. He needed time to think about it. He gently put Ha'ani down and watched as she calmly walked back to her seat.

The blue softly and slowly retreated.

The food was generous and delicious. It was more than enough for everyone. The energy of the party created good memories. Those in attendance slowly began to leave.

The palace guards were no longer needed for Arin. Three others at the table knew it was right. The smiles on their faces confirmed it. Pohii made it official with a rare handshake and a grin. Ho'uolo, Lokoihu, and Ferdinand all agreed.

"The elders will place you, Arin. You are welcome among us on this island." Pohii decreed. "Tonight, you stay in the palace until they decide."

Ferdinand translated. The traditional placement by the elders was the correct protocol. Pohii called upon the two remaining women in duty to the family to place him in one of the two unused quarters on the first floor of the palace. Pohii walked to the community lodge. He knew she would stay there overnight. He wanted to say good night to her—to both of them. He leaned over and gently kissed his precious daughter.

He hugged his wife, kissed her, and returned to the palace. The transformation for his daughter and the duty for his wife weighed heavily on him as he walked. The sunset began as he reached the bedroom. For the first time in a very long time, he ached in her absence. He reclined on the bed. His mind was racing. He closed his eyes in what he knew was the need for sleep.

As the sky darkened, the blue arrived. The swirling colors began. He had only seen it once before with Iliakahani at his side. He relaxed in the calming, centering, and nurturing. The thoughts of his duties subsided. He took a deep breath, exhaled, and slowly fell asleep in the blue.

Chapter 50

An hour before sunrise, Pohii opened his eyes. He saw the moonlight in the corridor. He had slept for a long time. The pains had not yet surged in his back. He turned to his right side and elevated his torso. He knew he had to go to the community lodge. He stood in the doorway and listened. He expected silence, but the feelings of family and duty began in a rush. He walked along the railing to the staircase.

As he was about to walk down to the courtyard, the images of the judgment room on Mokiki Island took over. He had dreamed of praying to God, giving thanks, and doing the right thing. Kai and the volunteers had seen it with him. Ferdinand had shown them. His guidance for the day was reverence to the highest degree.

Pohii reached for the railing and paused. He walked through the all-families room and out to the balcony. The stillness, silence, and calm gripped him. The blue increased as he walked out on the balcony.

He noticed the thin clouds barely moving in the moonlight. He looked toward Mokiki. He saw the mountain as it reflected the moonlight. The color of the mountain surprised him. The green had been replaced by the soft white of the moonlight. It was beginning. *Oh God!* He knelt behind the railing and prayed. His hands supported his head on the railing.

He heard footsteps behind him. They knew. The four of them stopped at a respectful distance. They knew their beloved leader was in prayer.

They calmly waited. Ferdinand placed his hands together and began his morning prayers. Ho'uolo lowered his head and prayed. Lokoihu moved slowly to the railing beside Pohii, knelt, and prayed. Kai stood next to Ferdinand with his head down in prayer.

Pohii raised his right knee and opened his eyes. He stood and enjoyed a deep breath. He let it out slowly. His mind was filling with the blue.

Lokoihu stood there for a moment. He knew that Pohii was assessing the gravity of the moment, the day, and the future. He nodded, smiled, and watched as Pohii turned.

Pohii paused in the all-families room. His heart felt the moment with humility and duty. His confidence returned as his mind relaxed. After a few moments, he went down to the first floor. The others waited at the top of the stairs. They knew their beloved leader had many things to do.

He walked through the garden as the sun rose above the horizon. He could see the sunlight in the tops of the trees as he walked to the community lodge. He saw the assembly outside, and Kenokeku was waiting anxiously outside. When he heard her, he knew to remain outside. The tradition was observed by all the men on the island.

Her final push was approaching. She breathed heavily as the contraction began. It had been almost twelve hours. She was exhausted. The last four hours had been grueling. Kenokeku was worried. His concern was evident on his face.

She screamed, and his child was born. The women were surprised by his cries. His ear-shattering volume was an inspiration to his mother. She knew his name would have to reflect it. The women with her attended to the newborn, cleaning and wrapping him.

Iliakahani presented the sleeping infant to his mother. She beamed and felt so very proud.

Kahania exited the lodge to tell the community. "Kenokeku, you are now a father. Come with me to meet your son."

Kenokeku screamed. It was the best news of his life.

Kahania offered her hand to escort him. "Ihilani is resting. She wants to see you."

He rushed to her side and saw his child for the first time.

Ihilani offered the boy to his proud father. "He looks just like you, my husband!"

He couldn't say a word. He looked at his son, rocked him gently, and kissed him.

Pohii finally entered. He saw his precious daughter. She was in tears. He knew he couldn't stay very long, but the sight of his new grandson filled him with the automatic love they all felt. Everyone in the room was smiling.

Pohii kissed his daughter and congratulated them both. He kissed his wife. This brief visit was the first of many. He walked back toward the palace for the meeting. The future of the islands would have to be debated.

They were waiting for him in the courtyard. He knew his beloved wife's spirit was with him as he entered the most important room in all on the islands. In that room, their future would be decided. The elders were sworn in as they entered.

"I have a new grandson," Pohii said quietly with a proud smile.

Olohu, the senior palace guard, nodded. He knew only seconds after the birth. The communication channels of the palace guards were working in tight order.

Pohii shivered as he walked to his seat at the table. He knew Kahania was coming to the palace. The two women in duty to the family were almost ready to serve the meal as Kahania entered and savored it. The aromas were very good. The fire-roasted fish smelled especially good. The vegetables and fruit were ready. Kahania knew that the meeting would be pivotal, and she began making the palace's exclusive drink. Within twenty minutes, it was ready to be served. She thought about its taste and aftertaste. She wanted it to be special this time. She thought about something to add to enhance its flavor.

Arin entered the kitchen, smelled the aromas, and watched her prepare the drink. He stopped, remembering the drink from the cafés in the central square in Marseilles. He gestured for her to wait a moment and grinned. He moved to the sideboard and gathered what he knew were the last two key ingredients. Arin had been the cook's assistant on the admiral's ship. She absolutely loved the result of Arin's assistance. She couldn't wait to see their expression after the first sip in the council room. She smiled a broad, loving smile to him after her first sip. It was so good she almost cried. She *loved* it.

Olohu welcomed the last person to the council room. The swearing-in protocols were observed. The torches in the four corners of the room were lit in a solemn ceremony reserved for high meetings.

The silence in the room signaled the anticipation of the meal. It was thought that satisfying the palate before deciding was the key to all meetings.

Olohu nodded, and the women in duty to the family began bringing in steamed vegetables, cool spring water, and fire-roasted fish.

Arin brought in the drink. He had a big smile on his face as he placed it on the table next to Pohii.

Ferdinand asked Arin to describe the drink.

"Goûts comme le chocolat," Arin said.

"Tastes like chocolate," Ferdinand said. *Here on these islands?* He had known the flavor for the past ten years after Señor Columbus had returned with huge treasures from the Spanish claims in Central and South America. "It's called chocolate," he whispered to Pohii.

Pohii sampled the sweet flavor and smiled. He was very impressed. He had not anticipated its sweet taste. He savored its taste. He wanted more of this new drink. He beamed with wide-open approving eyes, and Arin blushed.

The head of the palace guard stood silently. His demeanor was solemn as he raised his right hand in the protocol. The room went silent, and those around the table stopped eating and drinking.

Arin and the women exited.

The spiritual room had a domed ceiling, four columns, and double doors. It had the only oval table on any of the islands and polished chairs.

The hand-carved stone benches gently curved along the walls. A hidden ventilation system added to the grand feel of the room. The air current matched the inside to outdoors. The torches flickered with the wind.

Olohu stood. "This room is a sacred room. From this point on, we decide what to do on these islands and how we will face the future and all unknown to us who live beyond the sunrise and the sunset. We will all decide here in this room only. We must be careful."

Ho'uolo knew they needed to remain calm. It would have to result in comfort. His one-day trip to Loulu Island and the revelation after talking with Lokoihu had returned in the blue.

They *needed* to love without any changes in the emotion. He worried about the changes that could come.

The blue arrived in a slow and soft buildup for all in the room.

They all knew that this moment would be forever etched in their history. They relaxed as the blue calmed them to a centered emotion. They were friends talking to friends.

The meeting was extended another day when they could not agree on the course they must take. The ancestors had related the story on the sixth tablet of how remote and isolated these islands were, but they had not revealed where they had sailed from. That lacking detail caused a stir in the meeting. Without that one fact, the elders were no closer to deciding. The notion that there were others from faraway lands did not make any sense—even though Ferdinand and Arin could relate their knowledge to them.

The meeting was adjourned for the day.

After eight long days of meetings, the elders had agreed on most of the things that constituted their culture and resolved to maintain and protect their nation. Several critical issues remained. How would they protect themselves from another invasion and the unknown elements of the force that new enemy could unleash? What would they do as individuals and as a group? Did they have a cohesive national force of defense?

On the ninth day of meetings, Pohii was awakened by the waning moonlight just before dawn. In his dream, he felt something was missing in the discussions. They had overlooked something. He wrestled with it as he quietly left the bedroom. Iliakahani was still asleep. He walked to the door to the all-families room, but the balcony wasn't the inspiration he needed. He walked to the north corridor and turned right. He knew the chapel was the place. As he walked past Ferdinand's quarters, he knew Ferdinand was still asleep. He was relieved that he couldn't hear the thunderous roar of Ferdinand's snoring from his own bedroom.

The chapel door was open, and the interior door was also open. The guards checked the doors in the palace every night. He was startled to see someone praying. Nothing was wrong. His heart knew that the open door was an invitation.

A light breeze moved down the short hallway, and he briefly stopped to enjoy it. The feminine had arrived. The soft nurturing, the warm air!

He quietly entered the chapel and walked to the center aisle. He knew they were there before he walked in. Near the altar, they were deep in prayers. They knew he would join them.

He slowly knelt as Lokoihu and Ho'uolo completed their prayers.

Several minutes later, Pohii raised his head from his hands. They stood together and turned. They knew.

They exited the chapel and walked to the courtyard.

Pohii suddenly felt the need for caution. He knew the day would bring mental challenges. His duty was always first and foremost, but he didn't see the outcome yet.

As the sunrise was about to begin, Pohii said, "I have something to tell you. I must tell you what I saw in a dream last night."

A door closed on the third floor. A figure walked down the north corridor. When it reached the chapel, they knew it was Ferdinand. He entered the chapel for his morning prayers to the Lord and Savior.

The three of them silently waited for him in the courtyard. The morning prayers were always thought of as the most important element in beginning the day.

When Ferdinand returned to the corridor, he moved swiftly to join them. The solemn nods were all that was needed for a greeting.

"First, we will watch the sunrise behind the trees," Pohii said. He walked out into the north gardens. The first sunrise on this first day of spring was the moment Pohii knew they needed as inspiration for the meeting.

Ferdinand reached for the cloth in his pocket in anticipation of a sneeze. The palm pollen had begun. Alas, his effort to suppress it failed. It was loud, forceful, and shocking with little regard for adjacent eardrums or nerves. The three men with him felt a mild jump in their souls and thought the rest of the community was now awake. Then came two more sneezes in rapid succession.

"Are you all right?" Pohii asked.

"Yes, thank you," Ferdinand said. Sweat filled his face and neck. He wiped the perspiration and put the cloth back in his pocket.

They turned their attention to the sunrise. The unseen horizon beyond the islands hinted at the inevitable. The stars began to fade at first light. The moderate humidity beamed the light atop the trees. Next, the top of the palace's north wall received it.

All the elements of the islands were represented in the sunrise: the relentless calm, the inevitable, the blue.

The brilliant white provided the shadows. It was the welcome of the awesome power of life-sustaining light and warmth. The shade provided the cool protection. The light touch of the wind on their skin. God nurtured their souls. It was all there.

The soft arrival of the blue amplified it all.

Pohii knew words were not necessary. The perfect sunrise helped him decide not to talk about his dream there. He knew it should be said in the meeting.

Pohii knew with all his heart and soul that there was nothing to fear and nothing to fight. He knew that God wanted them to thrive and not just survive.

The concerns and complaints would be heard. Each of the islands and each citizen mattered. Each man, each woman, and each child were worthy and equal in his mind. To him, status was irrelevant. He felt love for them all. In his dream, he absolutely loved each and every living soul on the islands.

He felt a mild swelling of positive emotions as he pondered the meeting. The blue was surrounding him, but he hadn't felt it come to him. It had started in his dream state and had never really left. He knew they had to accept their own history. They had to accept their own past, present, and future—and they had the means to preserve it all.

When they assembled in the courtyard, Pohii, and the elders stood quietly in the sunlight.

Iliakahani stood solemnly next to her husband. Kai and Ihilani were on the third-floor corridor, watching the gathering of authority below. Their children were attended to in the third-floor all-families room.

The silence in the courtyard was broken by a small burst of the wind from the east. The blue arrived in a soft tone, a centered hue of blue. They all felt it.

The council room was filled with anxious leaders and the very real support of the women in duty to the family, Arin, Kahania, and Iliakahani.

Olohu felt something beyond his duties as leader of the palace guard. He watched the assembly as they entered the council room for the swearing-in protocols and reached to close the double doors. He knew food would be brought in, but something told him to leave one of the doors slightly ajar. He opted for leaving them both ajar.

"We are here today to decide the future of our nation. To decide how to meet the world, how to protect what we have and those that we love," Olohu said to set the tone for the meeting.

Iliakahani's mouth dropped open at such kind words coming out of his mouth. She knew he had accepted the blue. The shock turned to renewed respect for the man who knew his job and never quite loved anyone other than his quiet and close-knit family. His wife of twenty years was a soft-hearted personality who enjoyed listening and talking softly. Everyone admired her childlike voice and caring attentiveness. She wanted to participate in the event. She had gone to Ohluku Island with her husband for their marriage vows. He went to inspect the salvage operations, but she wanted to visit family and friends there.

After six days, it was time to return to Condonte Island. Her own mission had been a success. Two days later, eighty of her friends, neighbors, and family members took to the canoes at sunset and arrived on the northeast shore of Condonte. They had spent two nights sheltered with those she knew nearest her home just steps away from the beach and the seventh of many community lodges on the island. Not the one nearest the palace. Their group still wanted to practice a surprise.

Olohu and twenty guards brought back artifacts from the grounded fleet. Among the things he brought back were dangerous and heavy weapons he knew nothing about. They gathered some of the rigging, ropes, and wooden blocks from two of the ships.

They had removed anything that wasn't attached to the decks. They collected pots, pans, and implements from the galleys. A heavy barrel sealed with a wax coating was brought to the canoes. Six relatively small barrels sealed with metal rings and leather were brought aboard the canoes. The canoes and the outriggers were heavy with spoils. He would have the elders inspect it all.

Ferdinand and Arin knew about the outside world. Arin knew the latest naval warfare advances. Ferdinand's knowledge of the Armada in comparison to the French fleet intrigued him and had him worried about implementing and incorporating anything they found into this society. He knew it was the first time they would be filling the canoes. It could take months to fully strip the fleet.

The first day on the admiral's ship, they had spent more than four hours wrapping and hurling the dead sailors overboard. Olohu knew it would haunt his guards for years, but it had to be done with the spirits watching over them. It was a tradition of the island. The honor was bestowed on a citizen no matter who it was.

Olohu anguished over the power that he knew was the orange, and he wanted to talk to Ferdinand about it. The day before the last meeting, Olohu found him in the workroom. "Elder Ferdinand, may I have a word with you?"

Ferdinand was engrossed in the last tablet's translation. "Please come in," he said as he scribbled something on the bamboo cloth.

"I have questions that you may have the answers to," Olohu whispered.

"Yes, sit down here," Ferdinand said with a muted smile. He had a feeling that the questions he was about to hear were about to reveal the scope of the blue. He shivered. A short pulse of air refreshed the room. Ferdinand's shiver subsided.

"One moment please." Ferdinand stood and closed the door. "Now, what is your question?" His soft tone revealed the respect for his guest— and everyone on the islands.

"What is the blue and what is the orange?"

Ferdinand contemplated his answer. Olohu was asking for the academic approach, but from the text on the last tablet, Ferdinand knew the spiritual view was what the ancestors had intended. "That is perhaps the one question that deserves an answer. It also requires the sworn commitment to duty that permits that knowledge. You have that duty," Ferdinand said. "You are the first to hear this answer. The Cahbrean goal from your ancestors is supported by the Cahbrean laws, which were designed into the buildings on these islands. The blue and the orange were designed and engineered by your ancestors."

The frown on Olohu's face was replaced with disbelief.

"Thorn Mountain is the key to the concept. It's the nerve center of this nation. All the buildings on Mokiki Island work together. Each one of them has a purpose, and each one matters. And no—they didn't build the mountain," Ferdinand said

Olohu had not yet set foot on Mokiki and thought he had been last in accepting a small portion of the feelings he witnessed from the blue. The trust had not yet arrived for him.

"In fact, the total of those things they built enhanced the good and the bad. The Cahbrean laws were adopted with each new thing they discovered. Each effect was centered—good and bad—and recorded in stone," Ferdinand said. "Each thing was studied for years before they knew it was right. Each emotion mattered. Each fear addressed. Each discovery enhanced or rejected."

Olohu was stunned—even though he had heard of some of it before. The details of the "intent gathering" had forced his silence. A positive intent was assigned to the blue. A negative intent was heavily debated and ultimately assigned to the orange. Olohu was shocked to hear that the power and range of the orange were focused with mild power within sight of the mountain. They had measured its distant effect and had decreed no limit to the power of the orange beyond the horizon.

The dam they had built would supply the necessary power, especially at night, but they had not revealed how much power the dam was capable of making. Ferdinand felt in his heart and soul that the dam wasn't the single source of energy.

"Why did it not interfere with the raids between islands?" Olohu asked.

"Residency," Ferdinand said with startling authority. "For those who live here or were born here, your ancestors knew acceptance would require the least amount of time. They also knew, without a doubt, to expect limited internal strife and bickering. They knew any raids could not be sustained for very long and had decreed never to interfere with the full power of the orange. However, the orange would be used to deter long campaigns of the islands. That is why they quickly felt exhaustion in any raid or foreign invasion."

Olohu was trying to understand the concept. What civilian—indeed what citizen—should be made aware of it? He knew that Mokiki Island would have to be returned to a sacred and forbidden place in their souls. The sickness was the warning they must all obey. He knew they needed to decree that no one set foot on Mokiki Island. It would have to be forbidden forever.

He knew it would be too much to understand. Three other elders had also known this.

Ferdinand knew the blue was present, and he knew and felt Olohu's contemplation as it happened. He knew Olohu was the right person to proclaim it in the meeting. He was relieved that Olohu had felt it in the first level of the blue. It was the right decision.

The ancestral council room had been cleaned, and the torches were refreshed. The settings for the meal on the oval table were ready and had been thoroughly inspected. It was the highest protocol ever followed in the room. They had achieved a spiritual and elegant feel in the sacred room. They all felt a sense of high reverence and solemn duty.

Olohu presided over the swearing-in ceremony. The elders entered the room and stopped each time an elder was seated. Pohii, Kai, and Iliakahani were graciously seated together on the west side of the table. Olohu stood with four palace guards at the entrance.

They felt the tension of bravery and duty.

"We know what we must do," Olohu said. "We know each other well. This day is our traditional last day. Our laws say so. Our hearts say so. Today, we decide."

There was no doubt. The tenth day, by law, was the last day of debate. The customary order of hierarchy was in reverse on the last day.

Olohu would speak first, and Pohii would announce his decision last. Pohii had exercised his option to invite one more person into the room. He was waiting for him to be called in from the courtyard as Olohu recited the traditional swearing in of all those in the room. Olohu looked into the eyes of each person. They each responded with a simple nod and a hand held high. They vowed, by law, that they had accepted the duty to decide. They were each required to voice their opinions to agree or dissent; abstaining was not an option. They could briefly agree with the previous option, but dissent always required an explanation. The protocol called for all previous voices to be included in that debate.

It had always required courage to disagree on the tenth day. The opinions of each of the elders and Pohii were to be heard before any voting. The "hand-up protocol" to speak next was used in that part of the meeting.

Two rounds of votes around the table were always part of deciding. The first round encouraged further opinion, and the second round finalized the decision.

The seating around the table mattered when voting. Raising a hand was voting in the affirmative—and not the protocol to speak next. Debates would occur in the first round of voting but never in the second round.

The two rounds of voting would repeat until the decision was unanimous among the elders. When Pohii announced his decision, it would be final.

Just before they started the meeting, there was a knock on the door.

A single bamboo flute was joined by another. A pan flute accompanied the soft drums. Voices were singing in perfect harmony in the courtyard. It was a beautiful song for the leaders.

"Ohi i uhoi kaho', ohi'i lo'u kaho" *(We pray for us, we pray for you)*. The heartfelt song was sung slowly and lovingly.

Those in the council room stood with mouths agape and listened. The citizens, this land, this one heart, this experience was as beautiful and glorious as it was haunting.

Iliakahani stood with her palms together and tears in her eyes as she listened to the swelling of voices in the choir.

They all felt the blue together—for the first time in a meeting—and it mesmerized them. They felt reverence for God in the centered calm.

The song ended just as it had started—with a surprise. The salvage operation included a collection of ship bells. Five ascending rings—a bell for each island—ended the drum performance. The tears in the council room were unanimous.

Olohu opened the doors to see the smiles of the eighty-piece choir. That moment caused those in the council room to roar with applause. It was brilliant and unexpected. They felt the love from near and far.

Olohu's wife stood in the front row of the choir and beamed. Akaniha had arranged the most epic and most secret of surprises that gripped their souls and set the tone for the meeting.

Arin began the procession of food into the room. The stoic faces transformed to smiles as he placed the warm chocolate drink next to Pohii.

Kahania brought in two entrées. The vegetables and the fruit were placed, and spring water was brought in. This meal was lavish. The new dressings and sauces were exquisite. The aromas were nothing short of spectacular.

As Arin and Kahania exited, Pohii walked to the double doors and invited the last person into the council room. He pointed to a seat next to Ferdinand. "Please sit here, Arin," Pohii said with a calm smile. He told Arin that the others at the table had the duty to vote, but he wanted him there to speak and listen. Ferdinand would translate.

Arin was at a loss for words, but he obeyed. He sat at the table in silence. Being there to listen in on the meeting overwhelmed him. His nerves were causing him to force normal breathing. He placed his hands together to mask his shaking. His words would come from his knowledge, his heart, and his soul. He had already accepted the blue, but he had not known how it felt on the first level with any confidence. That was about to change.

"We eat," Olohu said.

The conversation focused on the meal. Ferdinand asked Arin to describe the flavors as the accolades poured in. He made sure they knew Kahania created the meal and that he had assisted her and gained her approval with each new flavor.

The crab and shrimp entrée had a sweet pepper taste; the flavor was a complete surprise to everyone. The savory fish fillets were cut thinly, breaded with flour, and sautéed in coconut oil. He learned the cooking technique in the Navy.

Pohii knew he had made the right choice to invite him to this meeting.

The spring water and fruit signaled the conclusion to the meal.

Olohu stood, "Thanks to God for this meal. Now we decide. I go first. We just heard it from the courtyard. The choir sang for us all. I feel it here in this room … now. My dear wife felt it when the first invaders left. The ones we feared. The ones we questioned. The ones I didn't believe. This next vote in this sacred room will set our goals as a nation. We will know of the next coming—another invasion—and it *will* come." He swallowed. "The first invasion filled us with fear, but the second invasion was worse. We didn't see it until it was too late … for them." His throat felt close to collapsing. "I felt it as it happened, but I didn't see it until the reefs of Ohluku captured their ships." He took several breaths and sat down. Pohii stood, paused a moment and said, "I want to hear from you before we vote. Ferdinand, Arin, and Ho'uolo,"

Pohii paused once more, "What should we know about these islands and the lands over the horizon?"

Ferdinand stood. "We know of the blue. We know of Mokiki. But some of you don't know of the orange. The ancestors came to these islands and built buildings and joined each together as one. I still don't know why, but I do know their intent was to guide and protect us. It doesn't watch over us—God does. Instead, it feels us. I do not know how. The orange was built to protect us. The blue centers us and guides us." Ferdinand sighed and sat back down.

Pohii said, "Arin, tell us what you know."

"Thank you for my rescue," Arin said. "I know you as one family—everyone on these islands. Thank you for your welcome." His confidence was returning. "I know some of the things that Ferdinand knows. I know France and Norway are places new to you—perhaps England, Spain, and Portugal. There are many, many more nations." The blue centered him and calmed him. "My hope is that other nations may learn from all of you, as I have." Arin sat down and swallowed. Ferdinand translated for Arin.

Iliakahani knew this young man's courage, and humility was stirring his emotions. He needed time. She knew it. She felt it. He was in the blue. Her tears had softly arrived as he spoke. She knew Arin loved it there, and she wasn't alone in that thought.

Ferdinand knew the other nations were powerful and experienced in war, and he knew they would come to the islands. He knew their intent would matter—and that the ancestors' experiment would respond once more.

Ho'uolo stood and cleared his throat. "My sons and daughters," he began. He cleared his throat again. He looked up at the ceiling. The blue intensified. For the first time, he saw the connection between spirituality and reverence in the room. The oval shape symbolized an embrace of all those in attendance. The six twin circles decoration on the ceiling represented the six most revered spirits.

His hands hit the table to steady him. He sat back down with weakened knees and open mouth. It was, _the_ moment, he had been waiting for. It was the moment he first saw the grand design of all the buildings as planned by the ancestors. *This building is part of the overall concept that included Mokiki!* Everyone had overlooked the designs in the ceiling—until now, Ho'uolo thought, his mind swirling in the blue as it burned in the answers.

Ho'uolo's mind was racing with questions. The images of their ancestors, their belief systems, their truths, and their love for one another were in a complete review. Their ancestors' beliefs had been devoutly practiced by the Islanders—from the beginning.

The blue focused on him and showed him images at a staggering speed.

Without saying a word, Iliakahani and Ferdinand ran to his side. His panicked breathing was the alarm. His eyes were still looking at the ceiling as his tears fell. His mouth was quivering. He hunted for the words, he couldn't speak.

They knew he needed time to recover before he could tell them what he knew.

Pohii stood, knowing that this momentous moment was cause for the meeting to go into recess. The blue reduced its exposure to the calm neutral.

The pause they needed lasted just less than an hour. All but three of those attending made their way into the courtyard.

Ferdinand, Ho'uolo, and Lokoihu remained in the oval room. Ho'uolo's nerves were recovering quickly. Ferdinand had his suspicions, but Lokoihu had no doubts.

Ho'uolo whispered, "Close the doors, please ... and tell Olohu to wait for us to open them."

Ferdinand looked at him and shivered in anticipation.

Lokoihu gave the instructions to Olohu, and they heard the latch click.

Ho'uolo's eyes moved back and forth between Lokoihu and Ferdinand for a moment. He was trying to decide where to begin. "This palace—this place, this room—has a different purpose than I ever imagined."

Ferdinand's mouth fell open. His thesis was about to be confirmed, and Lokoihu's secret knowledge would be revealed.

"I always wondered why it feels so good to be here in this palace. I have wondered why the west gardens are so lush and productive. I have wondered why the north and south gardens are so easily cared for. Now I know why the jungle on the east side touches the palace." Ho'uolo took a deep breath and swallowed. "It hides the stairs long buried by rock and soil. The entrance to the first headquarters the ancestors built. It is two floors below us ... below this room." He paused.

A whirlwind of images flew in with a precise order.

Ho'uolo turned his gaze to look at Lokoihu, and Ferdinand followed.

"It is not a door," Lokoihu said in a soft tone. "It is the east wall foundation. The stairs they built are a remnant of the construction that were never removed. They knew it would confuse whoever excavated it in the future. The real entrance is protected by disguise. Opening it must never take place. The design forbids it."

Ferdinand and Ho'uolo held their breath with their eyes on Lokoihu.

"I know, but it is forbidden," Lokoihu said.

For a moment, the wind accelerated through the ventilation. This time, they could hear it. The torches on the west end of the room flickered. Those on the east end were blown out.

Lokoihu moved quickly to light them again. The omen clearly forbid the discovery, but the lighting in the room never varied. It never decreased or increased during the event. It was as if the experience had been coordinated and anticipated.

Ferdinand and Ho'uolo were frozen in fear.

"Now you know," Lokoihu said. "We must not talk about it. We must not think about it. We must not search for it. Now you know it is forbidden. Our ancestors had known God before they built anything. They never *intended* for it to be found."

As Lokoihu's words finally sunk in, Ferdinand and Ho'uolo nervously agreed. Their silent breathing returned to near normal. The disguised entrance should not be discovered. Ferdinand had a vague notion of it in translating the fourteenth tablet, and it was not in this room. He knew he shouldn't try to verify its whereabouts. His natural curiosity on that one topic would have to quickly convert to absolute doctrine. He knew it, and then he believed. The ancestors' wishes would be honored.

Ho'uolo was still pondering the facts that the blue had shown him. The building was their first phase in experimentation—and it would serve as a retreat from the construction on Mokiki. They had always wanted to test their achievements. This island provided the place where the ancestors had proven their theories—the quest—before they abandoned it all.

Lokoihu walked to the double doors and grasped the handles. The light from the sunlit courtyard entered the room as the double doors were opened. Ho'uolo and Ferdinand were still in a state of shock as the air from the courtyard filled the room. The warm, gentle scent of the jungle mixed with the smell of the ocean and the room's internal ventilation.

Ah, what a good smell. Ah, the wind.

They all began to enter the sacred room again. Olohu knew that crossing the door's threshold meant they would have to be sworn in again. The strict protocol was performed with the utmost grace after the doors were closed.

One of the seats remained empty.

Arin's testimony had been heard, and he was relieved that he didn't have to return.

Ferdinand dreaded the last part of the meeting. His heart was still feeling the conflicts of new knowledge. He had always been fascinated by the desire to share it all versus the policies they would have to agree to in this room.

One by one, each elder voiced his heartfelt opinion. There was a loving tone to the emotional comments from each and every one of them. The details were different from the mouths of each of the elders. Each one expressed absolute trust for one another.

As Pohii graciously listened to the testimony, he knew what they would say. "The self-evident commitment to their flock," as Ferdinand would say. He knew it was what they needed to say. They cherished the people and the islands. He knew the undercurrent was the sworn duty to protect, preserve, and defend all of them at all costs.

"So here is what we must do," Pohii said. The weight of the nation was on him as he started his decree. "We will prepare our people with the news that there are other nations and other people. We must say that this is new to them and that it is good." He looked into the eyes of everyone in the room, especially his beloved wife. "We will tell them that there will be no changes in their day-to-day lives. Our citizens know it when we tell them that I work for all. I gather more than I can eat so that all can eat."

He swallowed and took a breath. "I don't think the invaders came from the east to find us. I don't think they know the ocean like we do ... or our ancestors did."

Pohii had a feeling that reading the waves was something the invaders did not know. They were looking up at the sky, not down to the waves to indicate directions to an island. The intricate and infallible wave patterns were the key to his society hiding from the rest of the world.

"The second invaders were not destined for our islands. They found us by mistake. I think the next invaders won't be coming for several years." Pohii said.

The faces around the room showed a mixture of hope, wonder, relief, and exultation.

Iliakahani knew he was absolutely right and that there was more to his decree. She smiled as he spoke. She knew he was correct. She was so proud of him.

He had told the elders about his dream in the blue—a forecast of sorts. A few days before the meetings had started, Lokoihu had taken him aside and led him to this announcement.

The elder of few words had told Pohii to expect the next invaders to be something that would change them all forever. Pohii was shaken. He knew that no one wanted those changes.

Lokoihu said something to Pohii that came close to his heart. He had already experienced it and had not found a true definition of it for himself. Lokoihu whispered, "The white is the answer. The White introduces the blue and the orange. With your intentions, the White will find you."

"So the white is the blue and orange?" Pohii asked.

"No," Lokoihu said softly. "It is all of them." He took a step away, knowing that Pohii now knew the full range of light into darkness. He also knew Pohii needed time to decipher it all.

Lokoihu had also said something else to Ferdinand. Ferdinand had asked him about the orange, but Lokoihu had learned the answer when his own father had disciplined him. "The orange finds you when you hate or when foreign invaders' intent is conquest. It's on a tablet that remains on Mokiki. Ho'uolo knew that he *dare* not tell you to bring it here. The ancestors knew that *that* one emotion was the worst among all traits. They were very close to reaching their Cahbrean goal. The orange is powerful indeed." Lokoihu walked away.

Oh dear God. He's right! Ferdinand hadn't felt hate since his rescue. The complete absence of hate—he hadn't thought about it for a long time. There was precious relief in the revelation. He had just realized one of the many parts of the Cahbrean goal.

Chapter 51

The oval room in the palace was silent as Pohii took several more breaths.

Iliakahani's tears fell to her chin, and her hands were on her lap.

Pohii said, "We will love, we will listen, we will live together, we will harvest, we will prepare, and we will be strong. When they come, we will be ready. We will know to love and defend us all." He took another breath. "We will decide to fight for our islands or lay down our defenses."

"No!" Ferdinand said. "We should not surrender to them. We should *welcome* them."

No one had ever dared to violate the sacred protocol and interrupt the leader.

Pohii said, "Ferdinand, you are my friend."

There wasn't anything more to say. The decree was final in the revelation from Ferdinand. They all agreed in silence, and they stood with broad smiles.

Iliakahani let the tears fall.

The blue elevated well beyond what anyone had ever witnessed.

Iliakahani knew something was about to happen. She felt it, and it was good.

They heard ferocious knocking on the doors. Olohu was shocked that another protocol was being violated and angrily reached for the door. He opened the doors with one eyebrow elevated in disgust.

"Come see. There are lots of them," Pohii's granddaughter squealed. "Come quick and see." She grabbed Arin's hand and dragged him as she ran. The moment was electric.

They followed the child—and her enthusiasm—to the northwest rocks on Condonte's shore. "See? Look!" She pointed out to the open channel. "Oh! There's a little one!"

Many pods of migrating whales were coursing in the channel. Their traditional beliefs told them about the majestic, enormous animals. The whales swam together as a family—and community. The whales were breathing and swimming together on their instinctive route north between Condonte and Mokiki. Their surfacing blows of breath were seen and heard by everyone. The gentle giants were breaching, showing their land-bound audience their size and grace in that small channel in the vast Pacific Ocean. It had happened a year ago to the day—just two days before the captain's ships had retreated for Europe.

It was powerful. It was the event that finally convinced Pohii and everyone else that they were not alone as a people or a nation. They had seen the unannounced spectacle many times in the past, but now they knew they existed together with people close to them and far over the horizon. Without any doubt, they knew there were others. With the sight of the whales, they knew they living with all the other living, breathing souls, all of them, everywhere.

About the Author

I have always had a fascination with travel. After visiting a small village, somewhere in the world, I became aware of the sense of community engendered among limited populations. Small towns nearby to me, or in Europe, Asia, the Pacific Islands. I've noticed the different feel versus a large city. I now think of a Metropolis as a jump point to explore a small town. And I'm so glad I discovered them and continue to find and explore more small towns.

I like to research historical data after each travel experience. When I decided to compose my first novel, I went all in. That jump into a literary endeavor was an intense experience. I was driven and committed to writing and researching, often every day.

Now, the adventure and the sharing begins.